MOTHERLOVE

SHARE YOUR THOUGHTS

Want to help make *MotherLove* a bestselling novel? Consider leaving an honest review of this book on Goodreads, on your personal author website or blog, and anywhere else readers go for recommendations. It's our priority at Brown Chicken Books to publish books for readers to enjoy, and our authors appreciate and value your feedback.

OUR SOUTHERN FRIED GUARANTEE

If you wouldn't enthusiastically recommend one of our books with a 4- or 5-star rating to a friend, then the next story is on us. We believe that much in the stories we're telling. Simply email us at pr@sfkmultimedia.com.

MOTHERLOVE

BY JANET HOGAN CHAPMAN

This book is dedicated to women who overcome horrific circumstances to become strong and whole, but especially to the real-life Louann Walker. You know who you are.

PART ONE

LOUANN

2017

M Y OWN MOTHER COULDN'T STAND THE SIGHT OF ME.
This was the raw truth I lived with for most of my life. Let me explain more of my life story. You think you know most of it, but there's so much more. Daniel, you saved my life. You're my husband, friend, counselor, father figure to my daughters, and grandfather to my grandchildren. I wouldn't be here today if it weren't for you.

Just my luck to be born on February 29th: Leap Day, 1964. Simple-minded folks like those in Albany, Georgia, believed the day was evil. Albany, not far from the Florida and Alabama borders, was stuck off in the southwestern corner of the state like a pushpin holding down the curling corner of an old map. It also happened to be one of the coldest days on record in that part of Georgia, and the cold served to reinforce the idea that this particular Leap Day was even more evil than others. Folks made up their minds that it was the Devil's day and nothing good could come from it. That included *me*. When I was told about this years later, the expression "when Hell freezes over" took on an entirely new significance.

My mother, Joycie, had still been six months shy of her fifteenth birthday when I was born, just a child herself. There was no baby daddy in the picture; I was always told he was some boy who ran off and left town once he found out she was pregnant. She didn't want me, and neither did Joycie's own mama and daddy, Lynn and Richard Walker. And so I was taken in by my great-grandparents. In those times and those kinds of places, the older generation believed in taking care of their own. Hampton and Bessie Walker were not about to give away their own flesh and blood. They were the only ones who seemed to care a fig about a new little baby with a child mama and no daddy. Truth be told, they'd been the only mama and daddy Joycie had known for most of her life, and now it would be the same way with me.

I never called Joycie "Mama," even after I figured out she was my real mother, and it never seemed strange that we both called Hampton and Bessie "Mama and Daddy." Joycie's real mama had been bad to drink, and one day, she'd run off and left Richard when Joycie was still a baby. That was when he let her grandparents take over her raising. Oh, he came around now and then, and he even took Joycie back to live with him when he got married again, but that didn't last long either. I don't recall me or her calling Richard anything—especially not "Daddy." He was just Richard, or more often, *that snake Richard*. It was just the way things were in those days.

Maybe those folks in Albany weren't so simple-minded after all. They had witnessed the past unfold for Hampton and Bessie Walker, their son Richard, and his daughter Joycie. Why should they think it'd be any different for me? Mamas, daddies, sons, daughters, grandparents, great-grandparents, brothers, sisters, and assorted other relatives. Evil would reach out with hot fingers and seize each of us and those we loved, no matter how hard we pretended it wasn't there.

RICHARD

1953

I WASN'T AROUND MUCH WHEN JOYCIE WAS A BABY, AND I NEVER DID love her mother, Lynn. Oh, I was fond of her, and she was a pretty thing, only sixteen when we started going steady. I always did like my women young and good-looking. When she told me that she was pregnant, we got married at the courthouse by the justice of the peace. No wedding. No promises of a rosy future—just giving the baby my last name so it wouldn't be a bastard. We moved in with my mama and daddy, and Joycie was born in August of 1950.

I kept going out the same as before I was a married man. No woman, baby, or piece of paper was going to cramp my style. If I wasn't much of a daddy, Lynn wasn't much of a mama, either. She stayed drunk most of the time and did her own fair share of gallivantin'. My mama and daddy were more like little Joycie's folks than me and Lynn were. One day, without a word to anybody, Lynn ran off and left us both. We'd barely been married a year before we were divorced. Truth be known, the baby most likely never missed her mother. I had more to do with her than Lynn had. Sometimes, when I wasn't on a bender and wasn't in a bad mood 'cause of Mama or Daddy harpin' on me about something, I'd coddle and coo with Joycie. She was such a pretty little thing. Sweet and pleasant to be around, too. She could always make me feel good.

"There we go! How's my pretty little darling? You're so pretty and sweet, Daddy's little girl. You're so soft and warm. Ride Daddy's rocky horse! There, now, doesn't that feel good?"

A baby's one thing, but a man eventually gets lonely for a full-time woman. After Lynn left, I took up with Lottie Sue. I'd known her all my life, and we'd enjoyed each other's company. The talk was we were related somehow, maybe distant cousins, but that didn't stop us from messin' around. After a while, she convinced me to get hitched, so we up and got married at the courthouse one afternoon. Didn't really think it through—just a spur of the moment thing. We moved to a little apartment and brought Joycie to live with us. Lottie Sue really took to Joycie, who was nearly three by then. Seemed to love her like her own child.

Lottie Sue worked at the laundromat most days, and I stayed home with Joycie. I loved stroking her silky blond hair and soft skin. I'd set her on my lap and settle her against me, her warm little bottom snuggled close, rocking her back and forth.

"There we go, my little girlie. I just love feelin' you up against me. Feels good, don't it?"

Woo-wee, her pretty little grin and big blue eyes really got my blood boiling. Of course, I was careful not to let anybody see me playin' with her that way. They'd say it was nasty when it weren't no more than a daddy having fun with his little girl. Me and Joycie had a grand old time when Lottie Sue was away at her laundromat job. I'd tell Joycie if she sat on my lap and played rocky horse a while, she could have ice cream or some other little treat. I could tell she liked our little game. Course, she was too little to know why it felt so good. She just wanted the ice cream. But that all came to a stop one day when Lottie Sue came in from work early.

"Richard Walker! What in the hell are you doing?"

I slipped my hands out from under Joycie's little T-shirt, where I'd been rubbing her tiny nipples. She started to cry.

"We were just playing rocky horse, weren't we, Baby Girl?"

Lottie Sue snatched her from me and held her close. "Joycie? Are you all right? Why are you crying, baby? Are you hurt?"

I shot Joycie a warning look. "Hush that crying. You know we was just playing. You're fine. Let me go get that popsicle I promised you." Glaring at Lottie Sue, I seethed. "Hell, woman, you're trying to make a mountain out of a molehill. Course she's not hurt. What do you take me for?"

She didn't answer.

HAMPTON

1953

IREMEMBER WELL THE DAY JOYCIE CAME TO LIVE WITH US FOR GOOD. It was a mid-July Sunday afternoon and hot as blazes. I was out in the garden to the side of the house, and Bessie was sitting on the porch stringin' beans. That porch was tacked onto the front of the meat market that we'd added to our little shotgun house years before. Shaded by huge old oaks, it was the coolest spot on a hot summer afternoon. Joycie jumped out from the car and made a beeline for me while Lottie Sue brought armloads of clothes and toys from her car and dumped 'em on the porch before she sat down by Bessie on the green metal glider. Something was up.

It wasn't unusual for Joycie to be in the garden with me, and at three years old, she was full of questions and wanted to help with everything. I was trying to hear Bessie and Lottie Sue, but between my old ears and Joycie's nonstop prattle, I couldn't make out what they was sayin', but their voices were rising and falling, their heads and hands moving back and forth. Joycie was ticking off questions one after the other.

"Granddaddy? Is this a weed? Can I pull it up?"

"Uh-hum, Joycie."

"Granddaddy? Is this a good bug or a bad bug? Can I stomp it?"

"What? Uh, yes, you can stomp it."

"Granddaddy? Can I pick this pretty flower?"

"What?" Glancing down at a squash blossom and trying to keep my eyes up towards the women on the porch, I answered. "Huh? Oh! No! Leave that one be. It'll turn into a baby squash."

I could see Lottie Sue and Bessie frowning like they was mad, then shaking their heads and dabbing at their eyes. When Bessie's hand flew up to her mouth, I knew something had to be bad wrong. I must have scared Joycie with my harsh tone of voice, 'cause now she was watching the porch, too. Lottie Sue trotted back to her car and took off, leaving Bessie standing on the porch, sobbing.

Joycie was suddenly still. She looked up at me, her eyes big and round.

"Granddaddy? Why's Grandma cryin'?"

I didn't answer. Joycie tugged at my pant leg.

"Granddaddy, Lottie Sue going? I go with her?"

"Not now, honey. You stay here," I answered.

I could see her little eyes get bright with tears, but she tried to be brave. She squared her shoulders. My heart hurt for her. She was actin' so grown-up to be so young. She shouldn't have to be dealing with such misery at her age. I bent down and spoke more gently.

"Here, sweetheart. See how this squash's nice and yellow? Pull off the ones that look like that, and I'll be back in a minute."

"All right, Granddaddy. I'll be right here." She rubbed at her nose and eyes, spreading dirt on her little face.

I stepped up on the porch and hugged Bessie to me, patting her back and wiping at my own face. I didn't know exactly what the problem was yet, but if it made Bessie cry like that, it had to be bad. I sat her down on the glider and got her calmed down where she could talk. That's when she managed to garble out what Lottie Sue had told her about findin' Richard "playing" with Joycie. I looked out to the garden, where Joycie was inspecting each squash plant. As I watched her little blond head bob around, barely as tall as the plants, anger rose up in me like vomit.

"Bessie, let's go on in the house. I'll get Joycie. She's safe with us. I'll make sure of that."

Bessie gathered up her pan of beans and went inside while I walked back out toward the garden.

"Let's see what you got there, Joycie! My, my, what a good job you done. Don't know how I'd manage this garden without you to help. Let's take these on in the house, and you can help your grandma in the kitchen."

Troubled notions don't stick long in a little girl's mind when she's barely more than a baby. Leastways not in her conscious thought. Now, Joycie was beaming like I thought she was the best picker in the world. She trotted along, carrying three of the biggest, hardest, yellowest squash you'd ever see. We went up on the porch and through the screen door into the meat market at the front of the house. We were closed on Sunday, so the long shiny cases and counter space where we cut and wrapped the orders was clean and gleaming in the pale light. We went on through a door in the back wall of the shop that led to our kitchen.

"Look, Grandma! I got three big squashes! Can I wash 'em? Granddaddy said I could help you." Joycie held up the squash with her grubby hands.

Bessie winked at me over the top of Joycie's head. "Oh, he did, did he? Well, I sure can use your help. It looks like both you and those squash need a cleaning."

I watched as Bessie got Joycie set up on the stepstool in front of the sink with a chipped white dishpan of cold water and a scrub brush. Joycie went to town on that squash in between Bessie swipin' at her face with a cold rag to get the dirt off. Not that Joycie minded. Not much a three-year-old loves more than playing in water. While she was splashin' and playin', I pulled Bessie aside.

"Bessie, you goin' to get Joycie down for a nap in a little while? I want you and her both inside. I got a feelin' Richard's liable to show up here, and I'd rather meet him outside and on my own. I've got some choice words for him."

Bessie's brow furrowed, and her eyes filled to the brim. "Oh, Hampton, what are you goin' to do? We don't need a scene, not with Joycie here."

"It ain't going to be a scene, Bessie, but you and Joycie just stay in the back, and I'll handle things. All right?"

"All right, Hampton. I trust you to know what's best."

About an hour later, he drove up. I was on the front porch, rocking back and forth, staring off into the yard, my hands locked tight on the shotgun across my knees. When he pulled up, I stood, still gripping the gun. The door to the beat-up old truck swung open.

"Don't bother gettin' out of that truck, Richard. Me and Bessie will look after Joycie. You got no business with that child. And don't go lookin' for Lottie Sue, either. She said to tell ya you'll get the divorce papers in the mail."

Richard stepped out of the truck anyway, slammed the door, and took two steps toward me. I raised the gun and pointed it straight at him.

"Now, Daddy, wait just a fuckin' minute—"

I came down the steps into the dirt yard and stopped with the end of the gun barrel about three feet in front of my only living son.

"I done told you not to get out of that truck. Now get back in and leave. And if you ever come close to that child again, I'll blow your brains out, so help me God."

Richard swore. "Hell, Daddy. You sound right pissed off. I'll come back some other time." He got back in his truck and drove so fast out of the yard the dirt flew up like a dust devil had took ahold of it.

"Don't bother," I said, keeping the gun steady until he was out of sight.

BESSIE

1953

T HAT SUNDAY, WHEN LOTTIE SUE TURNED UP AT OUR HOUSE WITH
Joycie and started telling me her suspicions, I got a dread in the
pit of my stomach, like I'd swallowed a rock. Somehow, I knew it was
true. When she told me she couldn't stay with Richard after finding him
messin' with Joycie like that, I knew me and Hampton would be taking
on the mama and daddy roles again. How we had conceived a son so evil
he'd take advantage of a baby, I would never understand.

Me and Hampton had a hard life in those days in South Georgia.
We'd married young, had our boys, and settled down to scratch out a
living near Albany. The Depression ruined the economy in the 1930s, and
along with it, everyone's spirits. Unlike bigger towns, Albany never recovered. Poor families like us scraped by as farmhands, backyard mechanics,
short-order cooks, and waitresses. A few nearly middle-class folks made
at least a decent living as tradesmen, teachers, and government workers. The upper crust, who lived on swaths of green land outside town,
owned the town's properties but did not do business there or mingle
with its people. They collected rents and bled us like leeches, leaving us
too broken-down to consider any other kind of life. It was like the rich
landowners had become ruthless carpetbaggers, leaving folks like us to
fend for ourselves.

I took in ironing from time to time; we kept a garden and ran a little
meat market out of a big front room that we'd added to our house, so

we managed to stay fed. Our first boy, Richard, was born in 1931, then three years later, Joey came along. Richard was a strong little boy with an independent streak. He could be downright mean at times, tipping over his milk just to exasperate me or pinching his baby brother to make him cry. And no matter how hard his daddy walloped him, Richard would not cry. He stood there and took it, then wandered off outside. A few hours after one of those whippings, we'd find a drowned squirrel or a strangled kitten on the doorstep and know Richard had acted out his revenge on the poor animal.

Joey was nothing like Richard. Loving and affectionate, but always sickly. When he was about six years old, the doctors told us he had the sugar diabetes. I s'pose we spoiled him, trying to keep him from getting sicker and protecting him from his older brother. When he died at barely fourteen years old, something went out of me. My baby boy was gone, and I was left with a hateful gangly boy who took every opportunity to make life hard on all of us, himself included.

A few years later, when Richard got Lynn pregnant and married her, little Joycie arrived in our lives. It was like the Lord had sent her to bring me back alive. Law, how me and Ham doted on that baby. Prettiest little thing you ever saw, and so good-natured. The day her mama left, I vowed I would take her in and she would never feel the lack of a mother's love. Hampton didn't say it in so many words, but I knew he felt the same, stepping in as her daddy while Richard ran all over town with other women. It near 'bout broke our hearts when Richard and Lottie Sue got married and took Joycie to live with them in a little apartment in town, but we knew Lottie Sue loved her and would be a good mama. We hoped and prayed she'd make up in the mama department what Richard lacked as a daddy. Turned out it didn't matter none anyway, 'cause by the time she was three years old, Joycie was right back with us.

JOYCIE

1962, Age 12

L ET ME TELL YOU A LITTLE BIT ABOUT MY DADDY. MY REAL DADDY, I mean. I knew my grandparents weren't my real mama and daddy, but I called them that anyway. Ever since I'd come to live with them when I was around three years old, they were like a real mama and daddy, but my real daddy was Richard. He didn't live with us, and we'd go weeks without seeing him, then he'd show up and stay a couple of days. Mama and Daddy never had much to say to him, and they kept me with one of them all the time Richard was there. They'd say, "Leave him alone and don't talk to him. He ain't right."

I knew that already. I'd known since that day back when I was about six years old.

It was a hot summer day, and Mama was in the meat market at the front of the house, cuttin' up a side of beef somebody had brought in. Daddy was out in the yard under the chinaberry tree, poking around under the hood of an old truck. I wasn't really big enough to be of any help, but big enough to be a bother, so they sent me out to play. I hid out under the porch wearing just my white panties; it was the coolest place I could find, playing in the dirt with rocks and sticks, creating a world of my own, a place that could have been anywhere but there. The space was about four feet high, just right for me. That was my favorite pastime—playing where nobody could see me. I'd spend hours under that porch, dragging sticks to make roads in the dry dirt, acorns and rocks my buildings and people. As usual, Richard wasn't around. It was weird for him to pay a visit unless he wanted money. When his car pulled into the yard, I moved to the edge of my shaded hideout and stayed quiet, so I could hear and see what was going on. I saw Daddy wipe his hand on a rag and watch Richard walk to the porch.

"Hey, Daddy," Richard said, walking up the porch steps. Daddy didn't say anything, just stuck his head back under the hood of the truck and kept clanging around. Then I heard Richard say, "Hey, Mama," as the screen door slapped shut. I couldn't hear them good from under the porch; it just sounded like a bunch of mumbling. I moved quietly up the sagging steps of the porch and tiptoed to the side of the screen door. They couldn't see me, but I could see them now. And I heard every word they said.

"So that's Mr. Philpot's meat? He still like it cut just so?"

"Yep, Richard. You know he's always real particular about how he wants it done."

"Oh, I remember. He likes it wrapped just so, too."

"That's right, son. I been working on this side near 'bout an hour. Probably take another hour to get it finished and wrapped just right." Mama wiped her brow with the side of her arm.

"Mama, it's really hot in here. You ought to take it easy. Why don't you take a break? Go in the back, sit down a while, and have some ice water. I can finish this for you."

The buzzing grind of the meat saw fell silent. I could see the look of surprise on Mama's face. Her mouth fell open and her eyes opened wide. It wasn't like Richard to be so nice to her, or to anyone else, for that matter.

"What? What do you want? It ain't like you to think of anybody but yourself. Why would you want me to do that, son?"

"Oh, come on, Mama, I'm just trying to be nice. Keep you from keeling over in this heat. Who'd take care of Joycie if something happened to you? I'll finish this up, take a few dollars for my trouble, and then be on my way to find some cold beer. Whaddya say?"

Mama didn't answer right off. She stood there looking at the floor, her shoulders slumped, breathing heavy. She rested her hands on the counter and leaned over. When she raised her head to look at Richard, he said, "Aw, come on, Mama, let me do something nice for you for once."

She wiped her hands on the bloody apron. "Well, it is awfully hot, and maybe I should get off my feet a little while. You could finish this up. Don't take any shortcuts, do it exactly right, and don't make a mess of it."

"I know how to do it, Mama. I ain't lived here my whole life and not learned how to cut through bone and meat. I'll do it up just right. You just go on and put your feet up."

Mama stepped over to the sink and ran the water, washing her bloody hands. I peeked around the edge of the screen and saw the piles of butcher-paper-wrapped packages stacked on the counter. I knew that just past them was the gory saw and what was left of the beef. Mama dropped her bloodstained apron into a corner and pushed through the door leading to the living quarters in the back of the shop.

Living behind the meat shop, I was used to the sight of blood, and it didn't bother me none. Still, something didn't seem quite right. It wasn't that I felt peculiar, because anytime Richard came around, I felt creepy. It almost felt good, in a way, but scary at the same time. I always tried to push the feeling under, but this time was different. Richard was being nice, like a normal person. My flesh began to crawl. I wanted to run but was frozen to that spot, like the blood covering the floor inside had seeped under the screen and dried around my bare feet, holding me in place. My eyes would not move, either. I wanted to tear them away, but they stayed fixed, staring through the screen as Richard, my real father, set the saw to spinning.

That was six years ago, when my real daddy became a one-armed man.

RICHARD

1958

"Hello, Mrs. White. My name's Alton Wakefield, and I'd like to talk to you about an important investment." I reached up to tip my hat with my right arm stump, and an audible gasp came from the little old lady.

While the lady was still staring in horror, her eyes wide and mouth open, I'd lower my eyes and paste a sheepish grin onto my mouth.

"Oh, pardon me, ma'am. Didn't mean to shock you with my arm. Those gooks in Korea might have got my arm, but least they didn't get all of me. Sorry to impose on you, but as you can see, my mechanic's career was done for, so here I am, peddling insurance plans."

The woman let out a deep breath and smiled kindly. "Oh, you poor dear. Come right on in. Let me get you a cold drink, and you can tell me all about it."

Before she knew it, I'd sold her a two-hundred-dollar plan. With my fake name scribbled on a fake receipt and a hundred real dollars in cash in my pocket, I said I'd be back in six months for the second hundred dollars.

She warmly patted my shoulder. "You do that, Mr. Wakefield. I look forward to seeing you again. Anything to help one of our former boys in uniform."

Of course, she'd never lay eyes on me or a penny of her insurance money again. With a jaunt in my step and a whistle in the air, I'd make my way to the next name on my list.

I'd been doing all right financially. Cuttin' off my arm hadn't yielded the big payoff I'd expected, but the money did last about a year. By then, the insurance scheme was bringing in the money. It turned out old ladies were particularly sorry for a one-armed man. Driving over to Dothan once a month, I'd make the rounds of the wealthy old widows, pouring out my story like molasses on cornbread with my nicest fake manners. By the time I was done talking, they were more than ready to trade cold hard cash for the fake policies. Just one trip a month earned enough income to last 'til the next time.

I didn't go around Mama and Daddy's house much. Daddy had made it plain I wasn't welcome back when Joycie had gone to live with them for good. Even so, I'd drop by from time to time, maybe once a month or so, just to see my baby girl. When Mama and Daddy wasn't looking, I'd smile, make kissy lips, and wink at Joycie. If they were out of earshot, I might even say something like, "Hey, Joycie, you sure are pretty!" or "Hey, Baby, you love your real daddy, dontcha?" She'd run off and never would say anything back.

After cuttin' off my arm, Daddy said I was downright crazy, and if I came back again, he'd have me committed. I made out with my insurance scam and staying around with different lady friends, sometimes staying in a motel or even sleeping at the bus station, if I had to. But that didn't mean I never saw my little girl Joycie. I just couldn't help myself. I might happen on her and Mama at the Piggly Wiggly, or see her with Daddy when he took her to town in his truck. Sometimes I would spy on her going to and from school.

One time when she was walking home, I rolled along behind her about half a block. Her skinny little legs poked out from a too-short faded dress, stretching right up to her tight little butt. Her long hair was halfway down her back and shone in the sunshine. Mama might not have money for fancy clothes, but she made sure Joycie was neat and clean. After watching her walk a ways, I pulled up alongside her.

"Hey, darlin'. Sure is hot for you to be walkin' all the way home from school. Can I give you a lift?" She didn't stop walking, so I let the truck keep rolling along right beside her. Her head down, hair covering her face, she did not speak or look my way.

"Hey! Joycie! Don't you hear me speaking to you? Where's your manners?"

Still no response.

"Aw, come on, honey, your daddy just wants to say hello and get a good look at you."

Still nothing. I was sure my folks had told her not to have anything to do with me. They had her scared to death to even say hello. I knew from times before she didn't even consider me her daddy. Called my own folks Mama and Daddy. That was a fine how-do-you-do. Takin' away my own daughter. But she knew I was her real daddy, and I wasn't about to let her forget.

"Hell—be that way, then. Don't speak to your own daddy." I stepped on the gas. As I looked in the rearview mirror, a cloud of orangy-red dust enveloped the scrawny girl. *Shit. My own daughter won't even speak to me.*

JOYCIE

1962, Age 12

I HATED IT WHEN MY REAL DADDY RICHARD TRIED TO MOLLYCODDLE up to me. I didn't tell Mama and Daddy about all the times he tried to speak to me on the street or around town. It would just make them mad, and I didn't want to be more trouble for them than I was already. They never explained why Richard didn't take care of me or why he wasn't welcome to come around. Of course, I remembered when he cut off his own arm—that would be etched in my mind forever—but I'd already been living with them years before that. I guessed it was just because he was crazy or drunk half the time. Even now that I was twelve, I didn't know exactly what he'd done or why I'd had to come live with Mama and Daddy all those years ago, but I knew it had to be bad, if they didn't want me around him. Maybe that explained the unsettling, creepy feeling that came over me anytime he was close by.

It got to where I wouldn't go anywhere if I didn't have to, except for school, and I dreaded even that. Other kids were so cruel.

"Hey, Joycie! Where're your old, gray-haired folks?"

"Hey, Joycie! Is that meat blood or man blood on your feet?"

"Hey, Joycie! Can't your real daddy take care of you with just one arm?"

I'd been living with the taunts for years.

Summers weren't as bad 'cause I could stay home, except for when we went to visit Mama's sisters in Florida. Going to see my aunts and cousins, not always having to look over my shoulder for Richard, was what I imagined being released from prison must feel like. Making the trip down there was an ordeal, like stories I'd read in school about children who had to sneak away from German soldiers.

We always left early in the morning, before daylight. Daddy said that was because it was the coolest time to drive. The back of the truck was loaded with battered cardboard suitcases with our clothes, the last of the food Mama had put up from the garden, and some castoffs to pass along to the relatives.

"Come on, Joycie, climb up in the front and stretch out here across me and Mama. Lordy, girl, you keep growing, and pretty soon, you won't be able to do this no more." Daddy would lift my feet and adjust them across his legs.

"That's all right, baby. There'll always be room on my lap for you," Mama would say as she smoothed my hair back.

With the windows rolled all the way down and me sprawled out over the both of them, I snuggled in, and we took off into the dark. The sound of the road lulled me to sleep for a couple hours. By the time the sun was up, we'd be at least halfway there, and I'd be waking up hungry and needing to pee. Daddy was the kind of man that didn't want to stop on the road unless it was an emergency, so Mama always came prepared. Mama pulled out the quart-sized Mason jar she always carried along on trips and unscrewed the lid.

"Squat down here to the floorboard, Joycie. Ain't nobody going to see you, and I'll hold your dress up out of the way. Just be sure not to knock the jar over or pee on my hand! I'll hold it steady for you."

"I'll try, Mama, I promise!"

I'd scrunch down in that cramped space and pee in the jar, just as nice and neat as a boy. Daddy would, of course, keep his eyes on the road, but he'd grumble: "I ain't never understood why girl children can't go more than an hour without needin' a bathroom break. What do y'all do at school all day? I know the teacher don't let y'all jump up and run out all the time.

That would drive a body nuts, with a room full of kids comin' and goin' all the time. My boys never had that problem. They'd hold it all day."

"But Daddy—I can't help it. We could have stopped at that gas station, but you just kept on going."

Mama chimed in before I could get Daddy too riled up. "Oh, Hampton, never you mind. She's just a little girl. Bladder barely the size of a walnut. It's different for males. They got extra room to hold it in. I could go, too, if you'd stop."

"I ain't stopping at no filling station. Filthy places. No tellin' what you'd catch in those bathrooms. Why, I've heard stories about—"

"Hampton! Hush. Little pitchers have big ears. Just forget it."

I'd heard Mama say that a hundred times, but I still didn't know what it meant. Pitchers like we kept the sweet tea in or pictures on the walls? Neither one had ears, big or small. What was she talkin' about? She always cut Daddy off just when the conversation was starting to get interesting. Mama dug in the wrinkled brown grocery sack she had behind the seat and brought out cold biscuits and bacon wrapped in pieces of butcher paper.

"Here, Joycie, I know you're hungry. Hold this paper good around the biscuit so your hands don't touch it, since you just peed. After you eat, I've got a jar of water, too."

I nibbled at the biscuit, being sure to keep my fingers on the paper and trying not to drop crumbs. Then Mama brought out another jar filled with water. I wrinkled my nose as I drank, 'cause I couldn't help but wonder if it had ever been a pee jar, too.

LOUANN

2017

YOU KNOW, DANIEL, LOOKING BACK ON IT, WHEN YOU HEAR WHAT a messed-up childhood my real mama, Joycie, had, you can almost understand why she had such a hard time in life. Of course, none of her childhood would compare to what happened during her teenage years. Who can say what all of our lives would have been like if Mama and Daddy had stayed right there in Albany? Hell, I might not even be here. Maybe it wouldn't have made any difference. What happened could have happened anywhere. They did what they thought best to protect Joycie, but it wasn't enough. Evil has a way of finding what it's after. The horrible things that happened to all of us over the next few years could have destroyed us, but they didn't—not yet, anyway. Yeah, we still live with the scars, but just look at the good things: I have you—and my own children. Thank God for that. It's taken me my whole life to discover the truth about my real mama.

JOYCIE

W E WERE STILL IN FLORIDA BUT WERE SUPPOSED TO GO HOME
to Albany the next week. School would be starting back in
two weeks, and I had a birthday coming up. It seemed like it ought to
be important. After all, I was going to be thirteen. A real teenager—
practically grown! Not that it would make that much of a difference in my
everyday life. I had no friends at school, and I certainly wasn't interested
in boys. My cousins in Florida were the closest friends I had, and I only
saw them a few weeks each summer. Staying overnight at their houses
for those few weeks was as close as I came to having girlfriends.

I learned quite a bit from those giggly, whispered conversations
in the dark. Marybeth and Sharlene were the oldest cousins at fifteen,
and the others trailed along at fourteen, thirteen, and twelve. There was
little Sally at eight years old, but she always fell asleep and wasn't party
to the nearly all-night-long talking marathons of us older girls. Mostly,
Marybeth and Sharlene kept the rest of us enthralled with stories of
boys, kissing, and periods.

Maybe it was because Mama hadn't had any girls besides me and just
didn't think about it, but she hadn't said a thing to me about what happens around twelve or thirteen. If it hadn't been for my cousin Marybeth,
I would have panicked that hot night at her house.

My Aunt Rene, Marybeth's mama, was my mama's younger sister.
Rene and her husband, Jimmy, both had good jobs and one of the nicest

houses around Williston. We were all laid out on quilts on their carpeted living-room floor, telling ghost stories. There was a small shaft of light from the kitchen; even at our ages, we were just too chicken to tell ghost stories in the complete dark. It was humid and sticky, and I'd been noticing the sweatiness under my arms and between my legs for a few weeks now. It hadn't been there before.

At one especially scary point in the story of the escaped convict, I just knew I would wet my pants if I didn't go to the bathroom, but I was too scared to go down the dark hall by myself. I nudged Marybeth and whispered, "Marybeth, I gotta go pee."

"Can't you wait? This is the best part of the story."

"I don't think so. It feels like I'm about to wet my pants."

"Oh, good grief, Joycie. Then just go on to the bathroom."

"But I'm scared. It's dark in the hall. Will you go with me?"

"What? Don't be such a baby. There's no convicts around here. It's just a story."

"But I really gotta go, and I don't know where the light switch is, and I'm scared, and I don't want to wet—"

"Oh, all right. I'll go with you. Sharlene, hold the story right there a few minutes. I gotta walk Joycie to the bathroom before she pees her pants."

A round of giggles from the others broke the tension in the dark living room.

When we got to the bathroom, Marybeth stood just outside the door while I went in. When I looked down to wipe, I noticed a brown stain on my panties. That was strange. The pretty green tile and fancy lights around the mirror made it so bright in there that I wasn't sure at first what I was seeing. I hadn't gone number two since wearing these panties. Ewww. I didn't think much about it, but I didn't want to keep wearing those panties, whatever it was. I called out to Marybeth in a hushed voice, hoping she could hear me.

"Marybeth? Can you hear me?"

"Yeah, what is it now, scaredy-cat? You need me to come in there with you?"

Tears welled up suddenly and were about to fall. I didn't want her to think I was a baby, but I didn't know what else to do.

"Not really, but could you poke your head in? I need to ask you something."

The door cracked open, and Marybeth's pink-sponge-rollered head appeared. "What? Hurry up! I wanna hear the end of the story."

"Uh, it looks like I got a little something on my panties. Could I borrow some of yours?"

Now Marybeth came all the way into the little bathroom. "What are you talking about? Something on your panties? You didn't . . ." As she came closer and bent to look down, her hands flew to the sides of her face. "Oh my God! That's blood! You got your period. You dummy— didn't you know what it was?"

The tears that had been brimming now spilled down my cheeks. I couldn't answer as sobs came wrenching up from somewhere far down in me. Marybeth put her arms around me. We must have looked an awkward pair, with me sitting on the toilet bawling and her trying to hug me at the same time.

"Oh, Joycie, it's all right! Don't cry. I didn't mean to call you a dummy. You really didn't know? Aunt Bessie didn't talk to you about this?"

Choking the sobs down into snuffles, I wiped at my nose.

"No, not really. I mean, I've heard y'all talk about it, but I tried not to think about it. Now what do I do?" The sobs returned, and I felt Marybeth's tears mingle with my own.

"Don't you worry, Joycie baby. I'll take care of you. I'll be right back. Just sit tight."

"Like where am I gonna go?"

We looked at each other and grinned. Suddenly, we broke out in an embarrassed laugh. She was back in a jiffy with a clean pair of panties, then rummaged around in the cabinet under the sink and brought out supplies. Showing me patiently what to do, she led me through the whole process, then hugged me again when we finished up.

"Now, Joycie, listen to me. I'm going to send you home a few pads in a paper bag, but you've got to tell Bessie about this soon as you get back to Aunt Lila's. She needs to know, and she'll get you all fixed up with everything you need. You're not embarrassed to tell her, are you?"

"No, I'll tell her. Maybe this explains all her comments about me growing up and becoming a woman. She's been looking at me funny for weeks now, and she brought me a training bra in a plain paper bag one day."

"All right, then. But there's one more thing about all this, probably the most important thing of all. Now that you're going to have month-lies, you can get pregnant. Just remember that."

"Get pregnant? Just from having monthlies? How come all y'all aren't pregnant?"

Marybeth put her hand on her forehead. "Oh, geez . . . there's more to it than just monthlies. Maybe you better ask Aunt Bessie about that when you talk to her tomorrow. Come on, let's get back to the story and then try to get some sleep."

I walked awkwardly back to our makeshift beds and squirmed around, trying to get used to the bulky wad between my legs. Didn't seem right that there should be anything down there, and the feel of it gave me a sick feeling in my stomach. The nagging, tickly sensation felt bad, and trying to pretend it wasn't there just made me that much sicker. It felt weird, and I wanted it to go away. This couldn't be the way it was supposed to be. What was wrong with me?

Sharlene went back to the story. I was scared Marybeth might tell everybody what had happened, but she just sat close with her arm around my shoulders, smiling secretively. She didn't know that my insides and my mind were roiling with feelings like monsters under a blanket.

BESSIE

August 1962

A COUPLE OF MORNINGS LATER, HAMPTON AND ME TALKED OVER breakfast. He commented about how nice it was being in Florida and away from the constant worry back in Albany, always looking over his shoulder for Richard. He also hadn't realized just how grown-up Joycie was now. He said, "Bessie, I talked to Jimmy about me working for him. He said he could use the extra help. I've been thinkin' maybe we ought to move down here for good. You'd be close to family, and Joycie seems so much happier here. It might be a good move for all of us."

"Oh, Hampton, do you really think we need to do that?"

"Yes, I do, Bessie. I think the change will do Joycie good, especially after what you said about her becoming a woman. Besides, we can use the extra money."

"Of course, I'd love being closer to family."

Hampton put his arm around my shoulder. "I know you'd like being closer, and getting away from Albany will be good for all of us. I'd feel better with her and us as far away from Richard as we can get."

"You're right, Ham. I couldn't believe it when she told me yesterday about getting her monthly visitor. I feel a little bad that I didn't prepare her for it. I just didn't think it'd be so soon, but she is turning thirteen, so I guess it's about time. I better have a talk with her about boys, too."

"It's not boys I'm worried about. Joycie ain't stupid. I just don't know how she'd handle it if Richard tried anything, and I don't want to find out, either. We don't have to scare her none. We can just say we're moving for the money. Don't see how there's much she'd miss back home. She might like it real well down here."

"All right, but I still think I need to have a talk with her about boys."

"Just don't mention the move until I'm ready to let her know. I'll need to get a few things in order, but we need to do it before school starts." Ham walked on out to the yard, whistlin' like a kid without a care. But I knew his heart was heavy.

The rest of the afternoon, all I could think about was how I was going to tell Joycie about the birds and the bees. I didn't have any experience raisin' a girl, and I didn't have much of an example from my own girlhood days. I'd grown up on a farm, and farm kids knew about the facts of life from the time they could walk and talk. Course, we didn't know more than a speckle on a frog about love. And nobody told us, either. Girls might get all moony-eyed over some handsome boy, but we never heard our mamas and daddies say "I love you" to each other. And we sure never said it to anyone ourselves. Weddings were not romantic events but social occasions fueled by lots of bawdy remarks.

The first and only man I ever heard the words "I love you" from was Hampton, and that was on our wedding night. Even now, over thirty years later, I remembered. I'd lain shivering and in pain, sure I was dying. I'd wanted to run home to my mama and daddy. As I'd curved away, tears rolling down my cheeks, Ham's arms had reached around me, and he'd turned my face to his. "I love you," he'd said in the most gentle and beautiful voice I'd ever heard. It would have to last forever, because he'd never said it again in all these years. But I knew he'd meant it then, and he meant it now, even if he didn't say so.

I went to track down Joycie. Back behind the trailer, I called out: "Joycie? You out here somewhere?"

A rustling came from the bushes. Fanning myself with a big elephant-plant leaf did not help the sweltering heat of the August afternoon, and neither did the unease about talking to Joycie. Sweat rolled down my face, the gnats flitted about, and my mind turned over words, and then she emerged from the scrubby hedges, tangled in honeysuckle vines.

"Mama? You need me? Are you all right?"

"I'm fine, baby, other than being about to burn up. Come around front, and let's sit in the shade." She followed me like a puppy dog to the big live oak out front. The same live oak where my sisters and I had solved all the problems of the world. Then it dawned on me. Land sakes, I should have asked my sister Lila about this. She had girls. She'd know what to say. Oh well, too late now for that. I'd just have to trust my instincts.

"You sure you're all right, Mama? You look kinda flushed to me."

"It's just the heat. I'm about burned slap-up, but that don't matter."

"Mama? There's something I forgot to ask you about yesterday morning, when we talked about . . . well, you know."

That got my attention. "Well, what is it, Joycie?"

"Well, um. Cousin Marybeth said that now that I have monthlies, I could get pregnant. I said she had monthlies and she wasn't pregnant, so how could that be? She said I needed to ask you about it."

I took a deep breath and swallowed the lump that was rising in my throat.

"Pregnant? You mean she used that exact word?"

"Yes, ma'am. Pregnant."

"Oh, Lordy. I didn't see this coming."

"Didn't see what coming, Mama?"

"All this talk about monthlies, and getting pregnant, and I don't know what all . . ."

"Oh, I know what pregnant is. I remember when Miss Jane at the grocery store was pregnant. She got really fat, and then little Wayne came out, and that was that. I guess she had monthlies, too, huh?"

"Yes, but there's a little more to it. You know, Joycie, every baby's got a daddy somewhere."

"Yes, ma'am. And I know you and Daddy are just my adopted mama and daddy. I didn't grow in your stomach. I know Richard's my real daddy, but I don't like him. He's scary. And whoever my real mama was got real sick and went away. But that's okay, 'cause I love you and Daddy."

"That's right, Baby Girl. And me and Daddy will always take care of you, we promise. Now, about the monthlies and getting pregnant." I decided to plunge right in with the seed story. "Once girls are old enough to get monthlies, like you, a man or a grown boy can plant a seed in their stomach, and a baby can start to grow. That makes the girl pregnant, and the man or boy is the baby's daddy. Understand?"

"I think so, but—"

"Now. Some boy might say he loves you and say he wants to show you love, but that might not be true. He really might just want to plant that seed, but don't you let him. You hear me?"

"But why not, Mama?"

Now what? How could I explain this?

"Well, honey, for one thing, it hurts for them to plant the seed. And it hurts to get the baby out. And it hurts real bad. That ain't love. Understand?"

"Yes ma'am, I think so, but—"

"That's all there is to it. So what you have to do is not let any boy or man get close enough to you to plant a seed in your stomach and hurt you. All right?"

"I guess so, but—"

I put my hands on the sides of Joycie's face and turned her to me, my voice hard and almost angry. "That's it. Don't take any chances, and don't let any man or boy get that close to you. Not even to give you a hug. Except for Daddy. He can hug you, and maybe your uncles or cousins. But nobody else. You understand?"

Joycie's eyes were wide as a wild animal's caught in a trap. I realized my hands were clenched on her face and let them drop.

"We don't ever have to talk about this again, Baby Girl. All right?" As hot as it was, I gathered her into my arms and patted her back. I was sure I felt tears that weren't my own mingle with the sweat running down my neck.

"All right, Mama. All right."

RICHARD
August 1962, Albany

DADDY WAS LOADING BOXES INTO THE BACK OF HIS PICKUP WHEN I pulled up to the house and blew the horn. He started walking back towards the house, and he stopped dead in his tracks but didn't turn around. He knew it was me.

"Hey, Daddy! Got a minute for your own son?"

His shoulders sagged, his head bowed, and he drew a circle with the toe of his workboot in the dust of the yard. Finally, he turned to look at me.

"How about it? Care for a little talk with your boy?"

Daddy came closer, stopping about three feet away from my truck door and crossing his arms over his chest, but not before I saw his fists clenching.

"Don't know that we have anything to discuss."

I spat out the window, into the dirt, purposefully close, but missing his boot by a few inches. "Oh, I think we do. I understand you're taking my daughter and moving to Florida."

"You might understand that, Richard. But what you don't understand is that I have legal guardianship of her. You never responded to the public notices, so she's not technically your daughter anymore. I can take her wherever I want."

"What in the hell are you talking about? I don't care about no piece of paper. She's my daughter and always will be. You got no right to take her away."

"Well, Richard, the law says different. You gave up your rights. Me and Mama are going to put her in school down there. Going to be a whole new life for her. And for us, too."

He turned and started back to the house. Mama stood at the screen door. There was no sign of Joycie. After a few steps, Daddy stopped and turned around. "You take care of yourself, son. If you need to get ahold of us, just get in touch with your cousin Jimmy, and he'll know how to find us. Goodbye." With that, he went up the steps and inside the house.

Mama was still standing at the screen. She brushed the back of her hand across her cheek, then raised it in the air in a silent, motionless wave. I put the truck in gear and sped away, never looking back.

They might think they'd got the better of me, but they were wrong. I'd show them. But first, I'd let 'em get moved and settled, let their guard down. Then I'd find them. If it took me forever, I'd find them and show them who Joycie's real daddy was. And I'd make sure Joycie knew it, too. I made my own plans to head south, and I was never more than a town or two behind them.

I picked up jobs for a few days here or there or ran a con, then left whatever little podunk town I was in for somewhere else. The towns and people were all the same: poor. Barely scraping by, like stray chickens scratching at the dirt to find a little something to eat. People and places like that should have made it easy for a man like me to show up for a few days and then disappear; drifters were part of the landscape. But there was something different about me: my arm, or the lack thereof. People tended to remember a one-armed man.

Drifting southward, I got a job pumping gas at a service station maybe ten miles from my mama's sisters. The owner had an old, run-down trailer out back that I rented. It didn't hurt that I knew Joycie was close by, and there were enough relatives scattered around that I could find out exactly where she was when I was ready to track her down. Even if they didn't care much for me, I figured I could play the "wronged sad-sack" well enough to wrangle some help out of 'em, and if that didn't work, I could rely on intimidation.

One Saturday afternoon, I managed to accidentally-on-purpose run into Uncle Buddy at the auto-parts store. "Hey, Buddy. How you doin'?" I asked. It took him a minute to answer, so I guess he was surprised to see me.

"Uh, Richard? I'm fine. What are you doing in these parts?"

"Well, you know we're all living around here now. Course, Joycie's still with Mama and Daddy, over in that little rental house of Aunt Lila's, right? I don't stay with them."

"Oh, that's right. That place would be kinda small for all of you. Probably best you're on your own."

"I thought so, too. Hey, don't tell 'em you ran into me, all right? I'm renting a little camper for now and want to surprise them when I get a nicer place. Don't want 'em to be worried about me, you know."

"Well, yeah, I guess so." Buddy scratched his head.

"It was good running into you, Buddy. You take care now."

I left him standing in the aisle of the store and skedaddled without buying a thing. Now I had my confirmation. I knew for sure where Joycie was.

I started back to my old ways, trailing after Joycie. But this time, I didn't let her see me. I knew all the places she went to and where she hung out. When she was by herself and when she was with somebody. She was thirteen now and getting prettier every day. Looking more like a sexy little baby doll, with her budding breasts, plump ass, and long blond hair. When the time was right, I'd make my move.

The gas-station job didn't pay enough to barely live on, but I managed to skim a little out of the register when the old man who owned the place wasn't around. The station only closed on Sundays, so in late October, I took advantage of my day off and headed over to Cedar Key to do some fishin'. But my old truck started to give out on me just outside of Dunellen. I cursed as it sputtered to a stop on the two-lane concrete road.

Hell no. Don't die on me now, baby. There ain't nothing out here on this God-forsaken road. That old truck didn't listen to me. It took one last gasp and cut off, rolling silently as I guided it to the soft sandy shoulder of the road. *Oh shit.*

I got out and raised the hood. Wasn't anything I could do. I'd known this had been comin' for some time. I lowered the tailgate and sat on it, swinging my legs. I had some coffee in a thermos, but now that the sun was up good, it was too hot for that. I'd planned on picking up something cold to drink, maybe some soda crackers and Vienna sausages when I got to a bait shop. They all had that in stock, just for us day fishermen. Just have to wait it out, I guess. If and when somebody came along, I'd raise my arms and wave 'em down. That was a big *if* out on this road.

I looked around; the palmetto scrub went on as far as the eye could see. I was no hunter, but I recognized the short, wavy parallel lines that followed in the sand beside the road. From the looks of them, it had to be at least a six-footer. Goddamned snakes. I couldn't stand 'em. I looked all around under my feet, then hopped off the tailgate and looked under the truck before I got back up there, bending my knees and putting my feet up on the edge. No more dangling my feet down for snake bait.

Maybe an hour later, after nearly dozing off, the sound of an approaching vehicle got my attention. As I squinted east into the sun, the dark blot got bigger and bigger. *Oh, hell. That's a big old Caddy. They ain't gonna stop for me.* Still, I stood up, waved my hat in my hand, and raised my stump in the air, too. Yep. Just as I thought. The Caddy barely slowed before accelerating faster, passing me by after getting a good look. I got a good look, too. A big white-haired man in a suit, smoking a cigar. On the passenger side, a beehived, brassy blonde with giant black sunglasses trying to smoke a cigarette in the wind from the rolled-down window. Both averted their eyes and pretended I didn't exist.

Didn't surprise me. I knew the type. Rolling in so much dough that they had no idea what it was like to scrape by. Didn't want to dirty up that nice Caddy with the likes of me. Probably scared I'd slit their necks, take off with the car and their money, leaving their bodies for the buzzards. They wouldn't be far off, either. Wouldn't bother me. This old world could do with a few less fat rich men.

The woman, on the other hand, I might have had a little fun with her first. It was often amusing how women weren't afraid of me. Didn't take me seriously. With my slight build and only one arm, how could I be dangerous? It always surprised them what I could do and what I could make them do. A knife, a gun, hell, even my one good fist could be pretty convincing. Spittin' on the ground, I got back onto the tailgate and picked up my feet. There'd be another chance. For a ride? For a woman? For a killing? Hell, maybe for all three.

JOYCIE

Fall 1962

I LIKED IT IN FLORIDA. WE'D ARRIVED A COUPLE OF DAYS BEFORE school was to start. Pulling up at Aunt Rene's, where we were going to stay for a few days, I was bouncing up and down. The truck barely stopped before I jumped out and ran into Marybeth's waiting arms.

"Hey, Joycie! I can't believe you're finally here." Marybeth hugged me tight.

"I am so wound up—I can't wait for school to start. Well, maybe I'm a little nervous, but I know it's gonna be great."

My other cousin Marsha had joined the group hug now and was babbling about school.

"It's going to be so much fun. You'll be in my same class. I can't wait to introduce you to everybody."

I was relieved to hear that. "I'm so glad I'll know somebody, at least. I hope your friends will like me."

"Don't worry about that," Marsha said. "They're going to love you just like we do." They both squeezed me tighter.

Being at Rene's was only temporary, but that was okay. I adored being with my cousins Marybeth and Marsha. It was like having my own sisters. We spent the rest of that day getting settled in. The next day, Aunt Rene took Mama and all three of us girls by the school to get me signed up, and then we went into Ocala for a shopping trip. New shoes, underwear, and then, to my surprise, practically a whole new wardrobe. Two dresses, skirts, blouses, shorts, and a bathing suit. Mama said I was a young lady now, starting out in a new place, and I deserved to have new things. I preened and turned as I walked out of the fitting rooms at the Lerner Shop, modeling each new outfit. I felt like a queen.

The big first day of school finally arrived. It was a relief that Marsha and me were in the same classes. It was like having a ready-made friend, even if she was outgoing and already knew everybody and I was the wallflower.

"Hey, y'all, this is my cousin Joycie from Georgia," she told everybody.

"Hello." I smiled but didn't say much. The other girls were nice enough, while some of the boys did seem to be checking me out. By lunchtime, the girls had warmed up. They were friendly but teasing me a little, too.

"Oh, Joycie, you're so pretty! You're gonna steal all our boyfriends."

Remembering what Mama had told me about boys, seeds, and all that hurtin', I just smiled and said, "Don't worry, not interested."

They exchanged sideways looks, and then this one girl, a very developed blonde named Peggy, giggled. "Oh, you will be," she said. "Just give it time."

I blushed and looked down, not having experience with that kind of banter. I was more embarrassed than flattered, remembering Mama's warning. Over the next few days, I kept my nose in my books and pretended not to hear or see any boys that came within ten feet of me.

After a couple of weeks, Daddy arranged for us to move into Aunt Lila's small rental house just about a mile away from Aunt Rene's. Not nearly so nice, but it was furnished decently, clean, and neat, and I'd have my own room. Most of the time, Daddy would take me to school on his way to work, but it was close enough that I could walk home if I couldn't get a ride. Mama got a job cashiering at the Winn-Dixie and was always bringing home something good to eat. Plus, she started giving me an allowance. That opened a whole new social life for me. I could buy lipstick or gum, but I was careful not to let Mama or Daddy see me with either. It was their opinion that both were of the devil. I went to football games, movies, and the skating rink with my cousins and new friends. On Sundays, we went to church. Surrounded by my now-big family, I was happy at school and happy at home. The move to Florida had been the best thing that had ever happened to me. Until.

One evening in January, I was walking home from the skating rink. Marsha and me had just separated at the corner, and it was only about a block down to my house. It was not yet completely dark, and the air was cool in the purpling evening, the smell of far-off rain promising a shower later. That was about the worst winter weather that could be expected in middle Florida. It seemed unusually quiet until the low purr of a vehicle came up somewhere behind me. Pulling my sweater close, I glanced around but didn't recognize the big black car and couldn't see the driver in the shadowy interior. Shrugging, I picked up my pace and kept going. I was home and in the door in just a minute or two. I would never have given that car another thought had it not been for what happened the next afternoon. Catching a ride home from school with Marybeth, who now had her license and a secondhand car, six of us girls were laughing and carrying on as she took the long way home just so we could cruise around our neighborhood. It was Marsha who first noticed the black car behind us.

"Hey, y'all, look at that creepy car behind us."

With that, all of us except Marybeth, who squinted into the rearview mirror, turned our heads to look. I couldn't make out much of the driver's face, but the car looked familiar.

Sharlene had a better view and chimed in. "Ewww. Even that old man driving looks creepy. How long's he been back there?"

"I really hadn't noticed," said Marybeth. "Let's turn up here and see if he follows us."

Sure enough, when we turned at the next street, he turned right after us. At the turn, I got a better look. Although I still couldn't see the face in detail, I thought the man looked a little like somebody I'd seen before. As Marybeth sped up a little, he did too. "Damn," she said under her breath.

Peggy, in the front passenger-window seat, gave the next direction. "Marybeth, turn again at the next corner. Don't put on your blinker. Just do it at the last minute."

"All right, Peggy. Girls, y'all hang on. We're gonna take this corner fast."

Despite bracing ourselves, Marsha, Sharlene, and me all leaned hard into each other at the next turn, then were thrown back as Marybeth stepped on the gas and the tires squealed. When she slowed up and looked in the mirror, we all giggled in nervous relief. "He's gone now. That'll show him not to mess with us."

"Probably some pervert, just trying to spook us," Marsha said nonchalantly.

"Well, I'm not spooked," said Sharlene. "But I'm glad he's gone just the same."

I hadn't spoken during this whole escapade. The familiarity of the car and the man's face were bugging me. There was a quiver in my stomach and an ominous throb in my head, but I couldn't put my finger on why it was bothering me.

"Oh, hell," said Peggy. "There he is again."

No giggling this time. The car had pulled out from a side street and was now following closer. Suddenly, the car sped up and passed us, nearly close enough to run us off the road. There was no mistaking what I saw then. A devious grin on a face I immediately recognized, and the stump of an arm raising a phantom fist.

BESSIE

February 1963

FLORIDA HAD BEEN GOOD FOR ALL OF US. I LOVED HAVING MY sisters Lila and Rene close by, Hampton was in good spirits working for Jimmy, and Joycie had come out of her shell. She liked school and had made friends. She didn't seem interested in boys, but that was fine with me. Plenty of time for that later. I liked my little part-time job at the Winn-Dixie. It gave me something to do and got me out of the house. The bit of extra income was nice, too. We were able to afford some things we'd never had before, like store-bought Sunday clothes for church. Instead of a wild turkey full of birdshot for Thanksgiving, there was a real Butterball. And at Christmas, the gifts were wrapped in shiny, printed colored paper instead of dull butcher-shop white.

All seemed fine and dandy until around the end of January. Joycie started complaining of aches and pains and didn't want to go to school. Sometimes it was her stomach, other times her head, and still other times unbearable cramps. And it wasn't just school. She quit going to the ball games, the skating rink, friends' houses, or cruising with Marybeth. She retreated back inside herself, like the nearly silent shadow she'd been back in Albany. It was like she was a tiny, cooped-up animal that had experienced a season of glorious freedom only to crawl back into its cage and huddle in the corner.

I decided I'd talk to my sister Rene about it after church on Sunday. Maybe Marybeth or Marsha knew something.

On Sunday, we made Joycie get up and come to church with us. She didn't want to, but I reminded her that was part of her allowance. She mumbled something about not needing an allowance anymore, but in a few minutes, she dragged herself out of her room, dressed for church, acting more like she was headed to a funeral. After the service let out, she went straight to the truck and got in while all the other young folks stood around their spot by the side door, cutting up, laughing and talking. It was one of the rare times the boys and girls mingled. There were more than a few shy grins, flirty glances, and even sometimes a brief hand-holding that disappeared as soon as an adult looked that way.

I managed to get Rene off by herself, no small feat in the traditional after-preachin' gossip-and-brag-fest of a small country church. The gravelly sand of the churchyard wasn't too hot this time of year, but I still pulled Rene over to the shade of a big oak dripping with Spanish moss.

"What is it, Bessie? Why are you dragging me over here? I wanted to hear about Old Man Johnson gettin' locked up last week. I heard his wife said he tried to shoot her daddy."

"Never mind Old Man Johnson, Rene. I got something more important to talk about. It's about Joycie."

"Joycie? What's wrong? Is she in some kind of trouble? Marybeth said—"

I grabbed her arm. "What did Marybeth say? I'm worried sick. Joycie was doing so well, seemed so happy, and all of a sudden, she's got aches and pains, won't come out of her room. She's missed days and days of school, too."

"Well, Marybeth said she wouldn't go riding around with them, or to the skating rink, or the Tastee Freeze, or the ball games. Said she won't talk much at school or lunch. Said she's acting like a different person. The other girls think she's turned stuck-up and don't give her the time of day anymore. They don't know what's got into her."

I tried to keep the tears that were brimming in my eyes from rolling down my cheeks. Hearing somebody else describe how our baby girl'd been acting made it a lot more real. It wasn't just me and Ham's imagination. I dug in my pocketbook for a Kleenex, finally finding an old crumpled one, and dabbed at my eyes.

"Oh, Rene, I don't know what to do. What do you think could be wrong? You have girls, but this is all new territory to me."

Rene patted my shoulder awkwardly. "There there now, Bess, it'll be okay. It can't be that bad. You know how teenaged girls can be. Remember when we were that age? All pouty and moody. Maybe it's just hormones. I wouldn't worry so much about it. That's what I told Marybeth."

"But that's just it, Rene. Joycie's acted like this before. Even way back when she was a little bitty thing. It's like she's hiding from something—like she doesn't even want to exist. Even when she does come out of her room and walks through the house, her feet don't make a sound, and she's all hunkered down, shoulders bent forward, head hung low, hair covering her face. Almost like she's trying to be invisible, and she nearly is! Not eating enough to keep a bird alive. I can tell she's lost weight. Her clothes are loose on her like they're on a wire hanger. Me and Ham have seen this before." Now my tears were falling freely, rolling like raindrops down a windowpane.

"Oh, Bessie, don't cry. It'll be all right. Just give it some time." She hugged me close.

"I don't know, Rene. I just don't know. I think there's more to this than winter blues."

"I'm sure it will be fine, Bessie. I'll tell my girls to try and get her more involved in something."

We hugged, and I gave my eyes a final dab. "Thank you, Rene. I'm so glad to be down here with you and Lila. I don't know what I'd do without y'all."

"I know, Bess. We're glad, too. I know it's not easy on you and Hampton raising a teenager at this point in your lives. Who'd have ever thought . . . well, nevermind that. We're here for you—just call me up if you need to talk or anything. I love you, Sis."

"Thank you, honey. I'm probably just being a silly old woman. Thanks for listening. You can get back to your hen party now." I gave Rene another hug and scooted her back towards the young ladies.

Rene tripped over to the group. Children darted in and out, aggravating their mamas.

"Mama, can I go over to Mary's house?"

"Mama, Denny pulled my hair!"

"Mama, I'm starving."

Across the churchyard, a group of older women whose kids were grown and gone stood and talked leisurely, enjoying their matronly status, my older sister Lila among them. Normally, I would have been over there with them. Lila gave me the stink-eye. I knew what it meant. What was I doing off by myself, dabbing at my eyes, having a private conversation with Rene? Her raised eyebrows meant I had broken an unspoken protocol. Well, so be it. I didn't feel like listening to those old women or adding my two cents' worth to their opinionated prattle. I sent Lila a halfhearted wave and trudged off to the truck. I squeezed into the front beside Joycie, and she scrunched up, making herself as small as possible. We did not speak a word. I let her be, the silence settling in between us as though neither one of us were there.

HAMPTON

February 1963

MOVING TO FLORIDA WAS ONE OF THE BEST THINGS THAT EVER happened for me, Bessie, and Joycie. At least it *had been*. Along about the end of January, Joycie started changing back to her old ways, but even worse than before. Me and Bessie talked about it but were at a loss as to what to do. The weeks crawled by as the house got more and more quiet. One evening after work, me and Jimmy had just finished making plans to complete a project when Jimmy said something that hit me like a lightnin' bolt out of a blue sky.

"By the way, Uncle Ham. There's something I've been meaning to tell you. Could be there ain't nothing to it, but then again, I know how you are about your boy Richard comin' around, so I thought you ought to know."

It felt like a grapefruit was coming up in my throat. A big breath whooshed out of me, and all my muscles clenched tighter than a wet knot. "What? What is it? What about Richard?"

"Well, one of my crew lives over near old man Dumas's gas station. He was telling me Dumas had a guy working for him, a small runt-like man he called Richard. Said this Richard fellow just had one arm. When my boy asked him if he lost it in the war, he said naw, it was a meat-cuttin' accident. I thought that was a mighty strange coincidence."

"Lord God! That can't be no coincidence. And it might explain a few things that's been going on at our house."

"Yeah, Rene told me how worried you and Bessie were about Joycie. I hate to be the bearer of bad news, but if that guy is your Richard, I don't have to tell you that can't be good. I'm sorry to have to be the one to tell you."

"No, Jimmy. You done the right thing. Wish I'd known sooner."

"We can't be sure, Ham."

"I'll damn well make sure. And if it is him, and it sounds like it is, he'll wish he never came within a hundred miles of here. Thank you, Jimmy. I've got things to do. I'll see you in the morning."

"All right, Ham, but you take care of yourself, hear? We don't need nothing bad happenin' around here. Promise?"

"Won't be nothing bad on my account. But I can't speak for nobody else. Goodnight."

I tipped my hat at Jimmy and wobbled my way to my truck. My muscles had let go, and I was limp as a dishrag. I couldn't do anything in this condition. I'd have to take my time and plot out what to do. If I were a drinkin' man, I'd head for the nearest beer joint, but I just wanted to go home.

It was quiet when I went into the house. Joycie's door was shut, so I figured she was holed up inside her room like usual. On the kitchen table was a plate with a dishtowel tucked around it. Clean dishes, pots, and pans stood neatly in the drying rack. There was a note by the plate.

"Here's your supper, Ham. Me and Joycie already ate. I'll be at Lila's for sewing circle and will get a ride home. Should be around nine."

I lifted the corner of the towel, and there was a cold pork chop, turnip greens, crowder peas, and a wedge of cornbread. A Mason jar with a lid was filled with golden-brown sweet tea.

It was a meal that on any other night would have me chowing down like I hadn't eaten in a week, but not tonight. All I wanted to do was go to bed. Pretend like Jimmy'd never told me anything. Go to sleep. Wake up and not have to talk to anybody, go anywhere, or do anything. I was gettin' too old for this.

In the short, shadowy hall, going to mine and Bessie's room, I passed Joycie's closed door. I nearly raised my hand to knock but thought better of it. Instead, I rested my palm flat against the frame and bowed my head. A revelation came to me. *Maybe this is how she feels. Maybe it's what's making her act this way—wanting to fade away, not exist in this time and place. Dear God, Baby Girl. I hope I'm wrong, but now I think I understand.*

RICHARD

January 1963

After my truck conked out on me last fall, I got a secondhand junker, a big ol' black Plymouth sedan. I knew where Mama, Daddy, and Joycie were living. They wouldn't be looking to find me driving something like that. Now I could take my time and figure out how I was going to get to her, my baby girl. I just wanted to see her and talk to her; after all, she was my daughter. The thing was, if I let myself think about her too long, my thoughts flowed back to those long-ago days when I'd cuddle her on my lap. It'd felt so good. She'd loved me, then, unlike now, when, along with my own mama and daddy, she wanted to disown me. If I could just talk to her, be with her, maybe I could convince her that was all I wanted, her to love me like she had when she was little. She'd look up at me and smile, her baby-soft skin smooth against mine and her hair smelling so sweet. Who could blame a man for getting excited? That was the kind of love you couldn't find just anywhere.

I knew I had to be careful. I didn't want to scare her off, and I especially didn't want her to let on to Mama and Daddy that I was around. They'd probably find out soon enough anyway. It's hard for a one-armed man to hide in plain sight. But if I could be alone with her, have some private time, I could convince her not to give me away. I could resort to pressure if I had to, but it'd be so much better if she could just relax and be with me without being scared.

I knew Mama worked at the Winn-Dixie every afternoon until about five o-clock, Daddy never got home from work before six, and Joycie was usually home from school by three-thirty. That gave me a window of about an hour and a half. I could have her to myself, and nobody would know. Meeting her at her own house, on her own territory, would probably be best in the beginning, then I could convince her to come over to my place.

One of those warm, sunny Florida winter afternoons, I decided it was time. I knew Joycie would recognize my car, since I'd been following her around for weeks. Even halfway waved at her that one time. About three o'clock, I pulled the car out of sight around the back of their house. Jimmying the lock on the back door, I slipped inside the little cinderblock house. It was neat as a pin inside; that was just the way my mama was. Better than the foul-smelling, junky trailer where I lived. I looked around and wondered if I should meet Joycie in the living room, or maybe in her bedroom? Maybe the living room would be best this first time.

I took advantage of the few minutes before she got there to take a look around. Not much to see, just the kitchen with the green vinyl dinette table and chairs, the living room, a front bedroom that had to be Mama and Daddy's, a plain, tiny bathroom, and the second bedroom that was obviously Joycie's. Pink ruffly curtains, pink bedspread, and a furry pink rug on the concrete floor. The dresser was covered with little-girl doodads, books, and a picture of Mama and Daddy. The bed was piled high with stuffed animals and pillows. I could just imagine her snuggled down in all that pink fluff, warm and cozy, maybe wearing little shortie pajamas with kittens or puppies or flowers or some none-such. I could settle right in beside her . . .

Snap out of it, man! This was what happened when I let my mind wander. She should be home any minute. I headed back to the living room and settled on the saggy couch. It wasn't long before a key turned in the front door. Not expecting anybody to be home, Joycie came in, shut the door, and turned the inside lock. She'd taken about three steps before she noticed me sitting in the shadows.

"Hey there, darling. Surprised to see your daddy?" A big grin plastered onto my face.

She stood in place like when kids played that swinging statues game. Even in the dim light, I could see the color drain from her face. Her arms were wrapped around a stack of schoolbooks, her fingers turning white as she gripped them in front of her like a shield.

"Been a while, hasn't it? S'pose Mama and Daddy thought they'd spirit you away down here to Florida and I'd never see you again. Is that it?" I stood up, and she took one step sideways. "Oh, come on, baby. Don't you have a hug for your daddy?"

I stretched out my one-and-a-half arms. She took another step sideways towards the bedrooms.

"Cat got your tongue? Say hello to your daddy." I advanced one more step. She bolted toward her bedroom door but didn't quite clear it before I blocked her way. "Now now, is that any way to act? Daddy just wants a visit with his little girl."

I reached my hand out and stroked her hair, then cupped her chin. I could feel and see her tremble. But still not a word from her sweet rosy lips. I rubbed my thumb across their silky plumpness. A single tear slid down her cheek. Damn! Maybe I'd gone too far, touching her like that. Then again, maybe it was a good thing she was a mite scared of me. I could use that to my advantage.

Dropping my hand and stepping aside, I shrugged my shoulders.

"I guess you're just not in the mood for a visit today. Must have took you by surprise. That's all right. You'll get used to seeing me around. In fact, I plan to see quite a bit of you. Course, Mama and Daddy don't need to know about it. You just keep those pretty little lips sealed, and don't tell anybody I was here. I'll leave you be for now, but I'll be back. And I'll expect you to be a little happier to see me next time. I plan on makin' regular visits. Okay, darling?"

I slipped out the back door, got in the car, and drove away. Hoo-wee, I needed a drink, and a woman, too. That little girl had me more steamed up than car windows at a drive-in movie.

JOYCIE

Spring 1963

ORE THAN EVER, I WANTED TO DISAPPEAR. MELT AWAY, SLIDE down into the earth and never return. I could live with the crabs, beetles, and tortoises that inhabited the sandy Florida soil—protected in a shell just like them, citizens of the dark, far away from the evil above. I had always been uneasy around him, but this was something else. The day that Richard had followed Marybeth's car and raised his phantom fist at me had been like an omen, a threat of the horror to come. When I came home from school and found him in our house that first time, I knew I was in the presence of wickedness.

The second time he showed up was when it happened for the first time. An unusually warm, muggy day, the sky was a yellowish green. A strange acrid smell hung in the air, the scent that meant a storm was coming—the kind of weather the old folks called a twirlywind. Richard appeared from nowhere, as he had before, just like tornados do sometimes. Except this time, he wasn't waiting in the living room. I got home, went inside, and dumped my books on the couch. Going into the bathroom to pee, I pulled my dress over my head so I could put on shorts and a T-shirt.

Grabbing a hanger off the hook on the back of the door, I took the dress and hung it on the doorframe of my room. I went straight to my dresser, opened drawers, and rummaged around, finding old shorts and a T-shirt. When I straightened up and looked in the mirror, there he was. My back had been towards my bed the whole time, so my first sight of him was in the mirror. I clutched the clothes to my chest. Richard was leaned back against the headboard of my bed, sneering. His arm rested on his chest, his legs stretched out, his sock-feet crossed. I had the inane thought that at least he had taken off his shoes.

Petrified, I could not move or speak. And I could not tear my eyes away from the mirror.

Richard slowly swung his legs over the side of the bed and turned his body to sit on the edge. "Well, now. What have we here? My little girl's wearing a tight brassiere and pretty pink panties? Looks to me, you're not much of a little girl anymore." He shifted over more towards the head of the bed and patted the space beside him.

"Come on over here, darlin'. Let Daddy get a closer look at you."

I did not move. I could not move.

Now he sprang to his feet, came up behind me, and put his arm around my back. The stump pressed into the side of my breast. His voice, close to my ear this time, growled low.

"I said, let me get a closer look at you."

I couldn't breathe. My eyes clenched shut. His one-handed grip on my other side was digging into my upper arm. He slowly walked me over to the bed and sat me down on the space he'd patted just moments before. I hung my head, not knowing how I'd gotten there. I didn't remember moving my feet or sitting down. Now he stood in front of me. His hand grabbed my chin and tilted my head up, my eyes still clenched shut.

"Look at me, you little bitch!"

I couldn't do it.

His hand released my chin, but the smack that followed came as sudden as a crack of lightning, flinging me sideways across the bed. Before I could comprehend what happened, he was on top of me, crooning.

"I didn't mean it, honey, I didn't mean to hurt you. I just want to show you love, that's all, not hurt you."

Mama's words came floating into my mind. *Some boy might say he loves you . . . wants to show you love . . . don't you let him . . . it hurts . . . it hurts real bad . . . don't let any man or boy get that close to you*—Oh my God! Was that what he wanted? I had to find the power to say no, to get away, to make him leave. I was sobbing now but couldn't make words come out of my mouth.

He continued to croon into my neck. His hand and stump stroking my hair, my face, my arms. The words he spoke seemed to float up to the surface from a long-ago past: *pretty little darling . . . you're so sweet . . . Daddy's little girl . . . so soft and warm . . . doesn't that feel good . . .*

Soon, his body was moving against mine. I wasn't here, but somewhere long past. Not here, not in my bedroom, not thirteen years old. And it did feel good. Then, all of a sudden, it hurt. It felt good, and it hurt . . . *It hurts . . . it hurts real bad . . . Doesn't that feel good.*

"*Please, God, no!*" I whimpered before passing out into a strange dream of pain and pleasure. Then it was over. When he came back, week after week, I knew the Devil walked the Earth.

PART TWO

LOUANN

2017

D ANIEL, YOU COULDN'T HAVE IMAGINED THE HORRORS THAT EVIL
man forced on his own child. It would be years before I would
know, myself. In those days, families didn't air their dirty laundry. They
just bucked up and kept going forward, best they could. What difference
could it have made, anyway? How could a little girl have made sense of it?
How would a body even begin to explain that your biological father was
also your grandfather? It's just too hard to wrap your head around. There's
no tellin' how many folks down South don't know their real origins. We
get told one thing or another, and maybe some of it's true—or none of
it's true. Even if somebody did tell the truth, the idea that a daddy would
do that to his own daughter is such a foreign idea to most people, they
can't grasp it. Easier to tell a lie and let it go—even if it gnaws and festers,
working its vile effect on generations.

It was easy for me to grow up thinking my real daddy was some boy
who'd had his way with Joycie and then run off and left her. After all, I
had Daddy, and he was all I needed. He was everything a girl could want
in a daddy, and I didn't think twice about him being old and gray-haired.
I knew he loved me, and I loved him, and that was enough. Nothing else
mattered as long as I had my daddy. I can't even imagine what it must have
been like when him and Bessie found out Joycie was pregnant. And the
circumstances of how she got that way? Talk about unbearable. I don't
rightly see how they managed to go on, but then, I guess it was because

of me they had no choice. Just like with Joycie, they wouldn't give up one of their own. Now that I'm a mama, too, I can understand that. I swear, Daniel, next to having a mama and daddy that loved me, being a decent mama was all I ever wanted in my life. I came pretty close to screwing that up, but with your help, I've been able to move on. Poor Joycie, she never had a chance.

HAMPTON

April 1963

I T WAS ONE OF THOSE SCENES YOU'LL NEVER FORGET AS LONG AS you live. Bessie was sittin' across from me at the little dinette table on a rainy April morning. For weeks, we'd both been gloomier than two hound dogs without a bone between them. Joycie was once again laid up on the sofa, sick to her stomach, the chipped metal dishpan, crackers, and Co-Cola on the floor beside her. She'd been sick every morning for three weeks. Bessie had finally taken her to the doctor the day before.

"Hampton, I know what's wrong with Joycie."

"You do? Why the hell didn't you say so before now?"

"Shh. Keep your voice down. Let her rest."

I glanced over at Joycie and lowered my voice, then reached across the table and took Bessie's hand in my own. "Well, what is it? What did the doctor say?"

"Promise me you'll stay calm. I need you to be strong, and Joycie does, too."

"I'll be calm if you'll tell me what's wrong. What is it? Is she gonna be okay? It's not the diabetes like Joey, is it?"

"No, it's not diabetes. And it's not cancer or leukemia or any of that stuff."

"Then what in the hell is it, Bessie?"

"Well, you know how she's been sick mostly in the mornings—"

"Oh God, Bessie, what are you trying to say?"

"I've been suspecting for a few weeks. It explains why she got so withdrawn. I don't know why we didn't put two and two together—"

"Damn it! Just say it."

Bessie took a deep breath. "Joycie's pregnant."

I jumped up and sent my chair skidding backwards. I couldn't help it. Bessie jumped up too and came around the table, putting her hands on my arms.

"Now, Hampton, you promised to be calm."

I gritted my teeth and clenched my fists. "Who? What? I'll kill the son of a bitch! I thought you had a talk with her about that. She hasn't even had a boyfriend. How could this happen? She's a good girl." My mind was going back over every boy I'd seen in the last three months. Not that there were many.

Bessie looked up at me. "That's not the worse part, Hampton." Her grip on my arms tightened.

"What do you mean? What could be worse? Isn't a thirteen-year-old being pregnant bad enough?"

"Oh, believe me, it's worse. She didn't do this of her own free will. She was forced."

I couldn't even form any words. I stood still and stared into Bessie's eyes. My heart was stone cold. The look in her eyes was like staring into a pit of grief so deep, I'd never seen such before, not even when our boy Joey had passed.

"There's more, Hampton." Her voice was flat and wooden. "It was Richard, Hampton. It was her own father. Our son. Richard."

I stumbled and sank into the chair. I wasn't usually a cursing man, but my head was filling with the vilest words I could conjure up. *Hell. Shit. Damn. Son of a bitch. God damn. Fuck. Motherfucker. Jesus H. Christ.* After a few seconds, I got up, got my gun from the bedroom, and started to the front door. Bessie could see I was about to boil over with rage. She pulled at my arm and tried to get me to calm down as I marched steadily to the truck.

"Hampton, where are you goin' and why do you need that gun?" Her voice wavered.

I didn't answer and pushed her hand off my arm.

"Hampton, please. Don't go. Come on back inside." Now she sounded panicked.

I stopped and looked at her. "Bessie, take your hands off me. I'm gonna take care of this like I shoulda done years ago. Now let me go."

I left her standing in the yard, hands on the sides of her stricken face, staring after me.

I headed to the other side of town and Dumas's filling station. The big black Plymouth was parked off to the side. I didn't drive over the ringer but pulled up next to the rundown building. That was when I saw him.

Richard strolled out of the building, wiping his hand on a work rag. As he came around to my driver's side window, I threw back the door, nearly hitting him, and stepped out.

"Whoa there!" He backed off and put both arms in the air, the pitiful stump greasy and grotesque.

I slammed the truck door and started walking towards him. My jaw was grinding, my steps heavy, my fists tight.

"Nice to see you, too, Daddy."

He barely got the words out before I landed a right hook that sent him flying backward, landing his ass on the ground. "Ain't nothing nice here, Richard. What in the hell do you think you're doing?"

Getting to his feet and rubbing his shoulder where the punch had landed, he kept talking like everything was normal.

"Doing? Why, I work here. Takin' care of things for old man Dumas. Got me a trailer out back to live in. This Florida weather agrees with me. Might be stayin' around a while."

"I don't think so, you son of a bitch. We know what you done to Joycie. If you don't disappear, I'll kill you myself. I'll take you out, even if you are my own boy. Do you understand what I'm sayin'? If you stick around, you're gonna be a dead man."

"Oh, Daddy, I understand all right. You and Mama took out Joey, filling him up on sugar 'til the diabetes did him in. Now you'd just as soon take me out, too, since you've got my baby girl. Pretty little thing she's turned out to be, ain't she? Only decent thing I've ever had in my life. All I wanted was to be a real daddy for her. But no, you and Mama wanted her all to yourself. Guess I showed you!"

He was babbling like an idiot. I threw another punch. Richard staggered back but stayed upright.

"You're not fit to be anybody's daddy, Richard. In fact, I don't know what you are fit for. You are one sick man. Stay away from Joycie, Bessie, and me. And once that new baby's here, you better stay away from it, too. Got it?"

I had his attention now.

"New baby?" The light dawned across Richard's face. "So that explains why Joycie ain't been feeling up to par." He rubbed his grizzly face with his one hand. "Well, what a surprise. Seems like I just can't help making babies." A sly smile slithered across his face.

That was when I lost it. Both fists came up, and next thing I knew, Richard was groveling in the dirt like the snake he was. He was down but not out. He squinted up at me, the sun right in his eyes.

"You touch me again, Daddy, and I swear I'll kill you. You, Mama, Joycie, and that bastard baby, too. I'll kill you all."

"Don't think so, Richard. 'Cause if I ever lay eyes on you again, as long as I live, I swear I'll kill you first."

BESSIE

Fall 1963 to Winter 1964

OUR GIRL JOYCIE, THE LIGHT OF OUR LIVES, THIRTEEN YEARS OLD, had been raped by her own father and was carrying his child. Of course, we didn't want to make it public knowledge about the baby's father, but close family members knew the truth. Lila and Rene were not surprised in the least. There was an unspoken understanding that it would not be acknowledged or talked about that Richard was the father. It also went without saying that we would see Joycie through the pregnancy and help raise the baby. Me and Hampton had serious decisions to make. Knowing Richard was banned by law from Houston County, we moved back to Albany. We wanted Joycie safe and under a doctor's care. She was so young to be having a baby.

We took up our old business running the meat market and settled in, waiting for the baby to be born, assuring Joycie we would take care of her and the baby, protecting them both from Richard. We let anybody who didn't know the truth think she'd gotten into trouble with some boy in Florida who'd run off and left her. Let them say what they would; we would protect our own. That was the way families did things.

Joycie was pitiful. Of course, she didn't go to school that fall, so she was at home with us. She never spoke. Her eyes were dull. Only a blank, unseeing expression. Her skin was pale, mostly because she rarely went outdoors. When she moved, she was like a phantom floating on air: no sound, no disturbance of the space around her. Her huge bloated belly on her thin little legs drifted around like a carnival balloon on a stick. If it weren't so hideous, it would be comical; she might as well have been the walking dead.

As the time drew near, the family rallied around us. Since Richard had threatened to kill all of us, even Joycie and the baby, we wanted to have reinforcements. The aunts, uncles, and cousins all came up from Florida like a motorcade of vehicles when somebody important comes to town. When the day finally arrived, we headed to the little county hospital where Joycie herself had been born, barely fourteen years before. It was one of the coldest days ever recorded in Albany. We had family members at the main hospital entrance, in the hallway where Joycie's room was, and at the nursery. Me and Hampton never left her bedside unless it was to talk to the doctor. Thank God, there was no sign of Richard.

On February 29th, 1964, our granddaughter Joycie, at age fourteen and a half, gave birth to our first great-grandchild, Louann. It seemed incomprehensible that the baby could be both our granddaughter and our great-granddaughter. To Louann, as we had been to Joycie, we would always be Mama and Daddy, and she would always be our baby.

Joycie did not fare well. After the birth, the doctor spoke to us in the hallway with a grim expression. "Mr. and Mrs. Walker, Joycie is only a child herself. She's had a difficult time and lost a great deal of blood. It took longer than usual for her to come out of the twilight sleep."

I tried to relieve Hampton of some of the more female-related talk. "I understand, doctor. I wasn't so young, but I know a new mother has special needs. I'll take good care of Joycie. You don't have to worry about that."

"I'm sure you will do your best, Mrs. Walker. But this is almost a criminal case." The doctor clearly intended to impress on Hampton the seriousness of the situation. "Mr. Walker, I know it's none of my business, but you ought to know how dangerous this whole birth was for both Joycie and the baby. I don't see how you can let the man or boy responsible for this off the hook. It could have easily cost Joycie her life, and still may."

His tone was chastising, and I got the feeling he was disapproving of not just whoever had gotten her pregnant but Joycie, me, and Hampton, too. This shaming just about broke me. The tears came, and I was wringing my hands, embarrassed and mad at the same time. I looked up at Hampton. He drew himself up and faced the doctor. His pinched face and set jaw told me he felt the same way, but he was going to defend us. Hampton Walker was a proud man and would not be talked down to. He knew the doctor was fishing for some confirmation about who the father of the baby was, and he was not about to let on. "Yes, sir, I understand your point of view. Thank you for taking care of Joycie and the baby. I promise you we'll look after them both just fine."

But the doctor wasn't finished with his judgmental attitude. "You can expect an unusually long recovery for Joycie. She's exhausted. It could take months for her to get over this. And she's going to be in no condition to take care of a baby, even if she wants to, much less herself. I know you and Mrs. Walker have your hearts in the right place, but it's not going to be easy on you two."

Hampton put his arm around me protectively and looked the doctor squarely in the eye. "For all practical purposes, Doctor, this is our baby, and Joycie is our child. I can assure you we will provide for them. We are prepared to give them the love and care they deserve."

The doctor gave a small sigh and stuck out his hand to Hampton. Then he patted me on the shoulder. In a kinder voice, he said, "I believe you, Mr. and Mrs. Walker, I really do. But I don't envy you. And I have no doubt you will do your best for these two girls."

JOYCIE

February 1964

"**C**OME ON, JOYCIE, WAKE UP, BABY. THAT'S IT, OPEN YOUR EYES! Time to wake up."

Through the lash-lined split of my eyelids, I saw bright white lights and blurry faces. The voices sounded like they were coming from somewhere far away, maybe down inside a damp, dark well. Then came a deeper voice, sounding closer, somewhere near my ear.

"Baby Girl, it's Daddy. Come on, now, wake up for me. You've been sleeping for days. Come on now, honey, wake up. Time to go home."

I felt Daddy's arms slip under me and wrap me in a cozy blanket. My eyelids closed. The rocking motion of Daddy carrying me as he walked down the hall of the hospital was pleasant, like floating in a boat on a lazy, slow river. I gave myself over to the muffled voices and the swaying motion. It wasn't until he stepped outside into the frigid air that I awoke fully. My eyes flew open, and I was blinded by rays of sunshine piercing the neon-blue sky. It's a light that only happens on the coldest, clearest winter days in the South: sharp, white, and flashing like a razor, but oh so cold.

I gasped as the light and cold hit my face. Mama reached over and tucked the blanket tighter around me. "It's all right, honey. You'll be home in just a few minutes, tucked warm and cozy in your own bed. Just close your eyes for now, and we'll be there soon."

Daddy laid me across the bench seat of the pickup. It was toasty warm where he'd had the engine running to heat it up. With my head in his lap and my legs stretched across Mama's, I started to dream of those trips to Florida. Only this time, something wasn't quite right. A dull, throbbing ache wracked my body. Every bump in the road felt like I was being pounded all over my body. I didn't realize that the harrowing moans I heard were coming from my own lips.

The next time I woke up, I was alone in my own bed. Lying on my side, facing the wall, awareness slowly came over me, and I realized I was home in our house in Albany. It was warm and quiet. It was daytime, but the curtains were pulled closed against the bright winter light. I opened my eyes, sensing something different. There was a dry, dusty scent mixed with the smell of clean laundry and a whiff of something sweet and oily. As I rolled over, the throbbing ache returned, and I winced, squeezing my eyes closed. When I opened my eyes again, my gaze landed on something foreign in my otherwise familiar room.

It was a funny-looking white basket-type thing over by the wall. It had thin stick legs and a rounded hood. On the dresser were stacks and stacks of white folded cloths, tubes, jars, and bottles of things. My eyes traveled past these to a piece of furniture. The old upholstered rocking chair that had always sat in the living room near the floor lamp, with Mama's sewing basket on the floor right beside it, was in my room. Definitely out of place. Why? What was it doing in my room? I never sat in it in the living room; why would I want it in here?

Realization began to dawn.

The door squeaked open, and Daddy's face appeared. "You awake?"

"I guess so."

He came in and helped me sit up, plumping the pillow and adjusting my cover so I could lean back against the bedstead. "I'll be right back," he said.

Daddy and Mama appeared at my door, Mama holding a wrapped bundle in her arms. She came over and sat on the edge of my bed, tilting the bundle up.

"Here she is. Here's your daughter, Joycie. Beautiful little Louann. She's perfect." Mama's voice was soft and reverent, almost as though she were praying.

I shrank back against my pillows and turned my head. I could not force myself to look. Every fiber of my being recoiled at the idea of that baby. I was supposed to love my own baby, wasn't I? Aren't all mothers supposed to love their babies? A mother? I was a mother? *But I'm only fourteen. I'm not a mother. It can't be. I don't want to. I couldn't help it.* The tears began to flow. Then the sobs. "Get it away from me! Take it out. I . . . don't . . . want . . . it." The words choked out. I turned to look at Daddy. His face was horror-stricken: mouth hanging open, eyes wide, tears brimming. "Daddy, make her take it away."

A deep intake of breath from Mama. "But Joycie . . . you don't mean that."

I looked her straight in the face, avoiding the sight of the bundle in her arms. "Yes, I do. Take it away. I don't want it."

Now Mama was as frightened as Daddy. They looked at each other, faces frozen. Couldn't they understand? I didn't want anything to do with that baby. All I could see when I looked at her was Richard's evil face. All I could feel was pain, hurt, and shame. My eyes pleaded with them to take her away.

Daddy's face softened, and, in a calm voice, he said, "Come on, Bessie, let's go."

"But, Hampton, the baby . . ." I could hear the quiver in Mama's voice.

Daddy's calm voice broke this time. "Come on, Bessie. We'll try again later."

As they left the room and closed the door, the tears rolled down my cheeks. *Don't bother,* I thought. *Don't bother.*

I couldn't remember anything about having the baby. I thought that maybe if I could, I might feel differently towards her, but it was a big black hole. I had gone to sleep with bad cramps, and when I'd come to three days later, they had told me I had a little girl.

Now, here I was, at home with Mama, Daddy, and a baby. I had to get away. *That's it, I'll run away.* As I struggled to stand up, the pain hit me. It hurt so bad.

"Please, God, no," I whimpered before drifting away into restless sleep.

HAMPTON

1965

M E AND BESSIE KNEW IT MIGHT TAKE A WHILE FOR JOYCIE TO warm up to the idea of being a mother, but we figured things would get better eventually. We figured wrong. As time went on, Joycie took even less interest in her child. In fact, she acted like she couldn't stand her.

When Louann was still a little baby and it was time for a feeding, Bessie would try to get Joycie to feed her. "Here you go, Joycie: little Louann is ready for her bottle. I got it all ready for you."

Joycie, sitting up in her bed, thumbing through a magazine, would sigh with exasperation. "I've already told you, I don't know how to feed a baby, and I don't want to learn. Take her away," Joycie would say as she pushed away the bundle Bessie was holding out to her.

As Louann got bigger, we'd try to get Joycie involved with her. I'd say, "Look, Joycie, Louann's sitting up by herself."

Joycie wouldn't even look. She'd just mumble, "Uh-huh." Joycie never spoke to her, played with her, changed a diaper, or gave her a bath. It was as though Louann didn't exist.

Of course, we hoped and prayed that things would change. Me and Bessie doted on Louann, giving her more love and care than any real mama and daddy. We still loved Joycie and tried to be understanding, but it was getting harder by the day. She was pushing us away, closing herself off as she had done in the past. We chalked it up to the horrors she had been put through by Richard. Who knew what kind of damage a thing like that did to a child?

Louann, on the other hand, was a joy. Given the circumstances, we were naturally concerned. I'd heard tragic stories of simple-minded idiots being born to parents who were closely related, so I kept an eye out for trouble without letting Bessie know that I was worried. I should have known better.

"Hampton?" Bessie said one night after we'd gone to bed.

"What is it, honey?"

"Do you think Louann is all right?"

"What do you mean, Bessie? Of course she's all right. She's sleeping sound in her crib."

"I don't mean is she asleep. I mean, you know, do you think she's all right?"

"Bessie, you're talking in riddles. What are you trying to say?"

"I mean do you think she's all right . . . in the head, I mean."

I sat up in bed and turned on the lamp. "Damn, Bessie. What are you talking about?"

"Well, I've heard that babies like her—sometimes they're not right in the head."

"What do you mean, babies like her? Ain't nothing wrong with her."

"You know what I'm talking about. Don't pretend you don't. I don't mean to be a gossip, but folks say that retarded baby of Mrs. Brown's is like that cause her brother is really his daddy. I get to thinkin' sometimes, what if Louann can't learn once she starts school, or what if she starts doing crazy things like banging her head?"

I looked at Bessie and put my hands on her shoulders. "Look, honey. I don't want you to worry. I do know what you're talking about. I used to worry about it, too. I've been keeping my eye on her for anything out of the ordinary. Far as I can tell, she's doing everything just like any other child."

"I suppose so, Hampton. But it still worries me. Now don't go gettin' mad, but last time we was at the doctor's for her check-up, I made sure to ask if she was doing everything she was supposed to do, you know, for a child her age. That doctor looked at me kinda funny and said of course she was, she was ahead of the timeline if anything, and why would I be worried about that?"

"You asked the doctor about her? Good God, Bessie. Leave well enough alone. We don't want to raise any suspicions or invite trouble where there ain't none."

"I know, Hampton, I just—"

"That doctor says she's just fine, and that's all I need to know. Quit worrying and go to sleep."

"All right, Hampton, if you say so. I just worry, that's all."

"Well, you can quit worrying. Go to sleep."

ONE SPRING AFTERNOON, not long after Louann had turned a year old and Bessie had relaxed about her being "all right in the head," a letter came, postmarked "Orlando." I recognized the handwriting immediately. I felt bile rise in my throat. I turned it over and over, wondering if I should even open it. There had been no word from or about Richard since we'd left Florida almost two years ago now. Why now?

I instinctively looked up and down the narrow little street where we lived. How did he even know our address? Was he in Albany? Had he been watching us? Had he seen Joycie or Louann? I went in the house, locked the doors and windows, and pulled the shades. Joycie and Louann were both sleeping. I called Bessie back to our bedroom, where I stood holding the unopened letter in my hands. When she saw it and recognized the handwriting, she sank down onto the bed.

"Go ahead," Bessie said. "Read it."

"You sure? We don't have to."

She rubbed her forehead. "Yes. Might as well. He can't do nothing worse than's already been done. At least, I don't think so. Go ahead, read it."

I ripped open the letter and started reading, silently, to myself.

"What? What is it, Ham? What does he want? It's not about the baby, is it? Or Joycie?"

"It's all right, Bessie. At least I think so. Here, read for yourself."

Handing the letter over, I sat beside Bessie on the edge of the bed. She adjusted her reading glasses and read out loud:

Dear Daddy and Mama,

I know you didn't expect to hear from me. Just thought you ought to know you have another grandchild. A little boy this time. His name is Richie and he was born March 18. Me and his mother, Helen, are taking him and moving to California, so you don't have to worry about me coming around. But I still know where to find you.

Your son,
Richard

Bessie and me looked at each other, and I spoke first. "I don't know what to say."

"I do," she replied. "He's going as far away as he possibly can. Praise God. Maybe he'll stay there forever."

"Maybe so. But another grandbaby? A little boy?" I rubbed at the burning in my eyes.

Bessie put her hand on my arm. "I know, Ham, I know. But maybe it's for the best."

I could only nod, but I saw the silent tear slide down her cheek, too.

"Hampton?"

"What is it, darlin'?"

"I think it best we don't mention this to Joycie, don't you?"

"God, yes. The less she knows about Richard, the better, as far as I'm concerned."

JOYCIE

August 1965

I WAS ABOUT TO GO STIR CRAZY COOPED UP IN THAT LITTLE HOUSE with Mama, Daddy, and that baby. Course, she wasn't a baby anymore. Just the same, I had no interest in being her mama. Every once in a while, I'd look at her and try to feel love in my heart, but couldn't bring myself to do it. What was I going to do? I hadn't gone back to school after she'd been born, and there were no jobs around Albany. Mama and Daddy didn't push me about takin' care of Louann, but I did try to help out around the house and in the meat market if it got busy. I knew it was exhausting for Mama to run around after the baby, and even though I felt bad about that, it wasn't enough to make me want to take care of her.

What would my life have been like if it weren't for Richard—if it weren't for Louann? It was all one big nightmare. Sometimes, I'd daydream about those few months before it had started. That had been the happiest time of my life. Living in Florida, close to my cousins, being a regular kid doing regular kid things. One day, I got an idea in my head. If only I could convince Mama and Daddy.

After Louann was in bed and the house was quiet, Mama and Daddy was sittin' in the living room, the TV on low and both of them about to nod off to sleep. I usually stayed to myself in my room, so I'm sure they were surprised when I walked in.

"Mama? Daddy?"

Daddy stirred, and Mama dropped her sewing on her lap. They both looked up at me, frowning in confusion.

In her tired voice, Mama said, "What is it, Joycie? Are you all right?"

I walked over and sat on the other end of the sofa from Daddy. "Yeah, I'm okay, I guess. I've been thinking about something, though. Can we talk?"

That got Daddy's attention. "Is it about Louann?"

Shit. Of course they'd think it was about that baby. Nothing was ever about me anymore. I was going to have to get straight to the point. "Well, not exactly. I know y'all are taking care of her, and I couldn't ask for more than that. That's why I was thinking. I know it's a lot, having me and her both here. I'm sixteen now, and I could be pretty much on my own, with a little bit of help."

Daddy's brows shot up, and Mama's mouth fell open. Mama was the first to speak. "Now wait just a minute, missy. Sixteen ain't grown. What are you gettin' at? This sounds like crazy talk."

Daddy started to say something, but I cut him off. "Just listen—I've got a plan." I jumped up from the couch and walked back and forth. I had convinced myself this would work, and the words came tumbling out, faster and faster. "See, I was remembering how the happiest time of my life was down in Florida in the summers and those few months we lived there before . . . well, before all that happened. Why couldn't I go down there and live? I'd be out of your way; maybe I could get a job, or maybe I could go back to school. I'm sure I could live with Aunt Rene or Aunt Lila for a while. I'd be willing to support myself. It wouldn't cost anybody anything. Every time I look at Louann, all I can think about is what happened. I'm going crazy stuck here. You've got to let me go, or I swear I'll run away. I've got to get out of here!"

The tears started streaming down my face. Mama pulled herself up and lumbered over to me. She put her arms around me and pulled me close. All I could do was sob out the words, "Please, Mama. Please, Daddy. Please. Let me go."

"Oh, Joycie, honey, don't cry." Mama was holding me and stroking my hair. She sat down with me between her and Daddy on the sofa. "You're just having a bad day. It'll be better tomorrow."

I threw her arms away from me and looked at Daddy. "No. It's not just a bad day, and tomorrow will be the same. I swear I'll run away. Then you'll never be able to find me. Just let me go live in Florida—I was happy there. You can call me, and come visit, even bring Louann. I know my aunts and cousins won't mind—they'll be glad to see us all."

Now I wasn't so sure I could convince them with common sense, and I was getting mad. How dare they try to keep me here? Saying I'd run away was only a part of my scare tactic, but now that I'd said it out loud, maybe it wasn't such a bad idea. Tears were still streaming.

Daddy was rubbing his grizzled face, his brow furrowed like he was thinking hard.

"Hmm. Sounds like you've given this quite a bit of thought, Joycie."

A glimmer of hope! "Yes, I have, Daddy. I know it'll work." I glanced back at Mama.

Mama, mouth open, was looking at me like she couldn't believe what she was hearing. "Hampton, you can't seriously—"

Daddy interrupted her. "Now, Bessie. Remember how happy Joycie was when she started school down there? She had friends, she went to church, she did good in school."

I'd only said that part about going back to school to help convince them to let me go, but I could play that up. "Oh, Mama, I'd love to go back to school. I promise I'll finish if I can go live down there."

Worry was etched in the wrinkles on Mama's face. "But, Hampton, what about—"

Daddy cut her off again. "I know what you're thinking, Bessie. But that won't be a problem. Remember the letter?"

I didn't know what letter Daddy was talking about, but I could tell he was leaning in my favor. He looked at me and said, "Joycie, are you sure about this?"

"Yes! Yes, Daddy. I'm sure."

Mama sighed like she was giving in. "Well, I'll have to call Lila and Rene and talk with them. If they say it's okay, we could consider it."

I threw my arms around her neck. "Oh, thank you, thank you, thank you! You won't be sorry, I promise."

I turned to Daddy and did the same thing. "Thank you, Daddy! Thank you."

BESSIE

Christmas 1965

I NEVER DID HAVE A GOOD FEELING ABOUT JOYCIE BEING DOWN there in Florida. Oh, Rene and Lila both said they'd love to have her and that their kids were excited to have Joycie back around. We sent her to Ocala on a bus the week before school was supposed to start. Rene said she'd get her enrolled and take care of everything on that end. We made plans to write and call and promised that we'd make the trip down over Christmas.

With Joycie out of the house, things at home took on a whole new outlook. Me and Hampton took care of little Lou, same as always. We were exhausted all the time, but what could you expect with two old folks in their fifties raising a lively two-year-old? We didn't have the specter of a solemn Joycie ignoring her own baby and moping around the house all the time. Louann didn't miss Joycie; after all, why would she? She seemed happier than ever. We all were in a better frame of mind, not walking around on tiptoes wondering what might set Joycie off or bring on a tirade directed at little Louann.

Still, I had that uneasiness about Joycie on her own. After all, Rene and Lila both worked and had their own kids to look after. Joycie wrote letters every week, and they were filled with what a good time she was having, how much she liked school, and all the new friends she was making. I scrimped and saved enough money to make a long-distance call to Rene about every three weeks just to check up and make sure everything was okay. She always reported that Joycie was doing well at school, helping out around the house, having lots of fun with girlfriends, and even starting to show some interest in boys. Nothing too serious, Rene assured me.

Christmas that year was one of the best. All of us gathered at Rene's house for two weeks of celebrating. One good thing about Christmas in Florida is the little kids can get outside and play, the men can go fishin' or huntin', and us old folks can sit around on chairs outside and enjoy visitin'. Louann was the youngest of the little kids, and they all doted on her, so I got a break from lookin' after her all the time.

I was hoping that after being apart for four months, Joycie might be glad to see little Lou. But I was disappointed; there had been no change in Joycie's attitude toward her baby, though she had changed in other ways. I tried to explain to Rene and Lila what was so different.

"Y'all remember how lively Joycie was that fall when we first moved down here? The way she's acting now reminds me a little bit of that, except it's even more. I ain't never seen her this way. Always laughing, jokin', and carryin' on. She never sits still. And her clothes—I've never seen the likes of such short skirts."

Rene laughed. "Oh, Bessie, you just haven't been around many teenagers these days. All the girls are wearing short skirts. We're all glad to see Joycie having some fun and enjoying herself. Lord knows she's been through enough in her young life. Let her be a kid."

Maybe she was just being a kid, but I was worried it was more than that. "Maybe so, Rene, but what do you think, Lila? Don't she seem a little too, oh, I don't know, *forward*, maybe? Wearing all that makeup and long hair down her back? And especially actin' so boy-crazy? She ain't never been like that."

Lila shrugged. "Oh, I don't know, Bess. I think she's just lettin' loose a little after all she's been through. I don't see that much difference in how she acts from any other sixteen-year-old. She's just having a good time for once in her life."

"Well, sisters, I know I'm an old fogey in a lot of ways, but it just doesn't sit well with me. I'm trustin' y'all to keep a close eye on her. I know y'all got kids of your own, jobs to go to, and men to take care of. It can't be easy to have another one to look after. I hate being up there in Albany and her off down here on her own. Seems like she's a different person down here, and maybe that's not all bad. I s'pose it's better than her moping around at our place."

As though on cue, a loud car pulled up in the driveway and honked. Joycie came runnin' over to where the three of us sat under the big tree in Rene's front yard. "Hey, Mama! Bye, Mama. Bye, Aunt Lila. Bye, Aunt Rene. I'm going off for a while—see y'all later." She turned and ran to the car before we could say a word. I watched as she climbed into the front seat and slid over up close against a long-haired boy. He honked again and waved his arm out the window as they drove off.

Bringing one hand up to my face and the other one over my heart, I said "Lord have mercy" to nobody in particular.

HAMPTON

Winter and Spring 1966

I KNEW BESSIE WAS WORRIED SICK ABOUT JOYCIE, AND I COULD understand why. When we saw her over Christmas, she was a different person. I know Rene and Lila had tried to convince Bessie that lots of girls acted that way, but I knew better. I didn't see her cousins acting all flirty and paintin' their faces up. Maybe they did think Joycie had needed to loosen up some, but I knew all too well what boys thought about a girl like that.

I tried to keep my worries to myself, not wantin' to trouble Bessie any more than she already was. She had her hands full enough raisin' a three-year-old. T'ain't no other toddler on Earth that got more love than little Lou. Oh, we didn't spoil her, but we did everything in our power to make up for her not havin' a real mother's love. As far as we could tell, she never missed out by not having Joycie around. Still, we wanted her to know that Joycie was her real mama. We made plans to go back down to Florida for the summer. Lila said her house would be available to rent again. It was a good thing we'd have a place to stay without barging in on family.

After we got back to Albany after Christmas, Joycie's letters stopped coming every week. We were lucky if we got one a month. Even then, they were short and didn't say much: *I'm fine . . . how are you . . . everyone says hello.* Money was tight, so Bessie stretched out the time between her long-distance calls. Maybe we were blind to what was going on, but with the distance and the lack of communication, we didn't worry too much.

One cold early-March evening after Louann was in bed, Bessie said, "Hampton? Do you think we ought to call and check on Joycie? We haven't heard from her, Rene, or Lila in weeks."

"Aw, Bessie, they're probably just busy. They're into basketball season at the school, workin' part-time jobs, and all that other stuff kids do. They've got a lot goin' on. Let's give it a while longer."

"If you say so, Hampton. I guess it won't hurt to give it another week or so."

As it turned out, all was not well, and a couple of weeks was not going to make a bit of difference. I answered the phone that morning at the end of March when Lila called with the news. "Hampton, I'm afraid there's some news about Joycie, and it's not good. She's not hurt or anything, at least as far as we know, and we think she'll be all right, but maybe I should tell you and let you tell Bessie. I'm not sure how she's going to take it."

"What in the hell, Lila? What's wrong? Just spit it out."

"Well, I waited a few days to call, just in case she came back, but then Rene said I better call and tell y'all."

"Tell us what? Came back? Came back from where? What are you saying?"

"Last Friday, Rene found a note Joycie'd left for her on the kitchen counter. It said she was goin' off with that boy she's been seeing—Ben, I think his name is. Said she'd be in touch, don't worry, she was fine, and don't bother lookin' for her, they'd be on the road."

"Last Friday? And you're just now calling? Are you crazy? She could be halfway across the country by now."

"Girls sometimes do these crazy things and then come back home in a day or so. We didn't want to worry y'all unnecessarily. Oh, Hampton, I'm so sorry. We never thought she'd do something like this, even after—"

"After what, Lila? What else happened?"

"Well, there was a couple of times she stayed out all night. At first, she told us she was staying overnight with a friend, but then she didn't come home after a date until the next morning, and we saw that boy dropping her off—"

"Oh my God, Lila. What am I gonna tell Bessie? Have you called the police? What about this boy's family? Have you talked to them?"

"The police said she's not a minor since she's sixteen, and since neither me or Rene are her legal guardian, there wasn't anything they could do unless her guardians wanted to file a missing persons report, and we didn't know if you and Bessie wanted to do that. They said most runaways come home after about a month and that we should give it some time. Especially since she was with somebody, not just out on her own. And that kid, he's from over in Ocala, but nobody seems to know much about him or how to get ahold of his family. I just didn't know what to do, Hampton, honest to God, I'm so sorry—" Lila started crying on the other end of the line.

"All right, Lila, all right. I've got to figure out what to do and what to tell Bessie. We're not going to panic yet. Try to calm down. Talk to your girls and tell Rene to talk to hers and see if they know anything. I'll get back to you and let you know what we decide."

I thought it'd be best if I had a plan before I told Bessie anything. I made phone calls. The first was to the police in Williston, and the second was to the police in Ocala. *Stay calm*, I told myself. I needed their help. At both places, they were reassuring and told me the same as what Lila had said. She'll turn up, they said. Try not to worry, they said. Wait to file a missing persons report, they said. She's not really missing if she's with somebody, they said.

I was frustrated as hell but couldn't do anything else as long as I was up here in Albany.

I decided we should go ahead and close up the meat market and get on down to Florida. It'd be easier to get information—if there was any to get—down there. After Louann was down for her nap that afternoon,

I called Bessie into the kitchen and sat her down at the table. Her eyes were following me with dread as I sat across from her and took her hands in mine.

"Oh God, Hampton. What is it? Something's wrong. I know it."

"Yes, darlin'. Something's wrong. But it's gonna be all right, I promise."

I started talking, beginning with Lila's phone call. I held Bessie's hands tighter as the tears rolled silently down her face. I explained about talking to the police. I told her we were leaving for Florida in the morning, that she should pack. She sat there looking at me, not saying a word.

Finally, she said it. "I knew something wasn't right. I told 'em. I told you. I knew something was wrong." She got up without another word, went to the bedroom, and started packing.

I called Lila back that evening to tell her we'd be there the next afternoon.

"Thank God you called, Hampton. I've got news. Joycie's okay!"

"What? How do you know?"

"She called Rene's house and talked to Marybeth. Said she was so sorry, she didn't want any of us to worry, she was fine. Said she was going to live with Ben for a while. Not to try to talk her out of it—she just needed to be on her own. Said we could tell you she was okay, but she wasn't going to say where she was because she didn't want anybody coming to find her. Said she'd call again when she could."

I let out a sigh of relief. Well, at least that was something. As hard as it was, I thought, *Fine. If that's how she wants it, that's how it'll be.*

LOUANN

1967 to 1971

O NE OF MY EARLIEST MEMORIES IS FROM THE SUMMER AFTER I
turned three. Joycie had been living that whole school year in
Florida, and we hadn't seen her in months. Mama and Daddy took me
and moved down there for a while that spring. Of course, at the time,
I didn't know anything about her having run off. I was happy living in
the little house near the aunts and cousins, and sometimes I'd stay with
them if Mama or Daddy was working. They were so good to me, Daniel,
all of them. If I couldn't have had a traditional family, at least I had them.

One hot July afternoon, I was home with Daddy when there was a
knock at the door. I followed Daddy to the door and was peeking around
his legs to see who it was. Daddy opened the door, and right there on the
doorstep was Mama Joycie. I couldn't believe my eyes. And right there,
slung on her hip, was a baby.

"Hey, Daddy, meet your new grandson. His name's Benny."

She barged right in, shoving the baby at Daddy. "Here, take him.
Where's Mama?"

She brushed right by me without so much as a word.

Daddy stood there, holding the baby, his mouth moving but no words
coming out. Finally, he found his voice. "What in the . . . ?"

Mama Joycie looked around and hollered. "Ain't Mama here? I want
her to meet Benny, too." Then she went straight back to the kitchen,
pulled open the refrigerator, and took out a cold Co-Cola.

Daddy followed, carrying that baby—and with me hanging on his leg. "She'll be home in a few minutes. But who . . . when . . . ?"

I was staring up in awe at baby Benny when Mama Joycie actually spoke to me. "So what do you think of your baby brother, Louann? Pretty cute, huh?"

I could only nod. I was transfixed, staring at my daddy holding that baby. Then here came Mama through the back door. She nearly dropped a bag of groceries as she stopped to stare at us. Joycie ran to Mama and threw her arms around her neck.

"Hey, Mama, look what I got. A little brother for Louann. His name's Benny. Isn't he the cutest thing?" Joycie took Benny from Daddy and thrust him at Mama, who was still holding the bag of groceries.

As it turned out, Joycie had left Benny's daddy, or he had left her. We never really knew which it was. She had come to stay. There we were, together again, with the addition of baby Benny. Joycie got a job as a checkout clerk while Mama and Daddy looked after me and the baby. Sometimes she wouldn't come home until midnight, and before long, there were times she wouldn't come home 'til the next morning. Then, she'd disappear for days at a time. I know it had to have hurt Mama's and Daddy's hearts for her to do them that way, but they were afraid she'd go on the run again, I suppose.

By the time I was four years old, it was plain that Mama Joycie couldn't stand the sight of me. I'm not sure how I knew it, but I did. Like most four-year-olds, I didn't try to figure it out; it was just the way it was.

After all, it was Mama and Daddy who really loved me. But when Mama Joycie was around, that hole in my heart would open up, and I wanted more than anything for her to step in and fill it up. It was probably good that she wasn't there all that much. She stayed down in Florida or shacked up with a boyfriend most of the time. Anywhere to avoid me. Being around Joycie always made Mama and Daddy sad, so maybe that was why it made me sad, too. But that didn't change the little girl in me wantin' her real mother's love.

"Please, Mama Joycie, take me with you. I promise I'll be good."

She'd answer without even looking at me. "Not today, Louann. Not today, and probably not ever." And out the door she'd go.

I just couldn't understand it. I'd run to bury my sobs in Mama's big, soft lap. She would pat my back and stroke my hair. "It's okay, little Lou. Mama and Daddy love you."

I tried hard to be a good little girl, pretty and sweet, just to make Mama Joycie love me.

"Mama Joycie, can I sit on your lap?"

"You'll wrinkle up my skirt."

"Mama Joycie, look how pretty my dress is."

"So what. Go on, leave me alone."

"Mama Joycie, I love you."

"Oh yeah? That's nice."

If I couldn't get her attention in a good way, there was always other not-so-good ways. Like the time I spilled chocolate milk on her white shoes.

I loved chocolate milk. Mama would make it up for me, stirring chocolate powder into plain sweet milk. I wasn't supposed to take it out of the kitchen, but when I saw Mama Joycie sittin' on the sofa reading her magazine, I couldn't resist.

"Hey, Mama Joycie, whatcha doin'?"

"Readin' my magazine. Leave me alone."

Her eyes never looked away from the shiny, slick page, so she didn't see me standing right in front of her with the tall glass of foamy chocolate milk. I watched her for a few seconds, and her eyes never looked up. Then I did it. I tilted the glass, deliberately and ever so slowly, and the light brown liquid landed right on her bright white Keds. She jumped up, shrieking. "Why, you little brat! Look what you've done." Her hand drew back, ready to fly, but Daddy caught it just in time. I didn't even know he was in the room.

"Now, Joycie, she didn't mean to do it. I'll pay for a new pair. Lou, you go on outside and play. I'll clean this up." Daddy was always stepping in, keeping me safe from Mama Joycie's tirades. Sad thing was, even though I couldn't put it into words or arrange the thought in my four-year-old brain, I'd rather have had Mama Joycie mad at me than have her pretend I didn't exist at all.

It wasn't long after the chocolate milk incident when Joycie got real mad one afternoon and packed up her and baby Benny's things, and some man came by and picked her up in a long station wagon. I remember standing at the door and waving. She didn't look back.

The really crazy thing is, about a year later, almost the exact same scene repeated itself. This time, when the knock on the door came, Mama Joycie was on the doorstep, holding baby Benny's hand, and slung on her hip was Barbie, my new little sister. For the next few months, it was just like the summer before. Joycie ignored me while Mama and Daddy took care of us kids when Joycie worked and ran around. Joycie would stay out all night, then for days at a time. When she got mad and packed everything up the next time, it was a different man in a different car who picked her up.

Then, unbelievably, the next summer, it happened again. Another knock at the door. This time, Benny and Barbie were hanging onto Mama Joycie's legs, and on her hip was another baby boy, Bobby. Just like with me, there was never a sign or mention of any baby daddies. By the time I was six years old, I had three half-siblings, and it was plainer than ever that my real mama didn't love me and never would.

BESSIE

1971

IT WAS GUT-WRENCHING TO SEE HOW JOYCIE TREATED LOUANN. With little Lou coming up on eight years old, she was noticing it more and more. The other babies had come along, and it just seemed to make things worse. It near 'bout broke my heart. Lou's little brow would furrow, and she'd hang all over Joycie, vying for her attention. Joycie had somehow come up with the money to rent the little house across the street from where we stayed every summer and for a couple of months in the winter over Christmas. We didn't know for sure how she managed to pay for it, but we suspected her boyfriends helped her out. She couldn't have made enough money as a check-out girl to afford rent and a car as well as food and clothing for three kids. No wonder she left 'em with us all the time, and even she stayed at our house more often than not. The things she said and the hateful tone of voice she used with Lou made me cringe.

If Lou said, "Mama Joycie, can I hold Bobby?" Joycie would sigh with exasperation and brush her away. "That's enough whining, now, Louann."

Or sometimes, Lou would ask, "Can I sit on your lap, Mama Joycie? Please?"

Joycie would rebuff her in a sharp voice. "Not now, Louann. Get off of me! Go sit over there."

When Joycie got ready to go, Louann would beg to go with her.

"Mama Joycie, can I go to your house with Benny and Barbie and Bobby? I want to go to your house with you. Please? Can I?"

A couple of times, when Joycie would give in and say okay, we'd agree to let Louann go, but only because she was so pitiful. She couldn't understand why the others got to go with her mama but she had to stay with us. It broke our hearts to see Lou cryin' after Joycie.

We had our suspicions about what kind of a mama Joycie was being to those babies. When they showed up at our house, they acted like they was starving. First thing they wanted was food. They were always dressed in secondhand clothes or hand-me-downs from the cousins and Louann. Nothing wrong with that, but usually they were none too clean—the babies or the clothes.

The first few days of each summer, Lou would knock herself out trying to get Joycie's attention. Then it was like reality set in: when Joycie came over with the babies, Lou would sit in the corner, sucking her thumb, watching Joycie every second with large, piercing eyes. Me and Hampton didn't want to give up on Joycie, and there were the children to consider. So we tried to help the best we could and not make Joycie so mad she'd run off again. Lord knows, every time she'd done that before, she'd come back with another baby, and that was the last thing any of us needed. We loved our new grandbabies and wanted what was best for them, but somehow it seemed like a betrayal to Louann if we showed the slightest interest in the little ones.

Bouncing Barbie on my lap, I'd say, "Come over here, Lou! Look at little Barbie giggling." Or, "Louann, show Benny how to stack those blocks. He would love that."

If Joycie was there, Louann wouldn't answer me or move from her corner. She'd sit and stare, her eyes fixed on Joycie, never even acknowledging the babies were there. It was like she thought that if she stared hard enough, she could force Joycie into loving her.

But Louann acted real different when Joycie left the kids with us and went off on her own, which was more and more frequent. As soon as Joycie was out the door, Louann turned into a little mother.

"Mama, can I help you feed Barbie?"

"Daddy, can I hold Bobby on my lap?"

"Mama, I think Benny's hungry. Can I give him a snack?"

She would talk to them, play with them, and carry on nonstop conversations.

"Here, Benny, let's play cars. You drive the red one, and I'll drive the blue one. Oh, you want the blue one? That's okay, here you go. Now, you go first."

With Barbie, she would crawl around after her on the floor or play patty-cake and peek-a-boo. Covering her eyes, chanting, "Where's Barbie? I don't see her! Where'd she go? Boo!"

Even though I knew that Louann loved having her little brothers and sister around, it wasn't always fun and games. One time when they'd been with us several days in a row, Louann was rinsing dishes with me when she got a serious look on her face.

"Mama?"

"Yes, honey?"

"When are the other kids going back to Joycie's?"

I set the dish in the drainer, dried my hands, and looked at little Lou, frowning.

"Why, Louann? I thought you loved having your little brothers and sister with us!"

"Well, I do, but it's just—"

I took her face in my hands. "Look at me, Lou. Me and Daddy will always love you, and we're going to take care of you, no matter what. Do you understand that?" I hugged her close.

Her lip trembled, and I saw tears about to spill over from her eyes. Hot tears started to burn in my own. Her small voice quivered.

"Yes, ma'am, I understand. There's just one thing, though."

"What, honey? What is it?"

"Well, at night, in bed, Benny does something."

I couldn't hold back a quick intake of breath. Hands on my hips, my smile disappeared as my heart raced and my mind ran ahead. "Louann.

What are you trying to say? What does Benny do that's bothering you so much?"

"Well, he uh, he—"

I grabbed her by the arms. "Tell me, Lou. Tell me, right now."

She bowed her head and said something in a hushed whisper.

"What? Louann? I didn't hear you."

She tilted her head up at me, looked me straight in the eye, and forced the words out loud. "He *farts*!"

My eyebrows shot up, and my eyes popped wide. I couldn't help but bust out laughing. I was laughing so hard I was shaking, and the tears that had been threatening ran down my cheeks. I squeezed little Lou up in a big hug. I had never felt such relief in my life.

She squirmed away, stepped back, and put her little hands into fists on her own nonexistent hips, indignant. She glared at me.

"What's so funny? It stinks! How would you like sleeping in a bed with a stinky boy?"

"Oh, sweetheart, I'm sorry. I don't s'pose I would. But we can fix this, okay?"

She didn't look so sure, but as I hugged her again, she mumbled, "Okay."

That night, when me and Ham got the kids ready for bed, I pulled out an extra sheet and blanket. Whipping the sheet over the old sunken-in couch, it made a popping sound before settling over the lumps and bumps. The kids stood off to the side, watching. I tucked the middle of the sheet into the crease between the seat and back cushions and called Benny over.

"Benny, this is going to be your very own bed from now on. You won't have to put up with those silly girls anymore, okay?"

Benny jumped right onto the covered seats and pulled the loose sheet from the back cushion over him. In typical four-year-old-boy talk, he hollered out. "Oh boy! My own bed to myself. Whoopee!" The next sound was a loud, long *pluuut*, and the smell of rotten eggs lifted into the air.

I looked over at the girls and winked. They squealed a high-pitched *Ewww* and ran from the room, holding their noses. It tickled me seein' the kids having fun together, like a real family. We would miss them when we went back to Albany for the fall, even though it wasn't easy making ends meet over the summers, takin' care of four kids and Joycie half the time, but we managed. Plus, me and Hampton weren't getting any younger. Now that we were in our sixties, it was all we could do to take care of those kids. Even so, that was what families were supposed to do: take care of each other.

JOYCIE

December 1971 to February 1972

C HRISTMAS WAS PERFECT. WELL, MAYBE NOT IN SOME FOLKS' WAY
of thinking, but far as the Walker family went, it was as near perfect as it would ever be. Mama, Daddy, and Louann were back from
Albany, right across the street from me and my babies. For the time being,
there was no man around to bully me or the kids. The last boyfriend had
thrown down a hundred-dollar bill, said, "Go buy your kids somethin'
to eat," and walked out. I hadn't heard from any of their daddies in a
year or more. Never did get any support from them. And Richard was
far away in California with his new wife and their kid. God, how we all
hoped he'd stay out there. And here I was, twenty-one years old, never
finished high school, had a crappy job, four kids, and no husband. What
in the hell was I going to do?

Across the street, Mama's house was decorated to the hilt. A silver alu-
minum tree with a red, yellow, and blue rotating light threw garish colors
around. Plastic green stuff draped everywhere. Knickknacks and candles on
every surface. Vanilla, cinnamon, and chocolate smells knocked you over
when you came in the door. I didn't have the money to do any of that at my
place, but at least my kids could spend their time at Mama and Daddy's.

Something about the season got to me. Hell, sometimes I wished
I could be a kid again and let Mama and Daddy take care of me. Then
I'd think about running away again, but that hadn't worked out so well.
Maybe the kids would be better off with Mama and Daddy. After all,

they'd done a pretty good job with me as long as Richard stayed away. But they had aged; they weren't going to be around forever to raise more kids. It was going to be up to me to straighten out my life and do the right thing by my kids. Even Louann. My head told me she was an innocent child and couldn't help who her real daddy was or how she'd gotten here, but all my eyes could see when I looked into her face was Richard. I'd just have to give it my best shot.

A few days before Christmas, I was helping Mama in her kitchen when she put her hand on my arm and said, "Joycie, I've been meaning to talk to you about something."

I didn't look up. "What is it, Mama? I don't want any bad news to spoil the Christmas spirit."

"Oh, it's not bad news, not really. I thought you should know Lou's been asking questions. She knows you're really her mama, of course, but she's been wanting to know who her daddy is. And she's asking how come the other kids live with you but she lives with us. She'll be eight in February, and she's starting to notice these things."

I stopped chopping pecans and set the knife down but kept my eyes lowered.

"I knew the day would come we'd have this conversation, Mama. I know I haven't been fair to Louann. She's my child, and I do love her in my heart, but I just can't get past what her real daddy did. When I look at her, I see him. You and me and some others *know* he's her real daddy, but she doesn't need to be burdened with that. I don't want her to know. Is that clear?"

I raised my eyes to stare defiantly at the only real mama I'd ever known.

"Well, I can understand that, but if you do really love her, maybe you should try—"

"Mama, I said I love her! I'll try to show her, but—"

"Joycie, just look at her as the pretty little girl she is. Those curls, her bright eyes, her sweet smile. And she's so smart. I swear she could skip a grade at school and do just fine."

"I know it's not her fault, Mama. She is pretty, and I know she's smart. Thank God for that. I've been so blinded by Richard's evil, and now I've got the other kids, too. If I could find the right man, maybe I could make it up to her."

Mama's eyes were sad as she put her arms around me. "Oh, honey, we love you, and Louann does, too. She just doesn't understand. And remember, a man isn't always the answer to every problem. Sometimes, us women have to pull ourselves together and do it on our own."

I knew she was thinking I ought to know that by now. And she was right; I should know better. After four children with four different daddies and not a cent of support between them, it should be pretty obvious.

"I know, Mama, I know. I promise I'll try to do better. Let's try to focus on the kids for now and make this Christmas a good one. Just like we used to have when I was little? Can we just do that, please?"

"Of course, Joycie. We can do that. That's what Christmas is all about, isn't it?"

I nodded and kept on chopping.

When I was a little girl at Mama and Daddy's, Christmas was an extravaganza, and now that I had my own kids, I wanted it to be that way for them, too. Now, between Mama and Daddy's and all the other relatives' houses, the grownups went overboard, but we loved to see the kids with their new toys, new clothes, new shoes, and stockings full of candy. When Christmas was over, the older cousins had to go back to school come January, but the younger ones could play outside all they wanted in the mild Florida weather. Louann was the oldest of the little ones, and she loved to mother the younger ones, acting just like a grownup most of the time.

I was trying extra hard to give her lots of attention. "Louann, you're such a good helper. How about a piece of gum for helping me with the groceries."

"Oh, thank you, Mama Joycie! You got any other jobs I can help you with?"

"Not right now, but tell you what. Would you like to play dress-up? I'll get out some of my things, and you can pretend you're goin' to a party."

Her little eyes would get big as saucers when I pulled out sparkly sequin tops, jewelry, and high heels. She squealed out loud when she saw herself in the mirror. "Look, Mama Joycie, I look just like you, 'cept you're prettier."

"Oh, honey, you're the prettiest little girl in the world. How about some makeup, too?"

Louann preened and pranced like the queen of the ball. She clomped over to me in those high heels and threw her arms around my neck. "I love you, Mama Joycie."

"I love you, too, sweetheart," I'd answer, hugging her close. "You're my biggest bestest girl."

But when things seem too good to be true, they usually are. It was exhausting putting all that effort into Louann and looking after the other kids, too. By the end of January, my holiday spirit, or whatever it was, had started to wear thin. The kids got on my nerves. First, I backed off from Louann, and then, before I knew it, I was distancing myself from the others, too. Then came that old feeling of wanting to disappear. I would leave the kids at Mama and Daddy's overnight and go out. Men's eyes would catch mine, and I wanted to go with them. Sometimes I did. There would be drinks, and dancing, and occasional one-night stands— anything to escape my real world.

Late one night, after pulling into my yard, I got out of the car and stumbled to the door. A man appeared in front of me and blocked my way. I froze in place. I couldn't move or call out. His hands pinned my arms to my sides, and he was shaking me violently. It hurt so bad! *Oh my God! Please, God, no!*

"Joycie! Baby Girl. It's Daddy. We need to talk."

Talk? I couldn't talk. I couldn't even move. I woke up in my bed. *How did I get here?* I hurt all over. In spite of the pain, I thrashed like a rabbit in the jaws of a wolf, being slung back and forth in its vicious grip. Hands, two hands, were holding my arms down.

"Joycie! Wake up! You're having a bad dream. Come on, girlie, it's Mama. Let's get you up and get some coffee in you."

Me, Mama, and Daddy were sitting around my dingy kitchen table, steaming cups of coffee in front of us. Coming out of my hungover stupor, I wasn't sure that I understood what they were saying. Mama's voice was calm but firm. "Joycie, this can't go on. You're neglecting your children—and not just Louann. Now it's the others, too. You're not fit to be a mother like this."

I didn't look up. Then Daddy took my hands. His voice was sharp. "Joycie, look at me! This is serious business. We're going to take your kids back with us to Albany. All of them."

That got my attention. Wide awake now, I opened my eyes, which searched the room wildly. I tried to pull my hands from Daddy's. "You can't do that. Those are my kids. You can have Louann, but the others stay with me."

Now Mama: "Listen, Joycie. If we don't take them, you're going to get turned in for neglect, and then where will they be? In some foster home where God knows what can happen. Is that what you want?"

"No! That won't happen. I'll take care of them. I promise. Just give me a chance."

Daddy, in a calmer voice now: "This is your chance, Joycie. Get yourself together, show us you can be responsible, and we'll bring them back. But you've got to prove to us you mean it. Stay sober. Get a decent job so you can support yourself and the kids. And no men. That's the way it's got to be."

Mama: "You've got to show us, honey, and we'll be glad to bring them back. But for now, we're leaving tomorrow, and they're all going with us."

I pushed my chair back and slammed the coffee mug on the table, splashing coffee over the scarred green vinyl. I screamed, "You don't care about me! You don't even love me. You just want to steal my kids so they'll love you and not me. I'll show you who really loves me. I'll find my real daddy! He loves me."

HAMPTON

1972 to 1974

WE TOOK ALL THE KIDS AND WENT BACK TO ALBANY. A MONTH went by, and we didn't hear from Joycie and didn't try to contact her. After about six weeks, we checked with Lila and Rene, and they both said her house was empty. There was no sign of her. We all presumed she must have run off to California to find Richard like she said she was gonna do. We never tried to contact her there and sure as hell didn't want to bring Richard down on our heads. What was it about that evil snake that drew her to him? For the life of me, I would never understand it. Still, I often thought about his little boy. A grandson I'd never even laid eyes on.

We had one picture Lila had sent us that she'd gotten in the mail a year earlier. In the photo, a glamorous, dark-haired, movie-star-looking woman with lots of makeup stood next to Richard, his stump on her upper arm as she leaned away from him. Had there been a hand on the end of that stump, it likely would have gripped her arm, holding her prisoner. Richard's other arm hung down to the little boy's shoulder, where his one hand was locked in a vise-like clench. It looked every bit like he was trying to hold them both in place. The little boy was sandy-haired and stared straight into the camera with a determined grimace. On the back, it said, *Richard, Richie, and Helen, California 1969.* So it was at least three years old. Sometimes, late at night, I'd see Bessie secretly take out the wrinkled snapshot and study our son and grandson. I'd see her lips moving, and I knew she was prayin' for that little boy.

After Benny, Barbie, and Bobbie were with us for six months and there was still no word from Joycie, I went through the process of obtaining formal guardianship. We'd already done that with Louann years ago, and we needed it to get benefits—having four kids was expensive. The meat market brought in some income, but it wasn't steady. Now that Louann was eight and Benny was six, they were both in school. Barbie and Bobbie, at only four and three, didn't go to school yet, so Bessie had her hands full with them. We kept to the same routine, spending summers and holidays down in Florida and coming back to Albany for the school year.

After two years had gone by, we got word from Lila that Joycie was back in Florida. Seemed she had taken up with a man named Dave and was living in Ocala. She didn't contact us herself, and we wouldn't have even known if Lila hadn't told us. We went to Williston for the summer, just like we always did. One day in late June of 1974, there was a knock at the door. Just like when she showed up all those years ago with babies on her hip, there was Joycie. There were no babies this time, and it was a damn good thing.

We almost didn't recognize her. She was alone, no sign of the man named Dave. Her hair was greasy, stringy, and blond with dark roots. She looked like she'd put on twenty-five or thirty pounds. Her clothes were wrinkled and ill-fitting. There were bruises on her arms. Joycie had always prided herself on her appearance, so it was a shock to see her like this.

"Joycie? Where'd you come from? I almost didn't recognize you."

She lowered her head and spoke softly. "I know, Daddy. I look awful. I'm so sorry. Can I come in?"

I held the door open, and she came in. Bessie walked in from the kitchen, the kids swarming behind her. They all stopped dead in their tracks.

Joycie looked up hopefully. "Mama? Benny? Barbie? Bobby? Oh my God, I can't believe it's all of you." She held her arms wide like she expected they would all come running to her.

Bessie was the first to make a move. She went right up and put her arms around Joycie. "Oh, honey, it's been so long. I can't believe it's you. Are you all right? Are you sick? What's wrong?"

Joycie's sobs were muffled in Bessie's hug. When they separated, they both turned to look at the kids, Joycie wiping at her eyes. Lined up like stairsteps, the children stood wide-eyed and still, like they weren't sure what they were expected to do. Joycie knelt down and put her arms out, but the kids didn't move. It was Bessie who understood. They hadn't seen their mama in two years, and with Joycie looking so different, they didn't even know who she was.

I spoke up to try to salvage Joycie's dignity. "Hey, kids, come on over and give your mama a hug. I know you've missed her, and she's missed you, too, haven't you, Joycie?"

She shot me a thankful look and answered. "Come give me a hug. I can't believe you're all so big. I've missed you all so much—"

Slowly, they moved towards their mother. Except for Louann. It hadn't escaped me that when Joycie had called out the others' names, she had left out Louann. I was sure Louann had noticed, too. Now she stood back, her arms crossed over her chest, her head down, and did not make the slightest move towards Joycie. As the others started to warm up and prattle with their mama, Louann turned and disappeared back into the kitchen.

Bessie followed Louann, and I swayed the others to go outside and play while their mama stayed inside. "Joycie, let's you and me and Mama have a talk in the kitchen while the kids play. I'll send Louann out to look after them."

It was like Joycie suddenly remembered her other child. "Oh! Okay, Daddy. I forget Louann's such a big girl now. She's what, ten now? I can't believe it."

I felt like saying if she'd ever taken care of her kids like a real mother, she'd know for sure how old they were, but I let it slide. Instead, I said, "That's right. And she loves those younger kids, just like a little mother. Let's go on in the kitchen."

BESSIE

June 1974

H AMPTON SENT LOUANN OUT TO PLAY WITH THE OTHER KIDS, then him and Joycie sat down at the table. I couldn't help myself, so I started in with the questions: "Joycie, what's happened? Where have you been? You never called or anything. How could you just desert your kids like that?"

"If you recall, Mama, you and Daddy took my kids. I didn't have any say-so in the matter. But I'm ready to have them back now. That's why I'm here. I'll even take Louann."

Hampton took a deep breath. "Now wait just a minute, Miss High-and-Mighty. You weren't fit to look after those kids. And from the looks of you, I'm not sure you're fit now. Besides, we have legal guardianship, so you can't just waltz in here and demand that we hand them over."

I tried a calmer approach. "Joycie, honey, are you all right? You look different from two years ago. What about this man Dave? Are you with him?"

"Yes, Mama. I'm with Dave. We're getting married soon, and I want the kids to come live with us. That's what I came over here to talk about. How about it?"

She was looking at me, and I could tell she thought she'd get farther with me than Hampton. "Honey, it's not good to jerk kids from one place to another without any warning. Can't we take this a little slower?"

Hampton snorted. "Slower? Or how about not at all? Joycie, I've got to be honest here. You don't look fit to take care of any kids. What's happened to you?"

Joycie bowed her head for a moment. There was a sniffle, and then she looked up, ran her hands over her face, pushed her hair back, and squared her shoulders. "Oh, Daddy, I'm all right, I promise. We've just been down on our luck a little, that's all. But Dave's starting a new job up in Jacksonville in a couple of weeks, and things are going to be so much better. Good money, a nice house, and closer to where his kids live with their mother. God, it's been two years. I just want to be with my babies." She smiled brightly. I couldn't be sure if she was trying to convince herself or us that things were going to be better.

I could understand a mama wantin' to be with her kids, even if Joycie hadn't always been the best mama. But there had been times when she'd truly seemed to love those children. Maybe we should give her another chance. I approached the idea carefully. "You know, Hampton, the kids do talk about missing their mama from time to time. Maybe we could consider a visit?"

Before he could answer or I could say any more, Joycie jumped in. "Oh, Mama. That's a perfect idea. Just let them come spend one night. Dave really wants to meet them. That wouldn't be hard, would it? It could be like an adventure for them. We're just a half-hour away in Ocala. I could take them with me now and bring them back in the morning. What do you think?"

Me and Hampton exchanged looks. Joycie wasn't waiting for a response.

"Please, Mama? Daddy? Just one night. Please?"

Against our better judgment, we relented. The younger kids were excited. They jumped up and down and acted like it was a big adventure. Louann, on the other hand, flatly refused to go.

We put overnight things into paper sacks for each of the kids and sent them out with hugs and kisses and promises all around to be good, have fun; we'd see them tomorrow. They weren't babies anymore: Benny was eight, Barbie five, and Bobby four, but still, we prayed they'd be all right. It was just the one night, after all.

When Joycie showed up the next morning, we knew there was something bad wrong. She tried to drop the kids at the door and get away, but we made her come inside. We could see immediately that both of her eyes were blackened. Benny had marks up and down his legs. Barbie's face was all swole up from crying. Bobby was silent, but he held his little arm in a funny position by his side.

Hampton's jaw twitched. He paced the floor, and his hands were clenched into fists.

"Joycie, go sit down in the kitchen. Kids, y'all go out back. Louann? Where are you?" he yelled.

"I'll get her, Hampton; she's in the kids' room. Go on out, kids. Louann'll be out there in a minute. Louann?"

She came out, and we sent her to the backyard with the kids. She didn't look at Joycie as she passed by the kitchen table.

Once all the kids were out of the house, Hampton exploded. "What in the hell, Joycie?"

She started to sputter out some excuse, then broke down into sobs. Between blubbering, she told us what Dave had said. "I thought he wanted the kids to come live with us. But he said hell no, that was just him talking. I tried to convince him I needed my babies. That's what started it."

I never could stand to see Joycie crying. My mama's heart always won out. "Oh, Joycie, it's okay, honey. They're fine with us." I was patting her back, trying to get her to stop cryin', but it only got worse.

"But, Mama, he said no. The more I tried to talk him into it, the madder he got."

Hampton swore under his breath. "Why, that son of a—"

"I know, Daddy. Then he got so mad, he hit me first and then started on Benny. Oh, God! I didn't know what to do. He jerked Bobby up, threw him on the couch, and then dragged Barbie off to the other room. I was so scared."

Nausea rose in my stomach. My mother's protective instinct kicked in. Why had he taken Barbie to another room? How could a man beat a child? I couldn't believe Joycie had let this happen. "Joycie, honey. You're their mama. Why didn't you call us? We would have come. We could have brought you all back here."

"I know, Mama, I know. I'm so sorry. I was scared, and embarassed, and ashamed. What if I'd made it worse? I was so afraid." Joycie broke down in sobs, and her whole body shook. I truly believed she'd been scared to death. Like one of those stories where somebody wants to fight back but is paralyzed and can't move or speak. She'd had to watch, helpless, as her babies were hurt. I even wondered if it had brought back nightmares of her own experiences.

Hampton was silent. I sat and cried with Joycie while Hampton stared. When he finally spoke again, all he said was, "It'll be over my dead body before you ever get those kids back again. Now, get out."

LOUANN

1975 to 1978

I LOVED MY MAMA BESSIE, AND I LOVED MY LITTLE BROTHERS AND sister, but my daddy was my whole world. His old pickup wasn't so good for driving four kids around, so he bought an old Falcon station wagon. All of us kids were in school by then. In Albany, during the school year, sometimes, when the school bus dropped us off in the afternoon, he'd be sitting on the tailgate of the station wagon. He'd send the other kids inside and call me over to where he was, fishing poles by his side, waiting just for me.

Once we got settled on the bank of the creek, he'd say, "Tell me about your day at school, Louann." Our cane poles were stretched out over the green water, the red and white plastic bobbers floating on the surface.

"Aw, nothing much happened, Daddy. Laura got in trouble for talking too much, and Eddie hit Mikey at recess and was sent to the principal's office."

"What about you? What did you do?"

"I didn't do nothing. Teacher said I did real good when she asked me to read out loud to the whole class. That was about it."

Then we'd just sit there, not talkin', enjoying each other's company. Most days, we didn't catch a thing, but that didn't matter none to me. There was something special about sittin' out there, just me and Daddy, being together. Now that the little kids lived with us all the time, I especially treasured those times alone with Daddy.

Me and Mama had some special alone times, too, usually in the kitchen, gettin' supper ready. If me and Daddy had caught any fish, Mama would let me help clean 'em. The blood and guts didn't bother me none; I was a little sad for the fish, though. Their shiny scales, sparkly like sequins, made me think of a picture I'd seen once of a mermaid. What if the poor little fish was a mermaid in disguise, and here we'd gone and cut off her head and tail? I put the thought out of my mind when Mama fried up the fish and we ate them with hot hushpuppies. Nothing better than fried fish on cool fall evenings for supper.

Course, there were plenty of times me and Daddy didn't catch a thing. Then Mama would have a pot of beans, maybe some greens, and cornbread. If Daddy been able to sneak a few pork chops or ham slices from the meat market, it made a fine supper. During the fall, Mama usually had apple pie, too. Mama had shelves full of jars of every kind of vegetable and fruit. I learned all about cooking, canning, baking, and preserving standing at her apron tails in that little kitchen.

I should have realized something was bad wrong when Daddy didn't plant a garden in the spring of 1978. Mama and Daddy were in their late sixties by then, and taking care of us four kids while trying to make a living had taken its toll on them. I was fourteen, and I tried to do all I could to help, whether it was sweeping, scrubbing, or cooking supper next to Mama. Benny was twelve, and even though he wasn't too keen on housework, he was always willing to help Daddy in the shop or with outside chores. Barbie was ten that year, and Bobby was nine.

I didn't give it much thought when Daddy tried to teach me to drive his Falcon a few weeks before school was out. Country people often taught their kids to drive before it was legal, you know, so it wasn't that unusual. But what a joke that was! It was a manual transmission: three on the tree. First time behind the wheel, I hit a stump and tore the front fender off. Daddy was mad when it happened, but only for a minute. He never could stay mad at me long.

One day after school on one of our fishing trips, Daddy was unusually quiet. He wasn't askin' me a bunch of questions like normal. Then all of a sudden, he said, "Louann, I'm going to buy you a car."

That should have been another clue that something wasn't quite right, but I was excited, even though Daddy wasn't making much sense. Lately, he'd gotten to where he'd ramble sometimes, talkin' about this and that, none of it seeming to have anything to do with anything. Then he'd break down in a coughin' fit, slump over, and not talk for a while.

But the next Saturday, we went to town to look at cars. There wasn't a lot to pick from in the scrubby used-car lot. Daddy stopped in front of a blue Mercury Comet with black racing stripes and white vinyl high-back seats.

"You know, Louann, I might not live to see you get to sixteen. I figured we ought to go ahead and get you a car. How do you like this one?"

More crazy talk that went right over my head. I was enthralled with the idea of getting a car. "It's the fanciest car I've ever seen," I told Daddy. "Does it go fast?"

"Fast enough," he said. "But most importantly, it's an automatic. You won't have no problem driving this one."

Just to prove it, he let me drive it home. He had me park behind the house and toot the horn. Mama and the kids came hurrying out to see. When we got out and all of us were standing around, Daddy pulled himself up like a preacher in a pulpit and boomed out, "Now, you all listen to me. This here is Louann's car. Nobody—and I mean nobody—is to drive it except for her. Y'all got that?" Then he dissolved into one of the coughing fits that were coming more and more often.

Benny, Barbie, and Bobby all answered, "Yes, sir," while Mama dabbed at her eyes with her apron. As we went inside, I glanced back at my pretty car sitting in the yard, just waiting on me and only me.

That May, Daddy got considerably worse. There were days when he didn't get out of bed, and he coughed all the time. Sometimes there'd be blood on the handkerchiefs. Mama tried to hide 'em, but I saw it. She finally told me.

"Louann, honey, I don't want you to worry none, but Daddy's real sick. Cancer is eatin' him up inside. We ain't gonna be going to Florida this summer. He can't travel like this. The doctor said he may not even make it through the summer." There were tears ready to spill out of her eyes. She wasn't doin' so well herself. She was worn down, takin' care of Daddy. She moved slow and hardly left Daddy's side.

I couldn't believe it. My daddy? I'd thought he was invincible, but all the things that had been going on that spring pointed to this horrible realization: he was dying.

The weeks passed slowly. We kept him at home in a hospital bed in the living room. He had to be turned every four hours because the cancer had eaten a hole in his back. He would only let me or Mama do it. The other kids tiptoed around and tried not to look at him. I couldn't much blame them. He was shrunken and gray. He smelled bad. By August, he mostly talked out of his mind. But every once in a while, he would say something clear as a bell, out of the blue. One day, he took my hand and looked me in the eye. "Louann, you've been the best part of my life."

I could only cry and say, "I love you, Daddy."

Those were the last words he ever said to me.

Mama somehow managed to get ahold of Joycie, and she came up from Florida around the middle of August. Joycie tried to talk to Daddy. Mama, me, and Joycie were all standing around the bed.

"Daddy, it's Joycie. I'm here." She spoke softly, and tears were slowly rolling down her face. "I'm so sorry, Daddy. I know I've been a disappointment. But I do love you, and Mama, too. Thank you for looking after me and my kids. You've been a good daddy to all of us." That was it. No response from Daddy, but Mama hugged Joycie as she left the room.

Joycie actually acted decent to all of us. She made meals, looked after the younger kids, and did a few household chores while Mama and me sat with Daddy. Me and Benny pretty much took care of ourselves, and Barbie and Bobby had started to warm up to their mama. Mama tried but couldn't even get Daddy to drink sips of water or soup. He had pain medicine that kept him mostly unconscious, but we knew he was still hurting because of the moans and groans that came from his almost-lifeless body.

A few days later, on a Thursday, the ambulance came to take Daddy to the hospital. Mama hoped and prayed there would be something they could do there that we couldn't do at home, but I knew better. I knew if he went to the hospital, he wouldn't be coming home alive. Mama tried to get me to go with her and Daddy, but I wouldn't do it.

"No—I'm not going. I'm not going to the hospital. He's never coming home, and I can't watch him die." I held onto his hand, crying as they rolled him out. "Daddy, don't go. Stay here with me. Daddy, I love you!" I don't know if he even heard me, but I didn't think so. It wouldn't have mattered anyway. Mama was going, whether I did or not. She wasn't about to leave Daddy's side. She had packed a little bag for herself days earlier, knowing that this day was coming. It was Joycie who pried me away from him, the only time in my life I remember my real mama holding me.

Daddy was still alive on Saturday morning. Mama had been at the hospital with him the whole time, and I was shut up in my room. I s'pose Joycie was halfway looking after the kids until she took a notion to go up to the hospital herself. She took my car, the pretty blue Comet that Daddy had said no one else but me was ever supposed to drive. I'd only driven it myself a few times that summer, to go to the grocery store for Mama or the drugstore for Daddy's medicine. What possessed Joycie to do that, I don't know.

She told us later that when she pulled into the hospital parking lot, the car died and wouldn't start back up. She left it right there in the entrance driveway. When she got upstairs to Daddy's room, a nurse was just leaving. Mama was sobbing. Daddy had died just seconds before. He had been adamant that no one was to drive that car but me, and he meant it right up until his dying day. After that, nobody but me ever dared to drive that car.

RICHARD

1978

I F JOYCIE HADN'T CALLED AND TOLD ME ABOUT IT, I WOULDN'T HAVE even known Daddy was dead. She was the only one of the family that knew I was back in Florida. Good ol' Joycie. My sweet baby girl. I figured it was best not to let anybody know I was going to be there, so I just showed up. Me, Helen, and Richie came in the back of the funeral-parlor chapel just as the service was starting. None of the family knew we were there. I planned to wait until later at the house to have my say.

God, it smelled awful. Ever since Joey had died all those years ago, the sickly-sweet smell of carnations reminded me of death. The sappy organ music didn't help, either. Never did like any kind of church music, and this was the worst kind. The old organ wheezed out some sad, slow hymn. I wanted to run up there and strangle the blue-haired lady that was playin' it, but if I did that, I'd give myself away. I'd just have to bide my time 'til this part was over.

I studied the sad little procession as they made their way up the aisle. Mama was really bad off, barely able to make it to the pew, even with Lila and Rene on both sides holding her up. Lord, how she had aged. No skin off my nose. If they hadn't been so mean and run me off, I could have stayed around and helped her out. Joycie came next, with a trail of kids trickling after her. The last one, I knew, had to be that bitch Louann. She was the cause of all this. Her and Joycie's other brats. If it hadn't been for Louann, we coulda been one big happy family.

Having to take care of her and all those other kids was what had done this to my daddy. Old people like him and Mama shouldn't have to be lookin' after kids.

I should have offed Louann like I'd wanted to way back when she'd been born. Well, her time was comin', and it was comin' soon.

The service finally ended. I slipped out and followed at a distance so nobody would see me. Last thing I wanted was some busybody tryin' to make conversation. I had other things on my mind.

The procession from the funeral home to the cemetery wasn't but four cars and the hearse. I waited until they all got started before I pulled out to follow, keeping well out of sight. The sheriff had sent that young deputy Joe Moss to stop traffic for the procession, not that it was necessary for just the four cars. I hung back at the cemetery, too, and had Helen and Richie wait in the car. Everybody was focused on the hysterics playing out next to the black hole in the ground under the red funeral-home tent.

God, why would a funeral home have a red tent? This ain't no circus. There was wailing and shoutin' as the preacher made his last remarks, and the casket was lowered into the hole. When he was done, even from the distance, I could see Mama sink down in her chair. I figured it wasn't just the grief doin' her this way. She must have worn herself out, taking care of Daddy and all these kids. Probably sick from exhaustion.

Back at the house, there were people inside and out in the yard, talkin' and eatin'. I sent Helen and Richie around back and told them I'd be out there in a minute, I needed to go inside first. Richie was thirteen now and didn't always like to do what I told him, but he knew from the look in my eye I meant business. I sat in the car and watched as people trickled out to the yard carrying plates heaped with food. When I saw Louann come out and go sit on the yard swing, I knew it was time. Pausing at the screen door, I took in the scene inside. Mama's family hovered over her. There was food everywhere, even on the end tables in the living room.

Folks talked and laughed and cried. It all came to a dead standstill when the screen door slapped closed behind me.

It was late afternoon, hot and muggy, typical for August in Georgia. Storm clouds were building in the west, and the air was as still as Daddy had been in that box. You could have heard a pin drop in that house. Hands froze in midair with forkfuls of food. Every eye was on me. You'd have thought I was a dead man come back to life.

"Y'all don't mind me. I'm just here to pay my respects. Please, go right on ahead and enjoy yourselves." No one moved or said a word. As I sauntered over to Mama, their eyes could have bored holes in me if I cared enough to let 'em. Lila and Rene backed away from Mama. I stopped and knelt down right in front of her.

"Hello, Mama. I'm sorry for your loss." Her old rheumy eyes took a minute to focus. I was near 'bout ready to turn nice and give her a hug when a whisper escaped her flabby lips.

"Joey? Is that you, Joey? My baby boy?"

It was all I could do not to slap her face.

My knees creaked as I stood up. I looked down at my mama and pulled my little pearl-handled pistol from my pants pocket. I don't think she saw it, but everybody else sure as hell did.

I calmly turned away and walked out the back door, the gun pointing my way forward. Outside, there was Helen, Joycie, and that little bitch Louann sittin' in the swing. When they saw I was headed their way, Joycie and Helen both jumped up, dragging Louann to her feet behind them.

Helen stood directly in front of Louann. "Richard, stop. You'll have to shoot me first if you think you're going to hurt this child."

"Step aside, Helen. I'm going to kill the little bitch."

Helen looked him steadily in the eye. "No, you're not, Richard. She's an innocent child and I love her. I won't let you do that."

"Then I'm going to kill you all, but first, I'm going to kill that little bitch. She's the reason my daddy's dead." I aimed the pistol.

"Run, baby, run!" Joycie screamed.

Everybody started screaming and hitting the ground as I emptied six shots from the gun.

"You better run, girl! I'll kill you like I should have done when you were born."

When the bullets were gone, that was it. I threw the gun down in the dirt. None of 'em had landed where I wanted 'em to. Tears of loss, rage, and hurt let loose as I turned and ran. Hell if I knew where, but I couldn't stay there.

LOUANN

September 1978

I DON'T REMEMBER WHO GOT CONTROL OF RICHARD OR WHO FOUND me out in the woods and brought me back, but I do know it was my real mama and Helen who saved my life that day. Both of them were gone by the next day. I never saw Helen again, and, thank God, I never saw Richard, either. Joycie took her other kids and headed back to Florida. If I hadn't needed to take care of Mama Bessie, I don't know how I would have survived losing my daddy.

I don't know how she made it. She seemed half-dead herself. She lay in bed for days, and when I'd try to get her to eat, she'd turn her head away. She'd either sleep or stare off into space. What could I do? She and I were truly on our own now. Daddy had always handled all the household bills, yard work, and any little jobs that needed doing around the house. Not to mention the garden. Since he hadn't even planted it this year, there wasn't much put aside for the winter. I didn't drive, and my car was in a tow yard somewhere since Joycie had left it at the hospital, and Daddy's old station wagon was a stick shift that hadn't been started up since last May. Even with the little bit of Social Security money we had coming in, it was going to be hard to manage.

School was about to start up. I needed clothes, supplies, and a way to get there and back, since we weren't on a bus route for the high school. I didn't know a thing about our money, and neither did Mama. Daddy had always been in charge of that, but I knew it wasn't much.

I made up my mind: Mama had always taken care of me, and now I'd take care of her. One day, when she was alert and comfortable, I told her, "Mama, I'm going to take care of you."

"But what about school, baby? You've got to go back to school."

"I don't need to go to school. I'll catch up later."

"Honey, you can't do that. You're still just fourteen. If the county finds out you're truant, they'll come and take you away. You'll end up in some foster home with God-only-knows what kind of people. I can't let that happen."

"Mama, I'll tell them I had to take care of you. We can get Daddy's car started, and I'll learn to drive it so I can get groceries and take you to the doctor. I'm not going off every day and leaving you by yourself."

"But, Lou, I'll be fine. We'll figure something out."

"Now, Mama, you listen to me. I'm not going to school, and that's that. What if you fall down, pass out, or get hurt? I can't lose you, too. I just can't! You and Daddy took care of me all my life, and now I'm going to do the same for you. Even if you're trying not to act like it, I know you're sick, and I've got to take care of you. That's what mamas and their girls do for each other. You get some rest, and not another word about it."

"Oh, honey, but your daddy, he wouldn't want that. Just let me rest . . ."

MAMA SLEPT ALL that night and most of the next two days. The next day after that, she seemed rested. She ate the breakfast I made for her. I went to take a bath and get dressed, and when I got back to the kitchen, Mama was dressed and moving around. There were papers spread out on the kitchen table. I breathed a sigh of relief. The two of us were going to be just fine.

"Louann, come over here, and let's sit down. I need to tell you something."

I sat across from Mama. I figured she was about to explain something about money or the house. We were going to carry on together, just the two of us, and that made me feel especially grown-up.

She looked me directly in the eyes. "Now listen carefully, Louann. This is real important. You know Joycie's in Jacksonville now. She's got a nice place with Dave. A big house with a swimming pool and everything. She's finally going to make a nice life for those kids. She told Dave that he doesn't have any choice this time. With Daddy gone, I can't take care of them on my own. Joycie says Dave's changed over the last three years, that he'll be a decent daddy."

I nodded, thinking Mama was just trying to put my mind at ease about my little brothers and sister and maybe fill me in on how to contact Joycie in case anything happened. But then her eyes dropped away from my face. "And not just them, Louann. You're going, too."

I blinked. "What?"

"Now, Lou, honey, don't make this any harder for me than it already is. Tomorrow morning, Sheriff Johnson's going to send his deputy Joe Moss over to pick you up at nine-thirty and take you to the bus station in town. The Greyhound leaves at ten o'clock, and you'll be in Jacksonville by ten tomorrow night. Joycie will be expecting you."

"But, Mama, I can't leave you! Who's going to take care of you?"

"I'll be fine, honey. I've slept like a baby the last two nights. Once I had this figured out, my mind was at rest. Just have to get my strength back, that's all. Mrs. Maxwell down the road promised she'd check on me, and Mr. Pope, the mailman, will see me every day. I'll make sure of that, 'cause I'll be looking for a letter from you."

"No, Mama, I won't do it. I don't want to. Please don't make me!"

"Oh, Louann, yes, you will. I know you don't want to. But it's best for all of us. You'll be with Benny, Bobby, and Barbie. You can help look after them. You've always been such a good little mama for them. And you'll be with your real mama, too."

I looked at her through tears. "But you're my real mama. I want to be with you!"

Mama came around and stood behind me. She put her arms around my shoulders and pulled me close. "Oh, honey, you know that's not so. I'll be all right, but I won't live forever. You'll have to make it on your own, one day. Now's as good a time as any. One day, when you're a mother yourself, you'll understand. Children have a hard time understanding why their mamas do what they do sometimes, but it'll all make sense in the end."

The next morning, I was on a bus to Florida. It was a long, tiresome trip. Mostly, I sat off by myself and cried and cried. The driver ignored me. Every once in a while, another passenger would ask if I was okay. I'd mumble, "Fine, thank you," then turn my head away so they wouldn't bother me anymore.

IT WAS DARK in Jacksonville. The bus station was crowded with dark-skinned people speaking in what I figured must be Spanish. Not like our quiet little one-room bus station in Albany. I'd never been around any foreign people. They were loud, talked fast, and had crying babies and little kids running around everywhere. I felt like I was in a different country. I was scared that I might be at the wrong stop, but the driver had definitely said we were in Jacksonville, and that was what the signs said, too.

Unsure of what to do next, I stood near an exit. I hadn't actually talked to Joycie, but Mama had said she'd be the one picking me up. After half an hour, most of the other people had cleared out. It was getting quiet, and the attendants were sweeping up, checking the restrooms, and closing down ticket windows. I'd thought I had cried all the tears I could, but more began to flow down my face.

Suddenly, there she was. "There you are. How's my girl? Was it a fun trip? What's this? Are you crying? There's nothing to cry over. Here, blow your nose."

I was speechless as Joycie handed me a wadded-up Kleenex from her big purse. I couldn't have gotten in a word edgewise if I'd wanted to. My manic, overblown mother was hustling me out the door to her car. "Come on now, hurry. I've got to get back home. I don't like leaving Dave alone with the kids. He was sleeping when I left, and I sure don't want them to wake him up. There'd be hell to pay. Is that all you've got? That one bag? You poor thing. Don't have much, do you? Well, we can take care of that. Dave makes real good money, and I don't have to work. We'll go shopping first thing tomorrow."

I was staring, wide-eyed. Joycie was dressed in expensive designer jeans and a shiny blouse and had jewelry dangling from her ears, neck, and wrists. Her hair was bright red and poofed out in huge billows. She looked nothing like she had just a few days earlier.

"What's the matter? Cat got your tongue? Don't you have a hug for your mother? Here I am, coming out at night to rescue you, and you can't say nothing? That's a hell of a how-do-you-do!" She was walking at a fast, clipped pace towards the parking lot, her high heels sounding out rapid-fire beats.

I started to speak, "Hey, Joycie—"

"Are you hungry? Did you get anything to eat? You must be starving. We can stop at the Majik Market, if we can find one open. But you'll have to be quick about it. I gotta get home. I don't like leaving Dave alone with the kids. He was sleeping when I left and I—" She was repeating herself.

I tried again, louder and more forcefully this time: "Joycie!" But she kept right on walking about ten feet ahead of me. Then she stopped, shut up, and looked at me, startled.

"I'm fine. Not hungry. You can go straight home. I'm tired and just want to sleep."

We were beside the car, and she was staring at me, like a battery toy that had suddenly run out of power. Something about her stillness and silence after her frenzied ranting was sad. She stood there, looking lost. I inched closer and put my arms around her in an awkward hug.

"It's okay, Joycie. Let's go."

Her car was a fancy white Pontiac Grand Prix. We rode with all the windows down through the muggy night. Once off the main roads, all I could see were long, low houses snuggled into tropical plantings with landscape lights flaring up into palm trees. Wide flat lawns separated the houses from the street, and soft light shone from huge plate-glass windows too far away to reveal anything. As Joycie pulled into the driveway, I couldn't believe what I was seeing.

No one had let on that she lived in a place like this. Maybe Mama knew, and maybe she thought I would like a fancy house like this. As the driveway wound around, I saw it: the strange neon-blue glow of a curvy swimming pool sunk into the ground. We parked under a cover in back of the house and got out of the car.

"Come on, Louann. And remember to be quiet." Joycie bent down and removed her heels, and I followed her across an area covered in stone, then through a back door into a huge kitchen. The counters gleamed white and glass-front cabinets reflected the modern lighting. She cut off the lights and moved on to a formal dining room. A glass-topped table and upholstered chairs nestled into a furry rug. Floor-to-ceiling glass doors revealed the pool area again. Without slowing down and without uttering a word, Joycie kept moving into a living room, or at least that was what I thought at first.

In a half-whisper, Joycie said, "You can sleep here in the family room for tonight. We'll move you in with Barbie tomorrow. I don't want to take a chance on waking Dave going down the hall to the bedrooms tonight. There's a bathroom right over there. Just a half-bath, but that will have to do for now. I put you out a sheet to cover the couch. I guess you have everything else you need with you?"

Too stunned to speak, I nodded. I had no idea what a family room or a half-bath was, but I didn't dare ask.

"All right, then. I'm turning out all these lights. Nighty-night! See you in the morning."

She disappeared down the hallway, leaving me in the dim light from the bathroom. I was miles away from my real home, in a dark palace, alone, and terrified. In the little bathroom, I undressed and put on my pajamas. I walked in the darkness to the couch and unfolded the sheet. Snapping it out to float over the couch, I forgot Joycie's warning about being quiet. I froze in place, listening for footsteps or an irate voice from down the hall. After holding my breath a few seconds and deciding no one had heard, I let myself breathe.

The outside lights cast faint shadows in the dark room, and my eyes began to droop. Maybe I could sleep. Then I started thinking about Mama and Daddy. All I could picture was Daddy in that box and the sound of the dirt thudding down on him at the gravesite. The only way to get that out of my head was to think about Mama, but that didn't help, either. I knew she was putting on a big front about how much better she was. I could tell in the way she'd grimaced with every move she'd made that she was in pain. I could see the sadness in her eyes when she'd stopped talking mid-sentence and stared off into space like she'd been looking for Daddy. She hardly ate at all, and her skin had a sallow, yellow tone. I suspected she'd pretended about sleeping better, too. Thinking of her at home, all by herself, not well, made me even sadder. What was I doing here in Florida with people who barely knew me when my mama needed me? I hoped the couch cushions would silence the sobs I couldn't keep inside.

LOUANN

September 1978

"**WELL, WELL, WELL. WHAT HAVE WE HERE?**" **THE DEEP, BOOM-**ing voice woke me.

Squinting my eyes against the early-morning light, I peeked out from underneath the sheet that had managed to cover my face but not my body during my restless sleep. Looming over me, hands on his hips and a smirk on his face, was a large, dark-haired man. I was suddenly wide awake, scrambling to sit up, and pulling on the twisted sheet to cover myself.

"So, you must be Louann. Joycie said you were a big girl now."

I was too bleary to respond, but somewhere inside, I had a bad feeling about this man who stood smirking at me.

I was saved from answering as Joycie entered the room. "Oh, Dave, now you've gone and woke her up. I told you she'd had a long trip and needed to rest. Be quiet before you wake up the other kids."

Dave's eyes slid sideways at Joycie, but his body didn't move away. "You're not trying to tell me what to do in my own house, are you? I'll do what I want in here, by God."

Joycie walked over and put her hand on his back, rubbing up and down. "Of course not, honey." Her eyelids sank low, and her voice was husky. "You know I didn't mean that. Come on out to the kitchen, sweetie. I've got the coffee made, and breakfast is ready. Bacon's crispy, just like you like it."

Dave's eyes slid back to me. I scrunched into the corner of the couch, my knees drawn up, the sheet pulled close under my chin. He grinned. "Well, darlin', we'll just have to get acquainted later. I need to eat and get to work. Somebody's got to earn the money to pay for this place. Let's make a date for this evening, okay? I want to hear all about our new girl." He winked as Joycie led him away to the kitchen.

Oh, man, did he give me the creeps. I took my time getting dressed in the little bathroom, hoping he would be gone by the time I was done. He wasn't in the kitchen, but the other kids were all there. Benny and Bobby jumped up to hug me. Barbie was friendly but didn't get up. Joycie put a plate of bacon, eggs, and toast in front of me. All of us except Barbie chatted like we hadn't even been separated after the funeral. Barbie barely said hello before ignoring me the rest of the meal. What was up with her, I wondered. But the mania that had been in Joycie's conversation last night had disappeared.

The others stayed home while Joycie took me shopping. She bought me several new outfits and then took me to the big high school to enroll. During all this, she barely made conversation. It was like she was performing perfunctory duties with no emotion. I stayed quiet and worried. What kind of a man was Dave? Why was Barbie so standoffish? Did Mama know what kind of a situation she'd sent me into? Here I was, fourteen-and-a-half, the same age as Joycie when she'd given birth to me. I was miles away from my mama, my daddy was dead, and I was about to start at a huge high school where I didn't know a soul. The only sister I'd ever known was ignoring me, and the man Joycie was married to looked at me like I was a piece of meat. What was I going to do?

That evening at supper, Dave sat at the head of the table with Joycie on his right, Barbie on his left. Everybody sat silently without touching their water or flatware. I followed their lead. Dave bowed his head, and all the others followed suit. I did the same but glanced around first, not believing my eyes. We'd never done this back in Albany.

Then Dave spoke: "Dear Lord, thank you for this food. Bless this family. Thank you for bringing Louann to live with us. Amen." As soon as he was done, Joycie served his plate from each dish, then passed it on.

Then came the questions: "Joycie, did you take Louann shopping? How much did you spend?"

"Yes, Dave. I enrolled her in school, too."

"I asked you a question, Joycie. I expect an answer."

"I, um—I don't remember exactly how much it was. Maybe fifty or sixty dollars. She needed clothes for school. Everything I bought was on sale."

"Just make sure they last until Christmas. Now, Barbie, my little sweetheart, what did you do today?"

I noticed Dave caressing Barbie's hand as he asked the question. He looked intensely into her eyes, and she returned the look like they were the only two people in the room.

"Well, Daddy . . ."

I almost choked on my food. Daddy? When had she started calling him that? She sure wasn't looking at him like a daughter would a daddy, and she was only ten years old.

"And were you a good girl?"

Barbie lowered her eyes. "You know I'm always a good girl, Daddy. Just like you like me to be."

He was still caressing her hand. "That's right, honey. You know just what Daddy wants, don't you?"

"Yes, sir. I do. I know what you want."

Joycie and the boys kept their eyes on their plates. Was I the only one horrified by this conversation? What was in store for me when it came my turn to be put on the spot? The boys were next to be questioned. Trivial inquiries were made about their days. They responded with brief yes-sirs and no-sirs.

Dave had flicked his eyes at me in between questioning each one, but now his eyes settled on me. I could feel his penetrating stare, but I did not return his look.

He started off in a syrupy-sweet voice. "Now, to our newest family member, Louann."

I kept my eyes down.

Fast as lightning, the voice changed and boomed like thunder. "Look at me when I speak to you, girl!"

I looked up, terrified.

Syrupy-sweet again. "How was your first day in Jacksonville, Louann? Did you enjoy yourself?"

I mumbled.

Thunder again. "Speak up, girl!"

From somewhere deep inside of me, I summoned determination. I was not going to be intimidated. I thought about what Mama had said about mothers having to do hard things sometimes. And Daddy had always taught me to be brave but polite. I wasn't going to let this man put me under his thumb like he had obviously done the others. I put down my fork and cleared my throat.

"My first day was fine, sir. Thank you, sir, for the new clothes."

Dave sat back from the table, raised both hands beside his shoulders, and laughed out loud. "What have we here? No shrinking violet, this one. I'm glad to see you have a voice and manners. You'll be a welcome addition to our family."

"Thank you, sir. I appreciate it very much."

While Dave gave a smug smile, the daggers shooting from Barbie's eyes could have speared right through me. As for the others, they kept their heads down and didn't say a word.

When Dave was finished eating, the meal was over. Each kid, in turn, asked to be excused until it was just him, Joycie, and me left at the table. I stood up and picked up my plate.

"Joycie, may I help you with the dishes?" She didn't respond.

Dave smiled. "Good girl, Louann. That's the least you can do. Everybody earns their keep in this household, one way or another." Then he left the table.

Later, after Joycie and I finished up the dishes with minimal conversation, she put her hand on my shoulder. "Louann?"

"Yes, Joycie?"

"I'm glad you're here. Just don't cause any trouble. Be nice, keep Dave happy, and we'll all get along just fine. Okay?"

"Is that what you and Barbie do? Whatever it takes to keep Dave happy?"

Her face hardened, her mouth a straight line, her brows bent in a harsh scowl.

"Yes. That's what we do, Louann. And I expect the same from you."

Throwing the dishtowel onto the counter, I said, "We'll see about that."

SCHOOL STARTED, AND I settled into a routine. I went to school each day, stayed to myself, came home, did homework, helped Joycie in the kitchen, and retired to Barbie's room that we were now sharing. She was still giving me the silent treatment. She sulked and sighed, fumed and muttered at my every move. I could handle her rejection—and the boys and Joycie ignoring me. I could even handle Dave's leers and innuendos by avoiding him. What I couldn't take was the sick atmosphere in that house.

One night, amid pink ruffles and soft sheets in my matching twin bed in Barbie's room, I was scared and homesick. I sobbed into my pillow. There was a rustle from Barbie's bed, and I heard her pad over and sit on the edge of my bed, reaching her hand out to rub my back. I wanted to curl into her and cry my heart out, but I was frozen at this sudden change in her behavior.

"Shhh," she whispered. "Don't cry. I know you're miserable here. I was, too, at first. Now I just make the best of it. I don't have anywhere else to go, but you do. Go home, Louann. Go home."

BESSIE

Late September 1978

T HE PHONE WAS RINGING, BUT I COULDN'T FORCE MYSELF FROM the bed. Eventually, whoever it was gave up. Well, I might as well get up to pee while I was awake. Now somebody was knocking at the door. What in the world? The pounding on the door got louder.

"Mrs. Walker? You in there?" I recognized Mr. Pope, my mailman.

I managed to get to the door and open it just a crack. "I'm here."

"Well, you asked me to check on you, so when I saw yestiddy's mail still in the box, I was worried. Thought I better knock."

"Oh, dear me. I must have forgot all about gettin' it yesterday. My mind has been preoccupied. Thank you, Mr. Pope. I sure do appreciate your bringing it up." I reached out my hand for the envelopes he held.

"You sure you're all right, Mrs. Walker? I can get a message to somebody if you need me to."

"Oh, no, no. I'll be fine. Just a little tired. Thank you again, Mr. Pope."

Closing the door, I looked down. Only two envelopes, and no letter from Louann. It had been almost three weeks now, and no word. *Lord,* I prayed, *let this work out for her.* And now that dang phone was ringing again. By the time I got to the hall, the ringing had stopped. I collapsed on the phone bench. Oh hell. Maybe I'd just leave it off the hook after this. How was I supposed to get any rest with the phone ringing and people knocking on the door? I was out of breath. *Now, what was I doing?* Lord-amighty, there it went ringing again. I grabbed up the receiver.

"Hello? Who is this?" I answered sharply.

"Mama? Is that you? What's wrong?"

"Louann! Oh, my goodness. Has that been you trying to call me all this time?"

"Yes, Mama. Are you all right?"

I summoned all my strength to make it sound like I was as good as a kid with an ice cream cone on a hot summer day.

"Why, yes, honey. I'm just fine. I was trying to get some chores done, then somebody came to the door, the phone was ringing and then stopped, and I had water boiling on the stove. Everything happened at once. I'm just fine—how are you?"

There were a few moments of silence on the other end of the line, then what sounded like Louann trying to talk over a sob. "Oh, Mama, it's awful here. I have to come home. Please. I can't stand it . . . Dave . . . Joycie . . . Barbie—"

"Lou, slow down. Take a deep breath." I waited a few seconds and heard her breathing become a little more regular. "Now, calm down and tell me what's going on."

"Mama, I can't even explain it. They don't want me here, I can tell. I'm miserable. There's something going on here, I don't know what, but everybody walks around like they're on eggshells. They're all afraid of Dave. He orders us around and complains about money all the time. He gives me creepy looks, and I can't stand it."

Oh no, I thought. I could hear her voice getting worked up again. "Listen to me, Louann. Take a deep breath again and tell me exactly what's happening."

She started over. "That's just it, Mama. I don't know exactly. I can't put my finger on it. But something is not right here. I don't feel safe, and I don't think Joycie and Barbie are safe either. Please just let me come home. I promise I'll do anything. I've got money hid away, and I can sneak away and come by myself. If you don't let me come home, I can't stay here. I'll run away."

More sobbing on the other end of the line. Dear God, there was no other choice. Given what little I knew about Dave and Joycie's history, there was no telling what was going on in that house. I had to let Lou come home.

"All right, Lou, just listen to me. You get out as soon as you can. Call the bus station and get the schedule. Do whatever you have to do to get back here. We'll figure something out when you get back home."

"Thank you, thank you, thank you, Mama! I'll see you soon as I can."

"Wait, don't hang up yet. Louann, promise me you'll be careful. You know I love you more than anything. You keep yourself safe and come home to Mama."

"All right, Mama. I promise I will. I love you, too."

LOUANN

October 1978

PRAISE GOD, I WAS GOING HOME. I HAD TO THINK HARD ABOUT exactly how I was going to manage it, but I finally got a plan together. I didn't tell the other kids, and I hated to leave them so suddenly without saying goodbye, but I didn't want them to know anything that Dave or Joycie might try to weasel out of them. I stuffed a change of clothes and some snacks into my bookbag one morning, and when the bus dropped me off at school, I walked into the building like normal. Once inside, I hid in the restroom until the bells rang and the halls were empty, then I snuck out a side door and walked as fast as I could. I'd studied the public bus system so I'd know how to get to the Greyhound Station. I should have just enough time to get there, buy a ticket, and make the ten a.m. bus to Albany. I would be on my way out of town before anybody even realized I was gone. I'd left a note for Joycie explaining I wanted to go home and take care of Mama, that I was on the bus to Albany, and that I'd be fine. I added for her to tell Dave I appreciated his letting me stay with them but needed to get back to Mama.

That night, when I stepped off the bus at the station in Albany, I looked around and thought, *This really is a different world from the station in Jacksonville.* The little one-room block building with old plastic chairs and scraped-up linoleum floors was nothing like the big bright station down there, but it was home. I felt like getting down on my hands and knees and kissing the ground, then giggled to myself at the thought. How silly that anybody could feel that way about podunk Albany. But after those few weeks in Jacksonville, I'd never been happier to be anywhere.

I knew Mrs. Smith, who worked the ticket window, and she knew all us Walkers. She was a nosy old lady and always knew everything that was going on around town. She raised her eyebrows and looked at me over the little half-glasses that were perched near the tip of her nose.

"Louann Walker! What are you doing here?"

"I just got here. I've been down to see Joycie in Florida. Now I'm back."

"Well, I can see you're back. Is Bessie expecting you?"

As much as I wanted to ask what business it was of hers, I remembered my manners. "Yes, ma'am. She's expecting me."

"Well, all right, then." Like I needed her permission.

"Could I use the phone? I need to call somebody for a ride out to the house."

Mrs. Smith took off her glasses and rubbed her eyes, then put them back on. She leaned forward towards me, both elbows on the ticket window shelf. I took a step back. *Uh-oh*, I thought. *Something is not right about this.*

"Louann, let me call Joe Moss to come get you. He won't mind taking you out there. I know he brought you up here a few weeks ago."

I'd known Joe Moss since I'd been a little kid. He was only about eight years older than me, and now he was a deputy.

"Joe Moss? Sure, that's a good idea. He'll take me home."

"Well, Louann, who else is there? Bessie certainly can't come get you, and I know you can't afford a taxi. The sheriff won't mind Joe giving you a lift, and I'll be assured you get home safe."

"I guess you're right. I'll just wait over here." I sat on a hard plastic chair in the waiting area. An hour later, Joe finally showed up.

"Well, hey there, Louann! Heard you need a ride home. Come on, let's go. I don't have all night."

"Thank you, Joe, I sure do appreciate it. I can't wait to see Mama."

I don't know what I was expecting, but when we went outside the station, there was Joe's official deputy car at the curb. He went over and yanked open the backseat passenger door. He was grinning at me, his arm stretched out, indicating I should climb in.

"Sorry, but it's policy. You'll have to ride in the back."

Ride in the back of a cop car? I felt hot tears rising. "But Joe—"

"Aw, never mind, Louann. I'm just kiddin'. You shoulda seen the look on your face. Come on, you can sit up front with me."

I was so relieved I just about wet my pants. Under any other circumstances, I would have been asking a million questions, curious about all the gadgets in that car. As it was, I sat quietly. Joe drove along slow and tried to make conversation.

"So, Louann, how was it down there in Jacksonville? I heard the streets are lined with palm trees, and it's hot as summer all year long. Did you go to the ocean?"

Lord, did everybody in Albany know my business? "Yes, there were some palm trees; yes, it was hot; and no, I didn't go to the ocean. Just get me home, please. I want to see my mama."

"Oh, come on, Lou, we're friends. Don't get mad at me. I hate to be the one with bad news, but you do know Mrs. Walker's bad off, don't you?"

"What do you mean, bad off? I mean, I know she wasn't doing so good back around the funeral, but she was fine when I left. Has something else happened?"

"Well, I don't rightly know all the details, but I know the sheriff's been out to see about her a couple of times. He's been worried about her getting along by herself."

I could feel the dread growing in my stomach. Once again, I put on my grownup act. "That's why I came back. I'm going to take care of her. Nobody will have to worry about her but me."

Joe shrugged. "If you say so, Louann. Just glad I could help you out."

We finally pulled up into the yard at Mama's house. It was dark except for the pale yellow light bulb in the porchlight. Joe looked around.

"You sure she's expecting you?"

"Well, she probably got tired and went on to bed. Here, let me get the key from under this flower pot."

Joe stood aside as I got the door unlocked and opened it into the dark living room. I went around and turned on lights while he brought my bag in. The house smelled musty and a little bit like a mix of old pee and boiled cabbage. It wasn't like Mama not to have her house spic and span. Joe wrinkled up his nose. "You sure you're going to be okay, Louann?"

"Yeah, Joe. Wait here just a minute while I go back and check on Mama, okay?"

I tiptoed down the hall and looked into her bedroom. The light from the hall shone over her, mounded up in the bed, snoring away. Even though the smell was worse back here, I breathed my own sigh of relief. I wasn't sure what I'd expected after what Joe had said about her being bad off, but she seemed okay so far. Back in the living room, I told Joe that everything was fine.

"Thanks again for the ride, Joe. I don't know what Mama's got in the fridge, but do you want a cold Co-Cola or something?"

"Naw, that's fine, Louann. I'll be on my way. You lock this door after me, all right? Glad you're home." He tipped his hat as I shut and locked the door behind him.

BESSIE

October 1978

I T WAS THE BRIGHT LIGHT THAT WOKE ME. THAT AND THE SMELL. Something was different. I lay there and looked around. These days, it took me a while to get out of bed, so I'd taken to lying there and thinking 'bout things before I hauled myself up. As often as not, I'd fall back asleep. Was that what had happened? My eyes were fading, but I knew from the light it had to be almost ten. Lord have mercy. If Hampton Walker knew I'd lain in bed this long, he'd be convinced I was dying.

The strong smell of Pine-Sol was almost overpowering. How had it gotten there? I knew for sure I hadn't opened that bottle of Pine-Sol since . . . well, I couldn't remember the last time I'd opened it. As much as I loved a clean house, I just hadn't had it in me to do any cleaning since Hampton'd been gone. If the kids had been here, I would have made myself, just like mamas had to make themselves do things all the time for their kids, but since it was just me, why bother?

I heard noises, or was I just imagining it? My mind wasn't always too dependable, these days. Then I heard it again. Banging and bumping, coming from the kitchen. Maybe Louann was trying to cook? Oh, wait, that was right. Louann was in Florida with Joycie. It couldn't be her. Then footsteps in the hall came toward my room. Oh, hell! I had to get out of this bed. Somebody was in my house. I heaved myself up. Next thing I knew, I was on the floor.

"Mama! What are you doing? Mama? Are you all right?"

This time, I knew neither my mind nor my eyes were foolin' me. "Louann? What are you doin' here? You're supposed to be in Florida—"

"Is anything hurt? Can you get up?" Louann was passing her hands up and down my arms and feelin' my forehead.

"I think I'm all right. Just a little swimmy-headed, that's all."

She put her hands on either side of my face. In a stern voice, she said, "Mama, don't you ever try to get out of bed by yourself again, you hear me? I can't have you fallin' and breaking an arm or a leg or hip, God forbid. Promise me."

I smiled. Just the sight of Louann brightened my spirits. And here she was, tellin' me what to do or not do. "All right, honey, I promise. Just listen at you, tellin' your old mama what to do. Has it come to that?"

She smiled. "I guess so, Mama. Now let's get you up. Think you can make it to the bathroom? I'll help you get cleaned up, then make you a nice breakfast. How does that sound?"

I let her lead me to the bathroom. As I relieved myself, I thought about how our roles had reversed. She helped me get a spit-bath, combed my hair, and got my dentures in. Then she got me into clean clothes and settled me in the living room. I followed her every move as she went into the kitchen. In just a minute, she was back with a tray of coffee and toast.

"Here, Mama, let's tuck this napkin up around your neck. Do you need any help? Be careful with that cup; it's hot. Want me to hold it for you?"

"I think I can manage, sweetie." I looked around the room and saw that everything had been straightened, the dust was gone, and the windows were open with the fans going. "You've been busy." When had she done all this? How long had she been here? I couldn't seem to remember her coming home.

LOUANN

December 1978

WHEW! IT HAD TAKEN ME DAYS TO GET THE HOUSE CLEANED so that it didn't smell, and that was in between taking care of Mama. It was almost a full-time job making sure she ate decent, bathed, and didn't fall. I did the laundry, cooked the meals, and kept the house clean. Mrs. Maxwell was bringing the groceries, and Joe Moss came by a couple of times a week to check on us. It was tiring, but I was happy as a pig in a puddle. Never mind that Mama slept most of the time. Never mind that I wasn't going to school or talking to anybody. Never mind that we never heard from Joycie. Never mind that Mama slipped farther and farther away, rarely even realizing who I was. The days turned into weeks, and before I knew it, the weather was changing.

I hadn't given a second thought to how I planned to keep this up. I'd been pulling money out of an envelope I'd found in a kitchen drawer to give Mrs. Maxwell for the groceries. I could cook and clean and take care of Mama, but I didn't know the first thing about paying bills. The lights kept turning on, and the water kept coming out of the faucets. The telephone never rang, but that was fine with me. We didn't need anybody checking up on us. But that cold morning in December hit me like a slap in the face.

The house was freezing. There was frost on the inside of the bathroom window. I didn't know how to light the little gas heater in the living room. I'd seen Daddy do it, but the hissing gas and his warnings to stay back had always scared me. Mama shivered and shook when I got her up and dressed. She stared blankly as I settled her into her chair and tucked quilts all around her. I heated up soup from a can for our lunch and supper.

That night, after getting Mama into bed, I climbed under piles of blankets. For the first time since I'd been back, I was scared. How was I going to manage? I cried into the pillows. Maybe I wasn't so grown-up after all. Morning came, and with it, reality came calling.

Even though the house was cold, I was warm, snuggled into my mountain of covers. The house was quiet. Too quiet. *Mama?* I depended on her snoring to let me know she was sleeping peacefully. The icy coldness of the floor went right through my sock feet. When I got to the door of her room and looked in, shivers went up my spine. Her bed was empty! *Oh, dear God.* My eyes searched frantically, and then I saw her: on the floor, on her side, her face turned away from me, quilts wound haphazardly around her body, arms, and legs. I might have thought she was sleeping peacefully except for the absence of that noisy snore.

"Mama? Mama. Wake up." I turned her toward me. Her eyes were closed, and her lips were blue. Faint, wispy breaths blew into the air, so I knew she wasn't dead. I shook her shoulders and half-slapped, half-patted her cheeks. Still, her eyes did not open. "Mama! Mama!" I called over and over, but she would not wake up. *Oh, dear God.* I couldn't get her back into bed, so I put a pillow under her head and covered her as well as I could. I ran to the phone. No dial tone. "Hello? Hello?" I pressed and pressed. Silence.

I put on shoes, wrapped a quilt around me, and took off for Mrs. Maxwell's.

LOUANN

December 1978

"**H**ELLO, UM, LOUANN, IS THAT RIGHT?"

"Yes, sir. Louann Walker."

The big man in the uniform cleared his throat with a gruff, phlegmy scrape. "I don't believe we've met, Louann. I'm Sheriff Mann. I knew your daddy—a fine man, a very fine man. And I know your mama, too. It's sad Hampton is gone, and now Bessie's so bad off. But I tell you what we're gonna do." Sheriff Mann had walked away from the doctor and come over to sit by me in the waiting area at the emergency room. I had the quilt wrapped around me but still shivered like I was freezing. "Now, Louann, I'm sure everything's going to be all right. It's probably nothing serious, but—"

"What? What is it? Is my mama gonna be all right? Tell me now."

"Well, Louann, Bessie's had a stroke. She's going to need to be in the hospital a day or so, then it'll just take time to see how she does. She may have to go over to the Green Hill nursing home—"

"The nursing home? She can't be that sick. She was just fine yesterday—"

"Whoa, now, Louann. Don't worry. I'm sure she'll be just fine with time. There's nothing you can do for her right now. You don't need to be at that house out in the country by yourself, so we're going to have to figure something out. I'll take you back to the office with me and get you a little something to eat while I make some calls. How about a cold drink and a candy bar from the machine?"

I broke down and cried. Sheriff Mann patted my back. I wished harder than ever for my daddy to be here. None of this would be happening. I let the sheriff lead me out to his car and drive me to the jail where he kept his office. It was scary seeing all those bars on the windows. He took my arm and led me through the gate and inside a shabby little office. I'd never been in the jail, but I didn't like the looks of it: dingy pale-green walls, old linoleum on the floor, dim lights hanging overhead. It smelled, too. Like a mix of pee and boiled cabbage. Somewhere down a different hallway, I could hear rattling and clanging, conversations I couldn't make out, laughing and guffawing.

Off in a corner, Joe Moss was sitting behind a desk with his feet propped up, laughing into a telephone. He said a quick "I gotta go, doll" and took his feet off the desk when the sheriff and me walked in. He had a puzzled look on his face. "Hey there, Lou? How're you doing?"

Sheriff Mann looked annoyed. "How do you think she's doing, Joe? Mrs. Walker's over at the emergency room. Go get Louann a drink and a candy bar out of the machine. Bring it in my office."

Joe's face fell, and he got right to his feet. "Sorry, Louann. I didn't know. I'll be right back." He trotted off down the hall, and I followed Sheriff Mann through a glass door to his office.

He put out his hand to indicate that I should sit in a hard chair. Joe brought me a drink and a candy bar, winked at me, and then went back out and closed the door softly. The sheriff, in his rolling chair behind the desk, picked up the phone. I suppose I was stunned into silence. I couldn't think of what to say or what to do. It felt like the walls were closing in on me. I didn't touch the drink or the candy bar.

Sheriff Mann turned the chair away from me and was speaking in a low voice to whoever was on the other end of the line. I wasn't trying to listen, and if I was, I couldn't have heard clearly, anyway. Eventually, he placed the phone back in the cradle and looked at me with a big, fake smile, dusting his hands together like he was relieved to be finished with a nasty job.

"There, now. That's taken care of. They're going to be here in a little while to pick you up. Won't be but a few minutes."

"I just want to go see my mama. I'm sure she can come home, and I'll take care of her. Please, sir, could we go get her, and you could take us home?"

He sat back in his chair, hands on the desk in front of him, tapping his fingers. "Well, Louann, it's not that simple. Your mama's too bad off to be at home. In fact . . . well, never mind that right now. That presents us with a dilemma. You don't have any other relatives close by, and you can't stay out at the house by yourself. You're too young."

Tears were starting to build and sting my eyes again. I tried to swallow the hard lump that was coming up my throat. He'd said Mama was bad off. Was she going to die, too? And what about me? What would happen to me? I wouldn't go back to Joycie's. I'd run away first. I s'pose the sheriff could see I was about to fall apart.

"Now, don't you worry, honey. They'll take care of your mama over there, and we've made arrangements for you. There are people that help out kids when there's nobody else to take care of them. I've called Mr. and Mrs. Rogers. They've got a nice home with a room just for you. You'll like it there, and they live in a nice part of town, the best foster home we have. Nothing but the best will do for Hampton and Bessie Walker's girl. It's all set up, and they should be here within the hour to pick you up."

It felt like the blood had drained right out the bottom of my feet. I felt woozy and swayed in the hard chair. Sheriff Mann was looking at me, now, eyes wide as his fat face would allow. He raised both hands like he didn't know quite what to do. It sunk in what the sheriff was saying. I'd heard Mama and Daddy talk about foster homes when they'd taken Joycie's kids in, Mama saying how she couldn't let them put those babies in foster care. It had sounded bad.

All I could muster was a small, whispery tone. "You mean I'm going to a foster home?"

I couldn't hold back the tears, now. They spilled from my eyes and ran down my cheeks.

"It won't be so bad . . ." About that time, Joe Moss poked his head around the door.

"Mrs. Rogers is here, Sheriff. I saw her pull in in that big Lincoln of hers. Should I bring her on back when she gets inside?"

"Lord, yes, Joe. And not a minute too soon. Bring her back." The sheriff stood up now, reaching to a shelf behind him to pull Kleenex from a box. He came around to my chair and gave me a handful of tissues. "There now, girlie. It's going to be all right. Mrs. Rogers is going to take good care of you, you'll see."

LOUANN

December 1978

MRS. ROGERS WAS AN ATTRACTIVE LADY DRESSED IN SLACKS AND a sweater, with pearls around her neck and matching pearl earrings. Her light brown hair was beauty-shop fresh, and she smelled like Jergen's cherry almond lotion. She didn't try to give me a hug or anything when we were first introduced in Sheriff Mann's office. When we got into her big Lincoln Continental, she touched me lightly on the arm and set me at ease right away. Her soft voice was kind.

"Louann, I know this is hard for you. Mr. Rogers and I want to make you as comfortable as possible. First thing tomorrow, I will take you to see your mama. I haven't had the pleasure of meeting her, and I didn't know your daddy, either, but Mr. Rogers spoke very highly of both of them. He had a late meeting tonight and said to tell you he was sorry he couldn't come with me to pick you up."

"You'll take me to see Mama in the morning?"

"Of course, dear. It's perfectly understandable you are worried about her. I know you don't understand everything that's going on, and it may take a while to get things straightened out, but we want to help you however we can. Just ask me anything you want to know, and I'll do my best to answer. Mr. Rogers and I have helped other young people, and we'd like to help you, too."

"Thank you. That's nice of you. I want to know what's wrong with Mama. How sick is she? Is she going to die? Can't we just go back and live together at our house and let me take care of her?"

"Those are some good questions, Louann, and very understandable. I don't know all the answers yet, but I will find out as much as I can when we go tomorrow. I was told the doctors think she had a stroke because she can't move very well. She also has some kind of infection that has made her weak, and she's not eating or drinking fluids like she ought."

"So she's pretty sick? Is she paralyzed? Can she talk?"

"I don't know how paralyzed she is or if she's talking. We'll find all that out tomorrow and maybe get some other answers, too. But, Louann, it sounds like it is going to take a while for her to get better. These kinds of things don't usually go away in just a day or so. I don't want you to get your hopes up too much about going home. You will have a home with us as long as you need it."

Mrs. Rogers did have a very nice home. She got me settled into a pretty bedroom that had a door that led directly into an attached bathroom. I didn't even have to go out in the hall.

There was deep, soft carpet in the bedroom and in the bathroom that was the color of peach ice cream. The curtains, bedcoverings, and towels all matched in a vanilla that made the whole room look like peaches and cream. There was soft light from a bedside lamp, fluffy pillows, and pretty little soaps shaped like seashells in the bathroom. It smelled wonderful, like fresh laundry. Lo and behold, on a little table right by the bed, there was a peach-colored princess telephone. I had seen one of these years ago at Aunt Lila's house but had never dreamed of having my own.

Waking in the morning to the smell of bacon, I was surprised that I had slept well. I felt rested; like I could face whatever we were going to find out at the hospital. It was like a weight had been lifted off my shoulders, and I had a sense of peace that everything was going to be all right. Maybe not today or tomorrow, but eventually. And I could stay in this restful place as long as I needed to.

I met Mr. Rogers at breakfast. He was nice, just like his wife. He smiled and said some kind words about Mama and Daddy and that he hoped I didn't mind staying with them until things got worked out. Their own children were grown and married, and they missed having young people around. He said it was the least they could do to help others, since God had blessed them with so much. I did not get any inkling of a bad feeling about him. Even when he patted my shoulder, said goodbye, and left for work, it felt perfectly natural.

Mrs. Rogers and I arrived at the hospital and told the lady at the reception desk that we were there to see Bessie Walker. The lady looked at us doubtfully, raising her eyebrows as the corners of her mouth turned downward.

"Mrs. Walker? She's in the ward, but I'm not sure she's up to receiving visitors."

"We'd like to see her anyway," Mrs. Rogers said, firmly but sweetly. "I've brought her daughter, Louann. I'm sure she will want to see her."

The lady's doubtful look turned curious. "Oh, really? I wasn't aware Mrs. Walker had a daughter. Nobody's inquired . . ."

Mrs. Rogers interrupted the lady. "Just direct us to her, please."

"Down the hall to the left, the ward is at the end. I believe she's in bed four, but you can check with the nurse there."

"Thank you. We will," said Mrs. Rogers sweetly.

The hall was the same dreary green color as the jail, and it smelled even worse. The odors of pee, vomit, diarrhea, and alcohol all rolled into one disgusting scent. I wanted to hold my nose. How could people stand to work here, much less have to stay here as patients? We passed old men and women sitting in the hallway in wheelchairs, mouths hanging open, drool flowing, eyes vacant. Some rocked back and forth, swayed sideways, or moved their arms in repetitive motions. Some made noises as we walked by or reached out their hands. I was scared, and I moved close beside Mrs. Rogers, whose heels made a brisk clicking sound on the tiled floors. I was amazed that she smiled and spoke to every person we passed:

"Good morning! How are you today?"

"Hello! Why, don't you look pretty this morning."

"Good day, sir. It's a fine day, isn't it?"

We reached the end of the hall that opened into one large room lined with hospital beds. In each bed lay either a snowy-white-haired person or a nearly bald person, wearing a printed hospital gown and covered with a grayish sheet. It was hard to tell if each was a man or a woman. There was a constant murmuring of moans, groans, and snores, punctuated now and then by a sharp shriek. The drone of machines and beeping medical instruments accompanied the human sounds as an undercurrent. It sounded like a scaredy-house I'd once been in at a carnival in Florida. Mrs. Rogers stopped, and I heard her sharp intake of breath. I shrank even closer into her side, and she took my hand into her own.

There were nurses at some of the bedsides, but it was a nurse at a desk just inside the door who spoke. "May I help you?"

"I hope so." Mrs. Rogers smiled. "We are here to see Mrs. Walker. Bessie Walker."

The nurse's eyebrows raised. "Oh, you are, are you? And may I ask just who you and this child are? We don't allow underage visitors."

Mrs. Rogers's voice did not waver. "Oh, my, that would really be a shame. Especially since Sheriff Mann asked me to bring Mrs. Walker's daughter here to see her first thing this morning. I'm Mrs. Gambell T. Rogers, and this is Louann Walker, Mrs. Walker's adopted daughter."

"I see," the nurse responded. "In that case, I suppose it will be all right. Mrs. Walker is the fourth bed on the right."

"Thank you, dear. How very kind." Mrs. Rogers held my hand and walked softly so her shoes wouldn't be so loud. We stepped quietly to the side of the fourth bed on the right.

There was my mama. Her white hair was spread out against the pillow. Her face was twisted in what looked like a painful grimace. She did not have her glasses on, and her eyes were closed, but there were jerky movements under her thin eyelids. Her hands were folded on her chest on top of the sheet, and her fingers twitched. If I hadn't been told it was my mama, I would not have recognized her.

Mrs. Rogers slipped one arm around my shoulder. She leaned over and spoke in the most gentle and loving voice I think I'd ever heard before. "Mrs. Walker? Bessie?"

There was no response. She placed her other hand gently over Mama's own hands. No response.

"Mrs. Walker? I've brought Louann to see you."

The papery-thin eyelids flew open, and Mama's blue eyes fixed on me. "Mama, it's me!"

Mama's mouth twisted but made no sound. But her eyes—oh, her beautiful eyes—smiled and gleamed and glistened with tears.

"Oh, Mama, you do hear me. You know it's me."

The corners of Mama's mouth twitched, and I swear her eyes were laughing. I couldn't contain myself any longer. I threw myself over Mama and hugged her hard. "Oh, Mama, I love you."

I slowly realized I was the only one doing any hugging. I released her, stood straight again, and held her hands, still contracting and relaxing in spasms. Except for that and the screwing motions of her mouth, Mama lay still.

Mrs. Rogers spoke again, and Mama's eyes tracked over to her face. "Mrs. Walker, I want you to know Louann is just fine. My name is Margaret Rogers. My husband, Gambell, and I will be taking care of her until you're better. Gambell knew your husband Hampton and spoke very highly of both of you. You rest, now, and please don't worry. I'll bring Louann back to see you tomorrow, all right? You take care, now, and concentrate on getting better. Louann, give your mama another hug, and then we need to go, okay?"

I hugged Mama hard. "I love you, Mama. Please get better. I want us both to go home. Don't worry about me, I'll be fine. You just get well."

Mama closed her eyes, and I swear the corners of her mouth turned up.

As Mrs. Rogers and I walked away, I moved closer to her side. A comforting arm came around my shoulder, drawing me close like a warm fire on a cold night.

LOUANN

December 1978 to March 1979

MRS. ROGERS DID TAKE ME BACK, THE NEXT DAY AND THE NEXT, and when they moved Mama from the hospital to the Green Hill nursing home, we went there every day, too.

After going to see Mama that first day, Mrs. Rogers took me shopping. She explained that I would have to go to school once the Christmas and New Year's holidays were over and that we would be going to church on Sundays, so I needed clothes and all the other things a young teenaged girl needs to make herself presentable. I'd never had anybody take me under their wing like that. The shopping spree was fun. I'd never had so many new clothes at one time, along with shoes, underwear, jackets, purses, and just about anything else you could think of. She bought me shampoo, hairbrushes, curlers. Even some blush, lipstick, nail polish, and a light cologne.

"Nothing too garish," Mrs. Rogers said. "But a girl likes to feel pretty."

I wasn't sure how to take all this, but it didn't seem fake. More like she truly enjoyed spending time with me. I wondered if this was how a normal mother-daughter relationship should be. The Rogerses put up a real Christmas tree in their living room. There were strands of electric lights right on the tree, and they let me hang fragile glass ornaments on the branches. There were even a few wrapped gifts underneath with my name on fancy tags. I wasn't expecting anything since they'd already bought me so much, and I felt bad I didn't have a thing for them.

The holidays over, I started back at school. I knew many of the kids and wasn't too far behind. I always had been able to catch on to things easily. Each day after school, we'd go see Mama. She wasn't improving, but she wasn't getting worse, either. Mrs. Rogers communicated with the doctors, and she would tell me everything so I could know what was going on. I knew she was in contact with Joycie and Mama's sisters in Florida, too. Being underage, I had no say-so in Mama's affairs or decisions about her care. I was constantly worried about what they were going to do with her. What if she got worse? Would she go to a hospital again? She didn't have much income, only Daddy's Social Security benefits and veteran's pension, but I didn't know how any of that worked. What if she did suddenly get better? Could we go back and live together at her house?

Despite all these questions plaguing me, I enjoyed being with the Rogerses. Sometimes we'd play board games, or Mr. Rogers would show funny old movies of when their children had been little and they'd gone on vacations in a silver trailer they'd pulled behind a big station wagon. It was interesting to see a happy family traveling to exotic locations like the Grand Canyon, Niagara Falls, or the Rocky Mountains. I couldn't fathom having the time or money to take such trips. Mrs. Rogers had me help her cook, sew, and arrange things in the house. All along, she was teaching me, not making me do it like a chore. There wasn't much cleaning involved because she had a lady she called her housekeeper to come in three times a week to clean, do laundry, and iron. It was my first experience ever spending time around a colored person, and I was a little scared at first, but Nellie turned out to be so sweet, calling me her honey-chile and slipping me treats. She even liked to do my hair in the mornings and make sure my clothes were absolutely perfect before I left for school. I was a little embarrassed by all that at first, but secretly, I soaked up the attention and preened inside at being made over.

The months went by, and Mama did slowly improve. She wasn't her old self, but her garbled speech became understandable to the Rogerses and to me, and she was able to walk short distances, although she was feeble. I began to hope that it wouldn't be long before Mama and I could be together again. I wouldn't mind going back to our plain little house, just the two of us. I could go to school, come home, and make supper, and me and Mama would be just as happy as a dog with two tails. I had my fifteenth birthday in February of 1979, and by then, I thought I was practically grown. I just knew that by the time spring rolled around, me and Mama could be on our own. But it was not to be.

One afternoon in March, after our regular visit to see Mama, we got home, and Mrs. Rogers went to work in her sewing room while I was doing homework at the kitchen table. Then there was a loud banging at the front door.

"I'll go, Louann," Mrs. Rogers called from the sewing room.

"Yes, ma'am, Mrs. Rogers." I called back.

I couldn't see the front door from where I worked in the kitchen, but I could hear the conversation that took place.

"Mrs. Rogers?" a woman's raspy voice spoke.

"Yes, I'm Mrs. Rogers. May I help you?"

"I believe you can," the woman said. "You got a girl here, name of Louann Walker, dontcha?"

At the sound of my name, I dropped my pencil and went quietly to the front door, standing slightly behind Mrs. Rogers. I wasn't exactly sure who the woman was, but she seemed vaguely familiar. I sensed Mrs. Rogers stiffen.

"May I ask who you are and why you need to know about Louann?"

The woman laughed harshly, a laugh that ended in a craggy coughing fit. Finally, she hawked a huge loogie off the side of the front stoop and caught her breath. "I happen to be her grandmother, Lynn Walker, and I'm here to take her with me."

My hands flew to my mouth. No wonder she looked familiar. I hadn't seen this woman since I'd been maybe three years old. What did she want with me? Mrs. Rogers put her arm protectively around my shoulder. "I see. Won't you please come in, Mrs. Walker?" Mrs. Rogers opened the door wide, indicating with her other hand that this woman should step inside.

Lynn stepped inside and grabbed me by the shoulders. "Louann? Well, I'll be damned. Ain't you a big girl now. Give your grandma a hug."

She put her arms around me and squeezed tight. I recoiled from the smell of cigarettes, sour breath, and unwashed hair. When she let go, she turned around and let out a low whistle. "This is sure a nice place you got here, Mrs. Rogers. I hope Miss Fancy Pants here isn't too spoiled from livin' in a place like this."

"Thank you, Mrs. Walker. Let's go in the living room and sit down so we can talk this over."

"Why, sure. But they ain't no need to talk. She's comin' with me."

We walked into the living room. Lynn sat herself down in a cushy side chair, and I sat by Mrs. Rogers on the sofa.

Mrs. Rogers smiled graciously at Lynn and said, "May I get you a drink? Perhaps tea or coffee?"

"No, ma'am. That won't be necessary. Just get Louann's things together, and we'll be on our way."

I looked fearfully at Mrs. Rogers and shrank closer to her side. What was happening? Did I have to go with Lynn?

Mrs. Rogers cleared her throat and spoke kindly to Lynn. "Well, Mrs. Walker, I'm Louann's foster parent. Her great-grandmother Bessie is her legal guardian, and she's been unwell. That's why Louann is here to stay with Mr. Rogers and myself. Legally—"

Lynn stood up, walked over in front of me and Mrs. Rogers, and shook her finger in Mrs. Rogers's face. "I don't give a shit about legally. Louann is my granddaughter, and I'm taking her."

Mrs. Rogers did not flinch. She patted me on the leg, and, without taking her eyes from Lynn, she said, "Louann, go into your room and get your things together. Get my two big suitcases from my closet. Pack as much as you can inside of them."

I was horrified. "But, I don't—"

"It's all right, Louann. Go ahead and do as I say for now. I'll get this all straightened out."

I was crying now and hadn't moved an inch.

"Go on, honey. Don't cry. Everything will be fine," she continued in a soothing voice.

I walked a wide circle around Lynn as she watched me with squinted eyes. "Yeah, don't be such a crybaby," she spat out as I left the room.

I don't know what was said between Lynn and Mrs. Rogers after I left the room. I was taking my time, thinking that maybe if I took too much time, Lynn would just give up and go away. In a few minutes, Mrs. Rogers appeared in my room. I rushed into her arms, sobbing. "Please don't make me go! I don't even know her. I don't want to go. Please let me stay!"

"Shh, now, sweetheart. I know, I know. I'm going to take care of this, I promise. I think it best you go with her for now. It's the safest thing to do. If I try to keep you here, no telling what she'll do. As soon as Mr. Rogers gets home, we'll be in touch with the sheriff and get this straightened out." She helped me cram as much as I could into the two large bags.

From the living room came that crone-like voice. "Come on, girlie. I ain't got all night. Let's get this show on the road."

LOUANN

March 1979

I DID NOT KNOW THIS WOMAN, LYNN. SHE HAD NEVER WANTED her own daughter, Joycie, and she had never wanted me, so why did she want me now? Was she ashamed that her grandchild was in foster care? It had never seemed to bother her that Hampton and Bessie had adopted her grandchildren away from Joycie just so they'd have a decent home. She'd never shown up when any of us had been young, happy to let an old couple wear themselves out raising young children.

That late afternoon when she took me from the Rogerses', we drove out on a country road to a rundown trailer. There was a beat-up taxi cab parked in the dirt yard, and dim lights glowed through pulled-down window shades.

"Welcome home, darlin'," Lynn's raspy voice chuckled.

This wasn't my home. I swore to myself I would run away if I had to stay here.

"Ain't ya got nothing to say? This here is where me and Billy live. He's my boyfriend. Don't pay him no mind, and he won't bother you. He gets kinda loud when he's drinking, which is about every night, but he'll pass out, and I'll put him to bed. Come on, let's get on inside."

We went inside. The place was nasty. Billy was snoring on the couch, empty beer cans all around him; on the floor, a butt was smoking in a chicken-pot-pie tin with half the pot pie still in it. The smell of stale beer, man-sweat, and garbage made me gag. A television was blaring a wrestling match.

In a low voice, Lynn said, "Throw your bags over there in the corner, and I'll get him off to bed. You'll bed down here on the couch. The bathroom's that way, and you can help yourself to whatever you can find in the kitchen. I don't keep much groceries on hand, but you're welcome to whatever's there. Just keep quiet 'til I get Billy back in the bedroom."

I don't know why she would think I wouldn't be quiet; I hadn't said a word since we'd gotten in her car at the Rogerses'. Pushing Mrs. Rogers's suitcases into the corner, I stayed out of Lynn's way as she pulled Billy up. He grumbled I-don't-know-what, threw his arms around her, and started nuzzling on her neck. "Not now, Billy. Later," Lynn cooed. "Later, honey. Let's get you back in the bed." She nudged him along, half stumbling and half falling, but somehow managing to get him out of the living room.

I walked into the tiny kitchen. The source of the garbage smell was obvious. A plastic bag lay on the floor, garbage spilling out. Roaches scurried around the opening. I backed up and made a wide circle around the bag. The sink was piled with dirty dishes, and the scarce counter space was overrun by sour dishrags, spilled food, and another butt smoking in a saucer. I didn't want to eat anything from this foul place, but I was hungry. I was afraid to open the fridge, so at first, I cracked the door just a little and peeked in. Nothing jumped out at me, and no bugs scurried, so I opened it a little farther. It was pretty bare, but there were cans of Coke, some wrapped slices of cheese, and a few other odds and ends. I took out a Coke and a couple slices of cheese.

I found some crackers in a cabinet that were firmly sealed; no bugs had gotten to them. Taking the food into the living room, I sat on the edge of the couch. I stubbed out the smoking butt and scooted the beer cans away with my shoe. I would have to inspect this couch for bugs before I slept on it.

In a few minutes, Lynn came back to the living room. She sat on the other end of the couch and lit a cigarette. "All right, Louann. Here's the plan. I'm gonna take you in, and I'll get your Social Security payment switched over to me. Besides Joycie, I'm the closest kin you've got. I'll take you to school in the morning and then go see about that."

It finally made sense. It was all about the money. She wanted the payments that had been going to Mama to take care of me to come to her.

She kept on talking like I wasn't even there. "Yep, with that extra money, me and Billy can get a nicer place. You'll be at school most of the time, and you can help out around here when you get home. Billy's gone most of the day driving his cab, and I work a few hours at the laundromat in town. We won't bother you, and you don't have to pay us any mind, either. What do you think? It's about time you said something."

I wasn't worried about me, but what about Mama? I could barely eke out a whisper. "What about my mama?"

Lynn laughed out loud. "Your mama? What's your mama got to do with it? Joycie ain't never been a mama to you, and she's not about to start now. You can goddamn count on that."

"I don't mean Joycie. I mean my mama, Bessie, that's in the nursing home. I can't stay here. I've got to take care of her when she gets out."

More cackling from Lynn. "Oh, honey, she ain't long for this world. She ain't never gonna get out of there alive."

I was horrified, but I found my voice. Now I talked, and I talked loud. "That's not so. She's getting better. Mrs. Rogers takes me to see her every day. She's not going to die. We're going back to live at her house together, me and her." I jumped up from the couch, furiously stomping my feet and yelling at Lynn.

Next thing I knew, Lynn was up too and had her hands gripping my arms and pinning them to my sides. "Now you listen here, missy. That ain't gonna happen. You're stayin' here, and I'm gettin' that money. Now, we're all going to bed, and we'll settle this tomorrow. You hear me?"

She let go of me, stomped over and turned off the television, and went off to the bedroom. I threw myself down on the couch and sobbed, not giving any more thought to what might be crawling around in and on it. Somehow, eventually, I fell asleep.

I didn't see Billy the next morning, and Lynn and I did not speak. I got dressed for school and sat on the couch. Finally, she came out of the bedroom and said, "Let's go." We got in the car, and she dropped me off at the high school.

I tried to concentrate, but it was like I was in some other world. Other kids swirled around me, teachers talked, and I followed instructions like a robot.

"When you finish the test, you may turn it in, then read quietly at your desk." I finished the test, turned it in, and sat quietly at my desk, staring blankly at the wall.

"Hey, watch where you're going!"

"Sorry," I mumbled, and I tried not to bump into anybody else.

"Open your books to page one hundred and ten." I opened my book to page one hundred and ten.

"Hey, didn't you hear that bell? Move it! It's time to go home." I picked up my book bag and walked along the hall until I was outside of the building.

There was Lynn's car in the car line. She was blowing cigarette smoke out the window, and her other hand fidgeted on the steering wheel. I looked around, hoping to see Mrs. Rogers's big Lincoln. Of course, it wasn't there. Why wasn't she here? I'd thought she was going to fix this. I wanted to run in the opposite direction, but I had nowhere else to go. Slowly, I plodded towards Lynn's beat-up Buick and threw myself in the back seat.

"What?" she growled, looking at me in the rearview mirror, the cigarette hanging out of the side of her mouth. "You can't even say hello, how do you do, how was your day? Spoiled rotten, that's what you are." She stepped on the gas and took off.

I slumped down in the seat and tried to shut out her annoying voice. Why couldn't she just shut up? If I had to be with her, I sure didn't want to hear that voice all the time. She kept on.

"Well, you might be happy to know I've changed my mind. I was gettin' fed up with Billy's drinking, and his attitude sucks. Why should I want to share any money with him when I could have it all to myself? So I've packed our things, and we're heading to my sister's in Florida. We can stay there 'til I find us a place. It's all decided. Settle in, honey; it's a long ride to Lake City."

She was taking me to Florida? How would Mrs. Rogers find me? Nobody would know where I was. What about Bessie? What if they let her out and there was nobody to take care of her? What was I going to do in Lake City, Florida, other than be a slave to this crazy woman? It was too much. All too much. I tried to stifle my sobs, but it didn't work.

"Oh my God. You're not cryin' again, are you? Can't you do nothing but cry? Clam up, girl. I'm sick of this crying. I've a good mind to just put you out on this road. Tell people you ran off and I don't know where you are. Maybe some serial killer will find you and take you off my hands. Nobody'd have to know."

She laughed that creepy, coughing laugh like some wild animal was trying to scratch its way out of her throat. I put my hands over my ears, scrunched myself into the corner, and tried to block out the world.

LOUANN

March 1979

T HAT HORRIBLE VOICE CRASHED THROUGH MY SLEEP. I WASN'T sure how long I'd been asleep, but it was dark outside, and we were in the parking lot of a deserted-looking gas station.

"Hey, wake up! I gotta pee, and I need coffee and cigarettes. You want anything?"

I did need to pee, too, but from the looks of this place, it would be a reeking, nasty bathroom with a stopped-up toilet, no toilet paper, no soap, no paper towels, and a broken hand dryer. Oh well, I figured: when you gotta go, you gotta go. Better than a mayonnaise jar on the floor of the car. I mumbled "I guess so" and followed Lynn inside.

We both went to the bathroom, and it was exactly how I'd pictured it. I noticed Lynn didn't bother, but I rinsed my hands the best I could and shook them dry. In the store, while she was fixing her coffee, I picked out a Coke and a bag of chips and put them on the counter at the checkout. "Thanks," I mumbled when she came up and paid. Back out at the car, I got in the backseat again while she pumped the gas.

As soon as we were on our way again, she started up. "'Bout time you woke up. I need you to keep me company. I done almost fell asleep a couple times. Near about run off the road and killed us both." The horrible laugh. "We got a couple more hours on the road."

"Yes, ma'am." That was all I could muster. What was I supposed to talk to this woman about?

"And, hey, don't get those chips all over my car. I got ants in here once and like to never got rid of 'em. Damn things just wouldn't die. I sprayed and sprayed and got sick from smelling that stuff."

"Ants are hard to get rid of."

She prattled on about this and that, and I commented here and there. Maybe if I was halfway nice, it wouldn't be so bad. And, the more I talked, the less I had to listen to her.

We got to her sister's house in Lake City around one a.m. Couldn't tell much about the place with it being dark, but the house was small. At the door, her sister's first words were, "Now, y'all keep quiet. Don't wake up Danny or the kids." Then they hugged, and Lynn introduced me to Rhonda. "It's about time I met my great-niece," Rhonda said. "My my, ain't you the pretty one. Look just like your mama." Mentally, I had to translate that she was referring to Joycie, not Bessie.

"Thank you. Some people say I look a lot like Joycie."

Rhonda hugged me. "Spittin' image, if you ask me."

We exchanged a few more pleasantries, and Rhonda got sheets for me and Lynn to sleep on the pullout sofa bed. The house was neat and clean inside, thank goodness. We didn't bother to unpack since it was so late, just yanked pajamas out of one of the suitcases. Even though I'd slept a few hours in the car, I felt exhausted and fell asleep right away, never even noticing whether Lynn was in the same bed.

I awoke to little kid voices snickering near me.

"Who's that?"

"I don't know." Giggle giggle.

"She must be mama's friend."

"I've never seen her before." More giggles.

I sat up and pulled the sheet around me, immediately noticing that Lynn was nowhere to be seen, and her side of the bed didn't even look slept in. About that time, Rhonda came in from the kitchen.

"Good morning, Louann. This is Shane and Brandy, my kids. Kids, this is your cousin Louann."

The kids giggled and ran off to the kitchen. Rhonda sat down on the edge of the pullout bed, frowning.

"Where's Lynn?" I asked. "Doesn't look like she slept here."

"Well, she didn't sleep here."

"What?"

"She's gone. Said to tell you bye."

"What? Where's she gone? When's she coming back?"

"Well, Louann, I can't rightly say. She took everything and left. Didn't say where she was going, when she was coming back, or even if she was coming back. Lynn's kinda like that sometimes."

I tried rubbing sleep from my eyes like I could rub away the confusion in my brain. I looked around the room. The other side of the bed had clearly not been slept in, and as my eyes roamed, I noticed the bags and suitcases were gone from where I'd stuck them in the corner the night before. *Uh-oh.*

"Did you, by any chance, put my bags away somewhere?"

"No, honey, I didn't touch your bags. I think Lynn must have taken them with her."

Now I was scared. Here I was, in some woman's house that I didn't know, in a place I didn't know, with little kids I didn't know giggling at me, and I had nothing but the pajamas I was wearing. *Oh my God. Now what?* I felt the tears beginning to sting.

Rhonda just sat there, looking at me with a sad look on her face, like she was waiting for me to figure out what to do. My breath started coming fast, and I felt faint. I fell back on the bed, pulled the sheet over my head, turned to bury my face in the pillow, and tried to let it stifle the wail that was rising in my throat. Not that it did any good. I felt a hand rest hesitantly on my back.

"Don't cry, honey. Please, don't cry. You want me to call your mama?"

My mama? Who was she talking about? My mama was sick in the nursing home. Mama Joycie wouldn't be any help—she couldn't stand me. I had no daddy. There was nobody in this world I could turn to for help. Except . . .

I sat back up and wiped the tears from my face. "My mama can't help, but there is a lady I know, my foster parent, the one Lynn took me from. Maybe she could come and get me? But I don't know; she's all the way up in Albany."

Rhonda's face brightened. "Oh, good. I'm sure she'll know what to do. What's her name? I'll call information, get her number, and let her know what's happened."

Within the half-hour, Rhonda had Mrs. Rogers on the phone. It was obvious that Rhonda didn't want any part of Lynn's doings, as she handed the phone over to me without explaining who she was or what was going on.

"Oh, Mrs. Rogers, it's Louann!" That was all I could get out before I started boohoo-ing all over again. I handed the phone back to Rhonda, indicating she'd have to do the talking.

I listened as she explained who she was, where I was, and that Lynn had apparently dumped me and taken everything I'd had with her. Rhonda sounded childlike as she asked what we should do. Then she was listening and nodding.

"Yes, ma'am, Lake City."

"Uh-hum, I know."

"I can do that."

"Sure, here she is."

I had calmed down enough to listen and answer Mrs. Rogers. She said that she would come and get me, but she was at least six hours away. She wanted to see if she could arrange for someone else who could get to me sooner, but she needed to make a couple of calls.

"Louann, I love you," she said. "Don't worry. Give the phone back to Rhonda so I can get her number, and I'll call right back."

"O-o-okay. You're the only one I could think of to call. Thank you. Here's Rhonda."

They spoke briefly; Rhonda passed on her address and phone number, then hung up.

"There now," said Rhonda. "I'm sure she'll take care of everything. Let me find you some clothes to put on. One of my T-shirts, some sweatpants, and socks ought to work for now. Then I'll make you some breakfast." She trotted off, smiling and humming a bright tune, like it wasn't out of the ordinary for a fifteen-year-old girl to be dumped on her doorstep with nothing but a pair of pajamas.

Rhonda brought me the clothes, and I went into the bathroom to change. When I came out, the little boy and girl were parked in front of the television watching cartoons, and Rhonda was in the kitchen. Just as I walked in, the old harvest-gold wall phone rang near the kitchen door.

"Hello?" Rhonda said. "Yes, oh, hey, Mrs. Rogers."

"Who? Joyce Deutsch?"

"Around noon? All right, that will be fine."

"Thank you."

"And you have a good day, too, Mrs. Rogers."

"Goodbye."

I was frozen in the kitchen doorway. Joycie? What did this have to do with Joycie? Rhonda turned that cheery childlike smile on me.

"It's all set. Joycie will be here to pick you up around noon. She's just over in Jacksonville and can be here much faster than Mrs. Rogers."

I was dumbfounded. Rhonda sat a plate heaping with bacon, eggs, and biscuits on the table by a glass of milk and a glass of orange juice. "Here you go, honey. Hope you like your eggs scrambled. You enjoy your breakfast and make yourself at home while I get the kids ready for pre-school." She walked out of the kitchen, humming some happy little song.

I sank into the kitchen chair and stared at the food. All I could think was, *Oh shit.*

LOUANN

April and May 1979

THERE I WAS, WITH JOYCIE AGAIN. DAVE HAD LOST HIS JOB, AND with it had gone the fancy house. Now they were in a plain little concrete-block house with three bedrooms and one bathroom in a semi-commercial area in the city. At first, the atmosphere there was just like before—Joycie was disconnected, Barbie and Bobby ignored me, and Dave was always annoyed. Benny, more grown-up now, had become more of an ally. We both recognized what was going on and tried to stay out of Dave's way. Joycie's weight had ballooned; she was smoking and drinking and didn't keep up her appearance at all. She seemed about as miserable as a body could be.

Dave treated her like garbage. He'd say, "Can't you clean up this dump? Just because you look like trash doesn't mean we have to live in it." He never called her by name. It was either "bitch" or "woman." "Hey, bitch, make yourself useful and get me a cold beer." His insults were mean. "Woman, can't you put on something decent? You look like something the cat drug in." He acted like she was his servant and he was the king. "Oh, hell. Here we go again. Shit, woman, quit nagging. I'll get a job when I'm damn good and ready."

But worst of all was when he brought Barbie into it. "Look at sweet little Barbie here. At least she fixes herself up, and she's not fat as a pig like you."

It was that last comment that really got to me. I couldn't stand the way that man made over Barbie. Joycie never said anything when he made those kinds of comments, but Barbie would preen and prance over to give him a big hug. Sometimes there was even a kiss—on the mouth. I knew I was in the way. I would have helped Joycie if I'd known how. I went to school and got a job at the Jack in the Box around the corner, working every afternoon and on weekends. Dave was almost never home, and Joycie was usually piled up on the couch with the TV blaring. Even though I tried to help out with the other kids when I was home, I accepted that this was the way it was going to be for now. It didn't help that I constantly worried about Mama, off in Albany in that nursing home.

One night when Dave was gone, Joycie, me, and the other kids were watching TV. She always wanted us to watch shows about child abuse—especially sexual child abuse. I thought it was morbid and didn't really like those kinds of shows, but she would insist. We were watching one of those programs, and all of a sudden, Barbie started crying. She jumped up and ran off to the bedroom. Joycie followed her. Benny and me exchanged glances. I flipped the channel over to an animal show.

In a little while, Joycie came out. "Louann, come on back in the kitchen. I need to talk to you."

I followed her to the kitchen, popped open a Coke, and sat down at the table. She sat across from me, stubbed her cigarette out in a jar lid, and looked me straight in the eye. "I've got a question to ask you, Louann. If I made Dave leave, would you stay here and help me support the younger kids?"

I was dumbfounded. Of course, I knew Dave was an asshole, but I'd never pictured Joycie leaving him or kicking him out. I had a funny feeling in the pit of my stomach. "Uh, well, sure, I guess so. But why would you want to do that?"

She covered her face with her hands, rubbed her eyes, and then looked back up at me. She looked like a person barely alive. Her eyes had no spark of life. They were as dull as marbles that were scrubbed and scraped by years of use on rough ground. The pale folds of heavily made-up skin on her face drooped around her mouth, where her thin, cracked lips formed a tight line. "It's Barbie . . . It's Dave . . . I mean, it's Dave and Barbie. He's been messing with her."

It took a few seconds for the meaning of what she was saying to sink in. "Messing with her? Oh my God, Joycie! Is that why she ran out of there crying? What did she tell you?"

Joycie squirmed. "Well, she didn't have to tell me. I knew. The first time I caught him, she was only nine years old. It was back at the other house, before you came down to stay with us. He promised he would stop. I guess I wanted to believe him. At least he's not her real father." She got a faraway look in her eyes, like she was thinking of something from long ago.

"What's that got to do with anything? Is that why you always want us to watch that crap on TV? I know he's not her daddy . . ." I grabbed Joycie's wrists and dug in my fingernails. "Joycie, what does that have to do with it? Who's her real daddy? For that matter, who is my real daddy? You've never said anything to any of us about them. Not that it matters . . ."

Now she looked afraid. Her eyes were wild as an animal caught in a trap. She started jabbering. "Oh, Louann, I don't know—I mean, that's not what I mean . . . just . . . No, I didn't mean to say that. It's just that I thought he'd stop, and now, Barbie says it's still happening, so I've got to do something, before—"

"You're right about that. You've got to do something. I'll stay and help you if you make him leave. He always gave me the creeps anyway."

"Wait a minute, Louann. You don't mean . . . he didn't try—"

"No, he never tried anything with me. I think he knows I'd kill him if he did. If I'd been the one to find him with Barbie, I would have, too. And I don't understand why you didn't. Why didn't you?"

Rubbing her face again, Joycie looked like a child being scolded. She whispered, "I don't know, Louann. I honestly don't know. I just didn't have it in me. I love Barbie, and I love Dave. I can't explain it."

"Well, I won't stay if he's going to be here. Get rid of him, and I'll help you as best I can. But I'm not quitting school."

"All right. I'll do it. The next time he's home, I tell him."

Dear God. I'd had to be like a mother to Mama, and now I'd have to do the same for my little brothers and sister, and I was still just fifteen. It was plain that Joycie wasn't going to be a mother to anybody.

The next day, when I came home from school to change into my work uniform, it seemed unusually quiet. The younger kids were normally home before me and making all kinds of racket when I got home. I could hear the TV in their bedroom going, but Joycie sat on the couch in the living room. No TV, no lights, no music, no nothing. She held wadded-up Kleenex in her fists next to her face. I stopped in front of her, but she didn't look up at me.

"Well?" I demanded.

"Well, what?"

"Did you do it? Is he gone?"

"Yes, he's gone."

She pulled herself up, still not looking at me, and waddled off to her bedroom, closing the door behind her. I changed into my uniform and got Benny, Barbie, and Bobby together. "Come on, you're all coming with me. Your mama needs to rest, Dave's gone off, and I'm gonna treat y'all to a hamburger for supper."

They hooped and hollered all the way down the block. It wouldn't be the first or last time I parked them in a booth and snuck burgers, fries, and Cokes their way. When they finished, I told Benny to make sure they watched the traffic going back home, got their homework done, took baths, brushed their teeth, and went to bed. He was thirteen now, and he could manage to get the kids back home. I told them not to wake up their mama and that I'd check on them when I got home. My heart broke for them, poor little things having to take care of themselves. Even if Joycie never cared a damn about me, at least I'd had Bessie and Hampton to give me a decent home life. As sad as it was, my heart was touched when they all hugged me bye and said, "We love you, Louann. See you at home."

Benny hugged me especially hard and whispered in my ear, "Don't worry, Louann. I'll take care of them. You be careful coming home yourself." Bless his little heart.

LOUANN

May 1979

DAVE MOVED INTO AN APARTMENT DOWN THE BLOCK, AND JOYCIE still saw him. He'd pick her up, and she'd go with him. I didn't want to know where they went or what they did, and I didn't care. When she went off like that, I was left to look after the kids. Even Barbie and Bobby were old enough now at eleven and ten not to need a babysitter all the time, but Joycie didn't like leaving them on their own.

One evening when I was trying to get my homework done, the other kids were off in their rooms, and Dave had just picked up Joycie. It wasn't two minutes later when two cop cars, one marked and one unmarked, came screeching up in front of the house. Two uniformed cops banged on the door.

"Police, open up!"

I was scared and didn't want to open the door, but I cracked it and was about to ask what was going on when they barged in, knocking me down. The other kids came running from their rooms and cowered near the couch, except Benny, who came over and helped me to my feet. He stood there with his arm around my shoulder.

"What's your name, young lady?"

I was crying now. There was obviously some kind of bad trouble. Had Joycie and Dave been in a wreck? "I'm Louann Walker."

"And what are the names of these other kids?" The cop motioned over towards the couch.

"That's my brother Bobby, my sister Barbie, and this is my brother Benny."

Then all hell broke loose. One of the officers went over and took Barbie by the arm. She screamed. He must have recognized I was the oldest and somewhat in charge. He turned to me.

"Ma'am, I have to inform you that we're here to take this one with us." He pulled Barbie over towards me and the door. She realized he intended to take her and grabbed onto me, hollering and crying. Benny started to move towards them, but the other cop motioned for him to stay put.

"No, I won't go! I want to stay here. No!" Barbie screamed.

I tried to talk over her. "Why? What's wrong? You can't just drag her away!" I reached out and held onto her. Could they? Could they really just come in and get a kid and take them away? Now Benny and Bobby were crying, too.

"Ma'am, it's for her own good. We know she's not safe here." He raised his voice over Barbie's caterwauling. Then he gently reached around and removed my hands from Barbie's other arm. His voice and eyes softened. "You can tell her mama to call the police station when she gets home."

Barbie kept up the screaming and crying. "Louann, help me! Don't let them take me. I don't want to go. Please, Louann, help me!"

She collapsed on the floor, holding onto my legs. Benny and Bobby stood still on the other side of the room, holding onto each other, eyes wide with terror. I was trying to get Barbie to let go of me and calm her down at the same time. Like a key in a lock, it all clicked into place. They were only taking Barbie. Somehow, somebody must have informed the authorities about Dave messing with her. Now it made sense. If I could reason with the officer, maybe I could change their mind. "Barbie, honey, it's all right. Stop hollering. Officer, can't I go with her? She's afraid. The boys will be okay until their mama gets back. I could go with her, and she won't be so scared. Please?"

She quieted a little bit and looked up hopefully, but she still did not release her grip on me. The officers exchanged looks, and I had a glimmer of hope, but then the one who'd done all the talking shook his head. "I'm sorry, ma'am. We can't do that. We've got orders. We've got to take just her." He proceeded to pry her arms off me one at a time. "Come on, honey, you're making this harder than it needs to be. Come on, let go." Finally, the two of them got her loose. She dissolved into a desperate blubbering heap on the floor. The other cop picked her up and walked out. The sound of her sobbing as they took her away tore me apart.

Joycie and Dave apparently saw police cars coming onto our street as they pulled out and must have thought they'd better turn around and see what was going on. The unmarked car was at the curb with the motor running and a woman in the driver's seat. Just as the officer and another lady were putting Barbie into the unmarked car, Dave and Joycie pulled up. The woman jumped in after Barbie, and the car sped off almost before she got the door slammed shut.

Joycie jumped out of Dave's car, screaming. "What's going on? Where are they taking my baby? You can't just come in here and take my kid!" Dave stayed in the car with the engine still running and didn't make a move as Joycie started toward one of the cops.

"Ma'am, we're just following orders to take the child into protective custody. You'll have to contact social services for more information."

Joycie stopped dead in her tracks. She turned and looked at Dave, who was still just sitting there, staring straight ahead, gripping the steering wheel of his car.

She addressed the cop again. "What do you mean, protective custody? I demand to know what's going on here."

"Ma'am, a report has been filed with the Department of Children and Family Services that the child has been sexually molested and is not in a safe environment here. That's all I can tell you. You'll have to contact those authorities for more information. But I can assure you she will be well taken care of in a safe place."

Joycie was crying now and holding the sides of her head. Over and over, she kept moaning, "My poor baby, oh my God, my poor baby, oh my God."

The police officers got in their car and left. Me, Benny, and Bobby were huddled together on the front stoop. With a wild look on her face, Joycie broke into a run towards Dave's car. A screaming, crazy woman heading straight for him. Not wasting any time, he floored it and pulled away, tires squealing. Joycie yelled after him. "You piece of shit! You'll be sorry!" She fell to the ground, wrapping her arms around her body, curled up like a baby in the dirt.

Sudden silence. Strange, after all the commotion.

I had tried my best, but I hadn't been able to protect my sister. And now, here was this woman in the dirt. Had she really given birth to me? Was she really my mother? I looked at her pitiful form on the ground. In that instant, I became the mother. Just as Bessie had had to step in and take care of me, it was now my turn. I left Benny and Bobby on the stoop and walked over to Joycie. I bent down, put my arms around her, helped her to her feet, and walked her slowly and gently inside the house.

LOUANN

May 1979

OVER THE NEXT WEEK, I TOOK CARE OF NOT ONLY BENNY AND Bobby, but Joycie, too. When me and the boys got home from school, she'd be in the same place as when we'd left her that morning, sleeping on either her bed or the couch. She ate whatever I cooked. The boys gave her what they, in their little boy heads, thought would make her happy: a steady stream of chips, cookies, candy, and Cokes. In between eating and sleeping, she cried.

We came home from school one day, and there was no sign of Joycie. The house was picked up and smelled like bleach. Then her voice called out from the kitchen. "Hello—oh! Is that you, dear?"

I walked into the kitchen, and there she was. Showered, dressed, hair and makeup done.

"Joycie?" I stared suspiciously.

"Yes, darling?" She turned to smile brightly at me, the wooden spoon in her hand dripping. "How was your day?" Then she turned back to stirring a bubbling pot on the stove. "Supper will be ready in just a little while. I hope you have time to eat before going to work."

"But I'm not going to work. You know I haven't been going since they took Barbie. I've been here, taking care of you and Benny and Bobby."

"Oh, I know, dear. But that's all behind us, now. I didn't tell you, but the social services lady called yesterday, then she came by for a visit earlier this afternoon. She'll be bringing Barbie home this evening. Isn't that wonderful!"

So that explained it. Why Joycie was on this manic high, like she'd been at the other house that time. She could turn on remorse and put on a good show of being a capable parent when she had to. I wasn't so sure that she had Barbie's best interest at heart. What was to keep Dave from coming back? I couldn't protect them all. I knew that man was evil.

Joycie kept running off at the mouth as she salted, peppered, stirred, lifted lids, sniffed, and tasted. "Aren't you excited to see your sister? She's going to be so happy to see us. Why don't you set the table? Use the good dishes!"

"I hope so, Joycie; I've missed her. But if Dave shows his face around here, I'll be the one to call social services. And just so you know, like before, if he comes back, I'll be outta here."

Joycie giggled and waved the spoon in the air without looking at me. "Oh, Louann, that's all over now. I promise. Won't it be nice for us to be together again?"

"Not if by 'us,' you mean him, too. I swear, if he comes back, I'm leaving."

"All right, Louann, let's don't think about that right now. Let's enjoy this evening."

How could she think that we'd forget what Dave had done? I would never forget or forgive him or any other man who would take advantage of a child. There was no reasoning with Joycie in her frenzied condition, so I let it go. I'd bide my time and deal with whatever happened when the time came.

I got my homework done, and we ate supper as Joycie prattled on in artificial brightness about us all getting back together, how things would be different, and how she promised to be the perfect mom from now on. From Benny and Bobby's silence and sideways glances at me, I figured they weren't taking this too seriously, either.

We had all learned to see through Joycie's swings of emotion and knew it wouldn't last long.

The knock at the door came around six. We all gathered as Joycie answered. There stood the prim and proper social services lady. Barbie stood there at her side, leaning to peer inside the living room. Joycie reached out and pulled her in.

"There you are. My precious baby girl. We've missed you so much." Without giving Barbie a chance to say a word, Joycie chattered on. "Haven't we missed her, Louann? Benny? Bobby? Hug your sister. Aren't you glad to be home, darling? Give your brothers and sister a hug." Turning to the social services lady, still standing on the doorstep, she spoke apologetically. "Oh my goodness, where are my manners? Won't you come in? We're just so excited to have our Barbie home, I completely forgot you standing there."

The woman smiled tightly, her lips in a thin line. "That's quite all right. I understand. I'll be on my way now and will check in with you next week. Goodbye, Barbie." She dusted her hands together like she was glad to be rid of a piece of trash.

"Bye, now," Joycie called, and she closed the door. She turned to the four of us who were standing there awkwardly, not knowing what to say or do. Hands on hips, she declared. "Well, that's that. I'm sure you kids have some catching up to do. I'll be back in my room. Y'all can talk a while, then get yourselves ready for bed, okay?" We kept standing there, watching as she sashayed back to her room, the food and dishes in the kitchen completely forgotten.

When Joycie was safely out of hearing range, Barbie gathered us in a big hug and broke the silence. "Y'all ain't gonna believe this . . ."

We went in the kitchen, raided the fridge for ice cream, and sat around the kitchen table, listening to her stories. She had us all laughing so hard we cried at the same time. "You know, when those people took me off, I thought they were taking me to jail. I was so scared. But turned out, it wasn't so bad. It was a big building, not really a house but more like an office or something. There were lots of kids, all different ages. And we ate spaghetti every night for supper. It was good at first, but by the third night, I was sick of it."

"Every night?" Benny said. "I love spaghetti. I'd eat it every night."

"Not this spaghetti, you wouldn't," Barbie continued. "It was kinda gross by the third night." The boys dissolved into laughter.

She went on. "In the daytime, we had school lessons we were supposed to be doing, but nobody really worked on it. Some lady was supposed to be making sure we worked, but she never paid any attention, so mostly we talked and cut up."

"That sounds like the kind of school I'd like," Bobby said. "Can I go there instead of our regular school?"

Then, like good little children, we followed our mother's instructions and got ourselves ready for bed. I made sure they were all settled in, then came back and cleaned up the kitchen.

The next morning, there was no sign of Joycie, so we got ourselves ready for school and made our own breakfast. That evening, I marched us all over to Jack in the Box for burgers. We did the same thing for the next three nights while Joycie slept off whatever she was on back in her bedroom. On the afternoon of the fourth day, Joycie was not in her room. She showed up at about eight o'clock that evening, and she was not alone.

I grabbed Joycie's arm at the door as Dave went on into the house. Seething with anger, I hissed through my teeth. "I told you I would not live here with that man."

Joycie shushed me and said to come outside. We stepped out onto the stoop. "I know, I know, honey. But I have a plan."

"Your so-called plans never work. What makes you think they will now? Anyway, there's no plan that will get me to stay in a house with that child molester."

She put her hands on my shoulders. "I know, baby. Just hear me out."

I shrugged her hands off my shoulders. "So, what is this fabulous plan?"

Joycie took a deep breath. "Well, you know Dave's been living real close by in those apartments over behind the school?"

I didn't answer, so she went on.

"He still has the lease, and the apartment is furnished. We were thinking you could move over there. Wouldn't you like that? Being on your own? You're going to be sixteen in just a few months. You can use your Social Security payment from Daddy to help pay the expenses. It's close enough to the school and to Jack in the Box for you to walk, and you'll still be close to me and the kids."

I could not believe what I was hearing. My real mother was rejecting me—again. Not only that, but she was throwing me out in favor of a child molester. Rebuffing me and putting her other kids in danger just to placate that horrible man. My mind went round and round, spinning from anger to disbelief to sadness to concern for my brothers and sister. What was wrong with a mother who could do such a thing?

I should have known it would come to this. She had never wanted me, and she never would. What was so repulsive about me that my real mother rejected me time and time again? I had done nothing but care for her and my siblings, even if I did hate the evil men she always attracted. Maybe this was my chance to get away and get back to Mama.

Joycie put her hands together as though she were praying. Her eyes searched my face, trying to read my mind. "Well, what do you say?"

"All right. I'll do it. But don't expect me to be over here when Dave's around. And please, take care of Barbie."

She threw her arms around me and hugged me close. "Oh, thank you, thank you, Louann. I'm so happy."

It was bizarre. My mother was thanking me for allowing her to throw me out and abandon my sister to that evil man. She was back on an excited high and giggled as she continued to thank me. I removed her arms from around me and stepped back. "When can I leave?"

Reality seemed to come over her for a moment. "The sooner, the better, I'd think. Come on, I'll help you pack." Giggles overtook her again as she grabbed my hand and led me into the house.

Later that night, my clothes were hung in the closet and folded into the dresser drawers at the apartment. I turned on the TV and sat on the saggy couch, but my mind wandered. I hadn't been working much in the evenings so I could take care of the kids, but that wouldn't be an issue now. I could work every night if I wanted to, and nobody would care. The extra money would be nice, too. I turned off the TV, took a shower, laid out my school clothes for the morning, got ready for bed, and set the alarm. *I must be a grownup, now.* If I didn't think about Benny, Bobby, and Barbie, I was okay. Benny was the only one who seemed to miss me. He'd come by sometimes, and we'd talk. He was helpless to do anything to help Joycie or Barbie. He'd experienced Dave's violent streaks himself and knew better than to intervene. I told him to take care of himself and do the best he could. I even said that he could come to stay with me, but I knew he'd never leave the others with Joycie as long as she was with that man. I knew Mama was taken care of back in Albany, and Joycie had made her choice, so I didn't feel responsible for her. I had only myself, and that would have to be enough for now.

I could be my own mother.

PART THREE

LOUANN

1980

I GOTTA TELL YA, DANIEL, I REALLY DID THINK I WAS GROWN BY THAT time. How many sixteen-year-olds do you know that live by themselves in an apartment of their own? That go to school, work, and take complete care of themselves? I did real well, most of the time. It was only when I'd get to thinking about Daddy, and Mama up in Albany in that nursing home, that I'd get lonely. Oh, I had a few friends at school and work, but nobody I really wanted to hang out with. I was either working, saving my money, or at school. But that was about to change.

The apartment, school, and Jack in the Box weren't too far from the Naval Base in Jacksonville, and lots of navy guys came in. Most of them were nice, always friendly, and they didn't try to flirt or hit on any of us girls that worked there. If they'd tried to, our manager would have set 'em straight. He was protective of his workers. This one guy that came in regular was named Morris. He seemed younger than most of the Navy men that came in, and he always came by himself. I guessed he must not have many friends; he was kind of quiet and shy. Maybe that was why my mothering instincts took over.

At first, we'd just exchange a few pleasantries when he ordered. All of us workers had name tags, so he knew my name.

"How are you this evening, Louann?"

"Oh, I'm fine. Morris, isn't it? That's your name?"

"Yeah. How'd you know that?"

"I heard somebody call you that the other day. What'll you have? The regular thing?"

After about a month of talkin' at the counter, I'd go by his table on my break and see if he needed anything else. He always looked kind of sad sittin' there by himself.

"Need some more Coke, Morris? I can get you a refill."

"That'd be mighty nice of you, Louann."

"What about some ketchup for those fries? I noticed you didn't ask for it up at the counter like you usually do."

"Oh, I must have forgot. That'd be great, Louann. Thanks."

Then one time, just to strike up a conversation, I asked him where he was from.

"I'm a long way from home," he said. "I came here all the way from California after my basic training."

"California! Wow. I never met anybody from California. Some of my family lived out there a while, but I've never been anywhere but Georgia and Florida."

"Is that right? Well, can you sit down a minute? I'll tell you all about it."

"Well, for just five minutes. My break's almost over."

That was how it started out. It got to be a regular thing. I'd go over and sit with him during my break, and we'd talk. I never told him too many details about myself. After another month of talking almost every night, he asked if he could stay until we closed and walk me home. I'd told him I lived close by and didn't have a car, so I walked to and from work. I said sure he could walk me home, and that became our routine.

One night, when we said goodbye at my apartment door, he turned to go, then hesitated and turned back to me. He put his hands gently on my shoulders, leaned in, and kissed me on the cheek. "I like you, Louann. You're a nice girl. Goodnight."

I touched my cheek and smiled. "I like you too, Morris. Goodnight." That became part of our routine, too.

After a couple of weeks, we were kissing on the mouth and holding each other close, but still with closed lips. I decided I was ready to take a chance at getting a little more serious, so I invited him over to watch TV and have hot dogs and popcorn on my next night off. He was right on time, with a bag in his hand.

"Whatcha got in the bag, Morris?"

He looked sheepish, and I was afraid I'd put him on the spot. "Well, you didn't mention anything besides hot dogs and popcorn, so I stopped and brought us something to drink."

Warning lights flashed in my brain. I wasn't a drinker. He reached into the bag and pulled out a six-pack.

"I hope you don't mind, Louann. Let's put the beer in the fridge to get cold." He walked off, finding his own way to the kitchen. I followed him. Once he was inside my door, he was like a different guy. Not so shy anymore.

"That's awfully nice of you, Morris. I gotta tell you, though, I'm not much of a drinker. Don't know why. Just don't care much for it."

He looked at me and grinned. "That's all right. Means there'll be more for me."

He set the beer in the fridge and looked around.

"Nice little place you got here," he said. "Sure beats a bed in a barracks with a bunch of other guys."

Here was another side to the normally quiet, shy Morris. I didn't want to give away my life story, and he didn't know I was only sixteen and still in high school. What could I say?

"Yeah, well. It's okay. My daddy helps me pay for it. Let's find the channel for the movie, then I'll get the hot dogs started."

Morris shrugged. "Whatever you say, darlin'. You're the boss."

In the living room, Morris sat on the couch and propped his feet up on the coffee table. "Make yourself at home," I said.

"I think I just did." He winked. Something else he'd never done before. I walked back to the kitchen. "Don't take too long!" he called out.

"It'll only be a minute. There's some magazines there, if you need something to look at."

I could hear magazines being slapped around while I got everything ready. Then I brought the hot dogs, popcorn, and two canned Cokes into the living room on a tray. Morris sat up and put his feet on the floor. I sat on the couch, too, about two feet away from him. I didn't want him to get any ideas. He kept up a running conversation while we waited for the movie to come on. He talked more in that few minutes than he ever had at Jack in the Box.

Around the hot dog he was cramming into his mouth, he said, "So what do you do besides work at Jack's?"

"I go to school."

"School? So you're a college girl?"

"Not yet, but I will be one day."

"Mm, uh-huh." He shrugged as he chowed down on the hot dog.

Still not giving away my age, I invented a little fib. "I'm finishing up high school now, and then I'll probably help take care of my grandmother. My mother and daddy do their own thing, and they're busy with my step-brothers and step-sister. They just moved to Orlando, but I wanted to stay and finish school here, so we worked out a plan."

Morris talked about growing up in California, what he was doing in his Navy job, and how he'd be moving around a lot for the next few years. Then, he tacked onto the end of a sentence, "How about one of those beers now?"

"I'm good," I said. I'd seen enough of what booze did to Joycie to know that I didn't want any.

"Don't mind if I have a couple, do you?"

"You go right ahead."

When he came back, he sat down closer to me. I didn't move one way or the other. We settled back, laughed, and made silly comments about the funny stuff in the movie. It was a silly comedy called *Murder Can Hurt You* that parodied 1960s detective shows. Don Adams and

Marty Allen were hilarious. Almost every commercial break, Morris went to bathroom, and each time he came back to sit down, he moved a little closer. Eventually, we were right up against each other, our sides touching. Still, I didn't move.

When I got up to take our plates back to the kitchen, Morris followed. At first, I didn't realize he was right behind me. When I turned around, he was right there in my face.

"Oh, I didn't know you were there!" A nervous laugh twittered out of my mouth.

He put his arms around me in a gentle hug. I stiffened and kept my arms straight down at my sides. *What now?* I couldn't bring my eyes up to meet his. Abruptly, he let his arms go and put his hands on my shoulders. Through a crooked smile, he said, "I just want you to know this has been really fun tonight. I hope we can do it again soon."

I hoped he didn't notice my sigh of relief. "Sure, it has been fun. Maybe next time we could have pizza."

"And maybe next time you'll have a beer with me."

"We'll have to wait and see about that." I shrugged his hands off and walked toward the door. "I've got to be at school early tomorrow."

Again, he was right on my heels. At the door, he put his hand on the wall beside my head and leaned in. "I mean it, Louann, I had a real good time tonight. Will you be at work tomorrow? I can't wait to see you again."

I couldn't shrink back any flatter against the wall. "Uh, yeah. I work tomorrow, after school, until eight." This was definitely new territory for me. I was waiting for him to move in, anticipating a full kiss, maybe even with our mouths open.

"All right, then. I'll see you tomorrow." He put his hands on either side of my face and kissed me on the forehead. "You be a good girl at school tomorrow. Goodnight."

Feeling foolish, since I'd closed my eyes anticipating another kind of kiss, I giggled, mostly to myself. As he went down the walk, I waggled my fingers in a childlike wave. "I will. Goodnight."

Morris was what I thought a big brother should be like. Granted, he was only five years older than me, but five years can be a big difference when a girl is sixteen and a guy is twenty-one, a full-grown man. He had a real job, his own money, and was in the Navy. Not a mama, wife, or anybody else telling him what to do—only a real boss bossing him around.

Not that I was your typical sixteen-year-old, either; no real mama or daddy to speak of, living on my own, making my own money. Maybe that was why we seemed so well-suited for each other. As Morris and I got closer in that spring of 1980, I decided to get on the pill. I wasn't that keen on having sex, but I was determined not to end up pregnant like Joycie had. The more time he and I spent together, the more things progressed between us. Then other circumstances played right into our hands.

Just before school was out for the year, I got a letter from Joycie with a Coral Gables return address. *What in the hell?* I hadn't seen her or my siblings for weeks due to school, work, and seeing Morris almost every night and on the weekends.

Dear Louann,

Hope you are doing okay. Wanted you to have our new address here in Coral Gables. Sorry we didn't get to say goodbye. By the way, Dave will no longer be paying for the apartment when the lease is up at the end of May, so you might need to find a new place. Benny, Bobby, and Barbie say hello.

Take care,
Joycie

Abandoned again. My own mother had moved away and left me on my own. She didn't even bother to say goodbye. How was I supposed to find a place to live on such short notice, and how would I pay for it? I'd only been able to stay here because Dave had footed the bill. Even then,

I'd had to be careful with my money. Working at Jack in the Box ensured I wouldn't go hungry, but a steady diet of burgers, fries, and Cokes got old real fast. With school getting out in a couple of weeks, I could work more hours, but it wouldn't be enough to pay rent and living expenses. Shit! What was I gonna do now? I didn't tell Morris right away.

Finally, one night when I got in from work, Morris was there, as usual. He'd had a key to the apartment for a few weeks and usually came there now after work instead of sitting at Jack's all evening. Said he liked being there, knowing I'd be coming home to him. I sat on the couch beside him and put my head on his shoulder. My chin crinkled up, and tears weren't far behind. He knew something wasn't right. Lifting my head off his shoulder, he tipped my chin up.

"Hey, what is it, baby? You all right?"

That was all it took. The tears burst out, and I choked back sobs. He held me and didn't press for answers, waiting for the waterworks to slow down so I could speak. Eventually, I got up to get a Kleenex, pulled the letter out of my purse, and sat back down.

"No. I'm not all right. Here." I dropped the letter on his lap. "Read this. It's a letter from my shithead mother." I'd told him more bits and pieces about my dysfunctional family, deviating from the fib I'd made up in the beginning about my family being in Orlando and me staying to finish the school year, but he didn't know all the details.

He took the page and read to himself. "Damn, that's cold! What is it with her? How can she just move away and leave you like that?"

Sniffling and blowing into the Kleenex, I actually laughed. "Oh, boy. You don't know the half of it."

"Honey, I just don't get how a mother could abandon her child. There must be more to the story. What can I do, how can I help?"

Again, I laughed. "Well, get comfortable, and I'll tell you the story of my life."

We sat on the couch and talked late into the night. I explained what I knew about why things were like that with my mother, how Bessie and

Hampton were a real mama and daddy to me, and how I'd never understood myself why my own mother had never loved me and couldn't stand the sight of me. I told it all: how Joycie's kids each had a different father and how I was the result of some boy taking advantage of my thirteen-year-old mother. How Hampton had died of cancer and then Bessie getting sick. How Richard, my own grandfather, had tried to shoot me. How I couldn't stand Joycie's husband, Dave, and how she knew he was molesting Barbie but wouldn't leave him. How I had a sixth sense for men who were evil like that. Most of all, I told him how nobody loved me, nobody wanted me, and that I must be a worthless piece of shit to be treated this way.

When I finally stopped talking, Morris got up and paced the room. "Jesus H. Christ," he said. "That is some seriously fucked-up shit." He came back over to the couch and sat down, facing me. "Tell you what, Louann. There's a couple things wrong with everything you said."

I sat back and looked at him incredulously. "I swear, it's every bit the God's-honest truth. You think I can make up this kind of shit?"

"No, I don't think you made any of it up. I think it's all true, except the very last part, and even though you believe that part's true, too, it's not."

"I don't get it."

"Here's the deal. You may have the most fucked-up family I've ever heard of, but—somebody does love you, somebody does want you, and you are not a worthless piece of shit. You are a beautiful, caring, strong young woman, and I love you. I want you. And if you'll have me, we'll get married, and I'll keep on loving you, wanting you, and taking care of you."

"Oh my God, do you realize what you just said?"

"Yes, Louann. I do. It's not exactly how I planned to say it, but I love you, and I want to marry you. What do you say?"

"Yes, yes, yes! I love you, too. And yes, I will marry you!"

We made love that night for the first time. I learned what real love felt like and how to show love to someone else. Mostly, I learned what it was like to feel worthy of someone's love, even if it wasn't my own mother's.

L O U A N N

1980 to 1981

I FAITHFULLY WROTE LETTERS TO BESSIE EVERY WEEK AND HOPED somebody took the time to open them and read them to her. I never knew if they did, because I never got letters back. I also checked in with Aunt Lila from time to time. Instead of improving in the nursing home, Mama kept going slowly downhill. She couldn't recognize any-body anymore, and she was now completely bedridden. It made me sad to think of her up there in that nursing home, all alone, so maybe it was better if she wasn't too aware. Still, I wrote cheerful letters about working and going to school, mentioning Morris as a good friend. In case she did have any awareness, I didn't want her worrying or knowing that I was living on my own.

Neither Morris nor I had money for a wedding, and I didn't really care about one, anyway. Weddings had never been a big deal in our family. We were married by a justice of the peace two days after school was out. Morris moved from the Navy base into my apartment, and with both of our incomes, we were able to make ends meet. I let Lila and Rene know, and I told Bessie in a letter that Morris and I were serious and in love, but I didn't get into details about being married. I didn't bother to let Joycie know—she wouldn't care anyway. I had learned that no matter how much we wanted a person's love or to be a part of their life, even if it's your own mother, there are people who only cause us pain and trouble. Now I had Morris. I felt loved and safe. I'd only ever felt this way once before—with Mama and Daddy.

We were happy in our home, even if we didn't have much. I loved being our own little family. I talked to Morris about having a baby—it was the one thing I thought would make life perfect. I'd always loved mothering my brothers and sister when they'd been little. It was like I wanted to prove that I knew what a real mother's love should be. He agreed we could try, so I came off the pill and was pregnant by Christmas. I was able to finish high school, and our beautiful daughter Melissa was born the following summer, right after our one-year anniversary. Determined to make a happy home for my husband and baby, I put into practice every lesson I'd learned from Bessie. Like playing house, it was the storybook life I'd never had for myself: a spotless home, a happy baby, home-cooked meals, and whatever it took to keep my husband happy. What we didn't have in material things, we made up for with love. For a seventeen-year-old from a dysfunctional family, I couldn't have asked for more.

Morris was nearing the end of his current cycle that summer of 1981 and was hoping for a permanent change of station to California. By the end of the summer, things fell into place, and we made plans to move out to Anaheim, where his mama lived. I was excited to meet his mother and to live in a different place, all the way across the country. It made it even more real that I was starting a new life. There was no furniture to move since we had rented the apartment furnished, so all I had to pack were clothes and Melissa's baby things.

The Navy flew Morris separately, and I was going to meet him a few days later in Anaheim. The first airplane ride of my life was from Florida to California with Melissa on my lap. The stewardesses made a big fuss over her. "She's a real trooper," they told me. And she never did cry, just charmed everybody with her grin and long eyelashes. Me? I was scared to death and green with airsickness. More than once, I checked to be sure the airsick bag was within easy reach.

I was never so happy to get my feet on the ground as when I got off that plane. A three-and-a-half-hour flight with a baby on your lap was no picnic. When I came through the airport gate, there was Morris with a big smile on his face. I ran into his arms, baby, bags, and all.

We'd never been apart since we'd been married, and the four days had seemed like forever. I barely noticed the striking woman standing next to him. "Hey, sweetheart—how's my favorite wife and baby girl?" Morris took Melissa from my arms.

"Oh, we're great now that we're here—whew—that was some trip." As I smoothed down my hair and clothes, I noticed the lady. She had long blond hair pulled back in a ponytail, tanned arms and legs extending from her shorts and T-shirt, and a big smile on her face showing bright white teeth. Gold jewelry jangled on her wrists, neck, and ears. A perfect example of a California girl, except that she wasn't a girl. Taking a closer look, I saw the beginnings of face wrinkles and sagging muscles. She had a protective hand on Morris's arm, and her eyes were glued to Melissa.

Morris introduced us. "Louann, this is my mom, Georgette. Mom, this is my wife Louann, and of course, this is your first grandchild, Melissa."

"Call me Georgie, honey." She embraced me and gave me air kisses on both sides of my face. "I am so happy to meet you, Louann. My Morris has told me all about you. I am so excited for you to be here. And this darling girl, too." She reached her arms out to Morris for the baby and said, "May I?"

"Of course, Mom." Morris handed over the baby.

"Come to your Georgie, my darling. Let me see what a beautiful girl you are."

I was a touch nervous, but Georgette looked perfectly comfortable holding Melissa, so I relaxed. Morris and I exchanged looks as Georgette oohed and aahed over the baby, who studied her with big solemn eyes.

Morris grabbed the diaper bag and my tote bag, leaving me with my purse and his mom with Melissa. "All right, let's get this show on the road. We don't want to get stuck on the I-5."

I had no idea what he was talking about, but I would learn soon enough.

LOUANN

1982 to 1989

I WOULDN'T SAY THOSE FIRST TWO WEEKS AT GEORGIE'S PLACE WERE awful, but they weren't a walk in the park, either. She lived in a fancy two-bedroom high-rise condominium with her boyfriend. Not exactly my idea of a traditional family, not that I was an expert on what a traditional family was like. Morris was her only child, he'd never really known his father, and he'd left home at eighteen to join the Navy. Georgie spent her days off at various activities that didn't exactly fit my mother or grandmother images, either: yoga class, salon treatments, manicures, cooking classes, whatever. Her boyfriend, Eric, was never home until eight p.m. and was gone every morning by seven, so we rarely saw him. He had the chiseled good looks of a movie star, was about sixty years old, and apparently kept Georgie well provided for.

Morris was gone all day every day at work, leaving me alone to take care of the baby, find an apartment, and arrange for furniture, deposits, and everything else that went along with moving into a new place. He was hoping we could get on-base housing, but so far, no luck with that. Georgie would talk to Melissa and play with her for twenty minutes max, then she was on her way. "Got to run, Louann," she'd say. "Meeting my friends for brunch. Make yourself at home, and feel free to eat anything you can find in the fridge."

Of course, there was little in the fridge, and yogurt and hummus were not my idea of lunch. Georgie never offered to change the baby, bathe her, get her down for a nap, or babysit her if I needed to go out. It was clear she had a busy social life and was not about to let us hamper her style. Thank goodness I had the easy umbrella stroller, since I had to take Melissa everywhere I went, even though I could only go places within walking distance. It was late August, and the heat was stifling. I was used to hot, humid weather in the South, but the hot, dry temperatures in Southern California felt like actual fire was about to flare up, and sometimes, up in the hills east of town, it did exactly that.

About two weeks after we got there, Morris came home with great news. I was back in the guest bedroom where the three of us slept. He came in, chuckled at Melissa in the rented crib, and then came and put his arms around me. "Louann, honey? Guess what? I've been following the base housing availability, and we got one! A two-bedroom apartment. We can move in next week, and best of all—get this, you're not gonna believe it—it's furnished."

"Oh, Morris, that's fantastic. I mean, it's been okay here at your mom's, but our own place? I'm ready, aren't you?"

"Oh yeah, baby. I mean, I know my mom's not much company, and it will be good to have some privacy. Know what I mean?" He swooped me up in his arms and landed us both on the bed. "I've missed you, my beautiful wife. I can't wait to have some alone time with just you, and in our own place." He nuzzled my neck.

I snuggled him back. "You do realize, don't you, it won't ever be just us again. Melissa will be there, too—"

"Aw, baby, you know what I mean. We've got to make up for lost time."

Within a month, we were settled in. The apartment was clean with fresh paint, even if the furniture was a little worn. And it was easy to make friends with the other Navy wives. The weather was milder on the coast and perfect for spending time outside. Being outside with a baby in a stroller was a conversation-starter. There were plenty of other young moms and kids of all ages.

There was always something going on for us wives: Tupperware parties, Mary Kay parties, Mommy and Me exercise classes, even Bible studies. And everything was convenient on the base: the commissary, doctor's offices, playgrounds, a swimming pool. It didn't matter that we didn't have a car. Everything we needed was right there.

When the men were home, we'd have picnics or barbecues. They had a baseball league that scheduled games around their work timetable. There's something about being in the military that makes everybody feel like you're a part of one big family; we all looked out for each other. The only community I'd ever known was family, and mine was anything but traditional, so I loved the sense of togetherness. We were fortunate to extend at the same base twice, and those early years in California flew by.

Melissa had been born when I'd been just seventeen, and we figured I'd get pregnant again without any trouble, but it took over three years once we started trying again. We had our second little girl, Miranda, in 1986. I loved being a mother to two little girls. With two babies, though, money was more of an issue, and I wasn't always the perfect wife once I had to meet the demands of two kids. All of sudden, life wasn't so idyllic anymore.

After Miranda was born, I didn't bounce back like I had with Melissa. Morris would come home, look around, and say something like, "What in the hell happened here? Laundry all over the couch, no food on the table, and Miranda crying in her crib? Geez, Louann, can't you do better than this?"

"If you think it's easy, I'd like to see you try it. I'm up all hours of the night with the baby, have to take Melissa to and from preschool, feed her lunch, change the baby, feed the baby, wash clothes, and try to get food on the table. It's not as easy as it looks. Give me a break."

He'd put both hands in the air in surrender and say, "Okay, okay. I guess I don't get it. Seems like other women manage all right—"

"Other women? How do you know how other women manage? Is that what you men do? Sit around and compare your wives, is that it?

Well, just go out and find yourself one of those other women." I'd go off into the bedroom and slam the door, leaving him to deal with dinner and the kids. He'd come in after a while, apologize for yelling, and start cuddling up and sweet-talking. I'd say I was sorry, and we'd have make-up sex after the kids were in bed.

We didn't worry about my getting pregnant, since it'd taken over three years the last time, but maybe we should have. Miranda really was an easy baby and slept through the night by two months old. By the time she was four months, I knew I should have felt better and gotten my strength back. I was nursing her, so I thought maybe that was keeping me worn out. Then I started feeling sick—every morning. I hadn't been having periods because I was nursing, but I knew I must be pregnant. There was no mistaking the nausea and fatigue. Our third daughter, Mikayla, was born in 1987, just fifteen months after Miranda. I was twenty-three years old and had three children.

If I'd had a hard time bouncing back after Miranda, there was no describing how hard it was after Mikayla. The baby blues hit me hard. Both babies would cry, and I'd cry right along with them. Poor Melissa, she tried to help, but even she got put out with it.

"Mommy? Can't you make them stop? I can't hear the video."

"Mommy? Miranda's pulling all my books off the shelf."

"Mommy? Mikayla's got a poopy diaper, and it's coming out on her legs!"

There were always mountains of laundry, diapers to change, food to make, and a cramped two-bedroom apartment that smelled like baby spit-up and poop. It was all I could do to keep them fed and changed.

Now, when Morris got home, he didn't yell. He'd come in, go silently to the kitchen, and make himself and Melissa something for dinner. Melissa craved attention and was glad to have her daddy to herself. He'd put on a good face just for her.

"Daddy? Guess what I did at school today?"

"What's that, sweetheart?"

"I got a sticker for marking the right words. I'm really smart, Daddy."

"Yes, you are, honey. You're Daddy's good girl. Can you put this bread on the table for me?"

"Sure, Daddy, I'm a good helper."

Later, Morris would get Melissa and Miranda into the bath and put them to bed. Then he'd shove the pile of clean but unfolded laundry off the couch, onto the floor, and plop down by me, where I was nursing Mikayla. He'd turn on the TV, not saying a word. I should've let it go at that, but I never could.

"Morris? Can you turn that sound off?"

"Hell, Louann. What is it? Can't I at least watch TV in my own house after makin' my own dinner, givin' my kids a bath, and putting 'em to bed?"

"I was just going to ask if you could bring some crackers and a Coke. I haven't had a thing to eat except dry Cheerios early this morning."

"Yeah, well, join the club. I had dry Cheerios this morning, too. You can't even keep milk in the house. Why didn't you go to the commissary today? Hell, we ain't got no milk, bread, cheese, or beer. All I could find to open up for supper was a can of soup."

The tears were about to fall. "I know, honey. I meant to ask you to leave a few dollars this morning so that I could pick up a few things, but I was busy doing Melissa's hair for school, and I forgot."

Morris sat up on the edge of the couch and exploded. "What do you mean, leave a few dollars? I just gave you twenty bucks three days ago. Don't tell me it's already gone. I'm not made out of money, Louann. Shit!"

The tears were rolling down my cheeks by now. "I did get a few things. Some peanut butter, orange juice, hot dogs, and buns. And Melissa needed markers for school. Oh, and your beer. That took up the twenty dollars. Remember, you drank that whole six-pack?"

"Oh, so now you're accusing me of drinking too much? A man can't live like this without having a drink or two when he needs it. Hell, I didn't have any clean T-shirts the last two days, and I had to dig around in a pile of laundry for underwear. Then I go in the kitchen and can't even find a clean cup for my coffee. This ain't no way to live. Something's gotta give." He stomped off to the bedroom and slammed the door, causing Mikayla to open up with a scream. I paced the living room with her and got her calmed back down by letting her nurse. I stayed on the couch all night with my baby. And I never did get anything to eat.

LOUANN

1989

T HE WHOLE NEXT YEAR WAS A BLUR. BABIES, DIAPERS, LAUNDRY, food, money, and the lack thereof. Morris and I barely spoke. Aside from the drudgery of kids, housekeeping, and money, I liked it in California. I knew his next assignment was coming up, but he never said we'd have to move, so I assumed we'd be staying in California. I'll never forget the shock of that hot day in August 1989.

"Louann? Come in the kitchen a minute. We need to talk."

There were those dreaded words, *We need to talk*. I knew it couldn't be good, but I never suspected how bad it could be.

"I'm not gonna beat around the bush, Louann. I've been assigned to Rhode Island, and I'll be moving at the end of this month." He wouldn't look me in the eye.

"What? We're moving in two weeks? You never said anything about a new assignment. I can't be ready to move in two weeks."

"Well, um, you don't have to be ready in two weeks. You're not going." My jaw dropped. He still didn't look at me, just kept staring down at his hands on the table.

"What do you mean, I'm not going?"

"Just what I said, Louann. You're not going. You and the kids are staying here, or maybe go back to Florida, if you want. I'm going by myself."

"Hell no! You're crazy if you think I'm staying by myself with three kids and you all the way across the country. We're coming with you."

"Look, Louann, you know things haven't been good between us ever since Miranda was born, and now there's Mikayla, too. I love you, and I love them, but I can't live like this. Maybe it will help if we're apart for a while."

I slammed my fist on the table. Dirty dishes rattled. "I can't fuckin' believe what I'm hearing, Morris Babcock. You can't just go off and leave us here."

"Louann, I don't have a choice. I gotta go where the Navy says go."

"But Morris, I don't understand why we can't move too."

"Louann, you wouldn't be happy in Rhode Island. It's the North. People are different there. It's cold."

"We'll get used to it. Plenty of people do."

"I just don't think it's a good idea to drag you and three kids across the country. It will be easier all around if you stay out here with my mama and enjoy sunny California."

Although my mother-in-law and I got along all right, I knew that would not be a good situation. She had her own life. She wasn't any help to me. "Easier for who?" I screamed.

"Easier for me!" he yelled back, and he finally looked up at me. "Easier for me, Louann. I'm going, and you're staying, and that's it." He walked out and slammed the door so hard a picture fell off the wall, the glass shattering, just like the happy family picture I carried in my heart. I was stunned. He had promised he would never leave me, and now he was doing exactly that.

In two weeks, he was gone. My old feelings of worthlessness crept up again, like a cloud sliding in front of the bright California sun. I was miserable. The apartment was a mess, and the kids ate cereal for breakfast, lunch, and dinner. Melissa was in school, but being home all day with barely-turned-two-and-three-year-olds was a nightmare. Their cute little matching outfits hung in the closet while they stayed in pajamas, day and night, their curly hair tangled and dirty. They had the run of the apartment while I sat on the couch watching soaps and game shows. I have to admit, sometimes I nodded off.

I got a rude awakening one day when there was a knock at the door.

There stood my neighbor with my babies, each holding one of her hands.

"Hi, Momma!" grinned Miranda. "Pway outside?" Her baby talk would have been cute if I wasn't so mortified.

"What?" I was confused and embarrassed. I grabbed at the girls. "Oh my God. I'm so sorry. Rachel, thank you for bringing them home. I don't know how in the hell they got out. I just went to the bathroom—wasn't in there five minutes. Thought the doors were locked—"

Rachel looked at me with sad eyes. "Look, Louann, I know it's tough with Morris gone. I found them playing in the parking lot. They could have been lost, or kidnapped, or worse. I know in your heart you're a good mother, but you need to get your act together."

"I know, I know. I feel terrible. I'm so sorry. You're right. I promise this will never happen again. Thank you again, Rachel." I hugged my babies to me and closed the door. I made sure it was locked, turned on cartoons, sat the girls down with crackers and juice, and then sat on the couch, staring at my precious babies.

What in the hell was I doing? Was I no better than Joycie? I broke down and cried. *Oh, Bessie, what am I going to do? Look what a mess I'm in. God help me, what should I do? I'd give anything for your advice right now. You always knew the right thing to do and say. I miss you so much—I need a mama just as much as my girls do.* I thought back to the good times with Mama and Daddy, how I'd always felt loved and protected.

It was almost as though Mama was right there in the room with me. *Come home, Louann. Come home.* Home? Where was home? Mama wasn't in the nursing home in Albany anymore. Her money had run out, and now she was in Florida with Rene. Oh, how I'd love for my girls to know her, my aunts and cousins, maybe even my brothers and sister. We had a whole family in Florida. What was I doing out here in California, trying to manage on my own? I had no idea where Joycie was and didn't care, but Lila or Rene would know how to find Benny, Barbie, and Bobby. I made up my mind. I was taking my girls and going home.

LOUANN

1989 to 1990

M Y HOPE WASHED AWAY THE FIRST DAY I WAS BACK. IT FELT SO good to see everyone, and the best part was seeing Mama after all this time, but it was not what I expected. Tiptoeing quietly up to her bed, the girls trailing behind me, she turned her head towards us.

"Hey, Mama. It's me. I brought somebody to meet you." I pulled the girls around in front of me. "These are my girls—your great-great-granddaughters. Melissa, Miranda, and Mikayla."

Her voice was barely a whisper. "Joycie? Joey? Lou? Where've you been? Where's Daddy?" Her eyes sparkled, but she talked out of her head.

My heart fell. My beloved mama didn't even know who I was. I kissed her cheek. "You rest now, Mama. I'll be back in a little while." I herded the girls out. I was thrilled to see her out of that nursing home, but it was painfully obvious she would never live on her own again. She couldn't take care of her own needs, much less those of little children.

The first couple of weeks at Aunt Rene's went by quickly. Different cousins were always in and out, bringing food, taking the kids off on fun adventures, and making over my girls. They all wanted to hear about life in California. Aunt Rene had said that me and the girls were welcome to stay until I could find my own place, and she didn't press me about my nonexistent plans. I had no idea in Hell how I was going to find a place to live or get a job, and even if I did, who was going to look after my babies? The weeks turned into months at Aunt Rene's.

Me and Morris wrote and talked on the phone occasionally. He would send a little money now and then. When I asked him about putting in for a PCS back to Florida or letting us join him, he would brush it off. After another year, he wrote to tell me he was in Texas. When I insisted we'd come out there, he used the same lame excuses. Melissa would have to change schools, too much trouble, easier to stay where you are. I told him the girls had nearly forgotten who he was, and I was getting pretty lonely for him, myself. They hadn't seen him in over a year and had all grown—Melissa was nine and starting third grade, Miranda was almost five and starting kindergarten, and baby Mikayla was three, not even a baby anymore.

In his return letter, he said that he missed the kids and appreciated the snapshots I sent, but if I was getting lonely, he understood, and if I wanted to move on, it would be fine with him. I couldn't believe he was so nonchalant about it. What was I supposed to think that meant? He didn't miss me? He didn't love me? *Fine with me*, I thought. I'd been on my own well over a year now.

Without letting any of the family know, I filed for divorce. I didn't bother to tell the girls. I figured they didn't need to know and wouldn't understand. Morris was supposed to send child support, but it only came every now and then.

When school started, I found a job at a convenience store so I'd have some money coming in. Rene didn't mind me staying with her to help look after Mama, and her built-in help with my kids was convenient. She didn't have any little ones at home anymore and seemed to enjoy having the girls there. I eventually told them that me and Morris had gotten divorced, except for Mama. No point in telling her. She didn't know who I was, much less who Morris was.

I hadn't been out on my own in, well—I guess, really, I'd never been out on my own. I'd gone straight from being a kid to taking care of my brothers and sisters to being taken care of by Morris and then taking care of my own kids. Eventually, I started going out with some of my single cousins and their friends. I was learning what it meant to be young, be single, have friends, and have fun, and I liked it, even if a little voice in my head whispered now and then, *You don't deserve to have fun—you're a bad mother—worthless—unlovable.* The voice got louder, and the louder it got, the harder I tried to silence it.

I can't really explain how it happened, but in a matter of months, I was a different person. Going out with some of my cousins had turned me into a party animal. I met other girls and guys, and pretty soon, it wasn't just their group of friends. What had started out as a little social drinking and dancing turned into heavier drinking and going out with men for one-night stands. I had no experience with that kind of thing and didn't realize what was happening. Before I knew it, I fell in with a bunch of aimless drunks and dope-heads. They accepted me and made no demands. There was no struggle to prove my worth to them. I would sneak money from Rene's purse, use my child support, or lift a little something from convenience stores—at first just for booze and then for drugs. It got to the point that I'd rarely go back to Rene's. I'd pass out at a flophouse or with some guy, not thinking about my kids, Mama, or Morris. I don't remember thinking about anything at all, except my desire to disappear into nothingness. That void, where I felt nothing at all, felt far more secure than the real one where I was just a worthless piece of shit.

LOUANN

1990 to 1991

I'D ALWAYS THOUGHT THAT BEING IN JAIL WOULD BE THE LOWEST anyone could get. I was wrong. Jail was bad, but worse than that: I didn't have a dime to my name, missed my kids, felt ashamed to call my family, and was withdrawing from an addiction to cocaine all at the same time. I was too embarrassed to call any of my aunts, and I sure as hell didn't want to ask Morris for help. Of course, I couldn't have if I'd wanted to; I had no clue how to get ahold of him.

That only left one person who *might* be able to bail me out—dare I even think it? I had no idea where Joycie was living or what her circumstances were. If she never did another thing for me in my life, maybe she would help me.

I had talked to Benny from time to time over the years, just not in the last few months. He was twenty-four now and on his own, but he would know where to find Joycie. Marybeth kept up with him, too, and she would have his number. Plus, if I called Marybeth, she could tell me how my kids were. I called her and made her swear not to tell anybody where I was, but I was going to get clean somehow and be back for my kids. She said they were fine and gave me Benny's number. I finally got him on the phone.

"Benny? It's Louann. Thank God I finally got you."

"Hey, Big Sis. What's up? Are you all right?"

"No, goddammit, Benny. I'm not all right. I'm in trouble." I was practically screaming at him.

"Trouble? What kind of trouble? Are you hurt? Are the kids okay?"

"It's bad, Benny. I think the kids are okay, but I haven't seen them in days, so I can't know for sure."

"What? What do you mean? Where are they? Where are you? Why haven't you seen them?"

Sobs gushed out like a torrent through a broken dam. On the other end of the line, Benny said those words you should never say to a woman crying her heart out. "Calm down, Louann, stop crying."

The blubbering surged even harder.

"Hush, Louann! Whatever it is, we can fix it. It can't be that bad."

I finally got my breath enough to answer. "Oh, yes, it can. It's that bad and worse. I'm in jail, Benny. I'm in goddamn jail!"

He whistled out a big breath. "Okay, Louann. Let me get this right. You're in jail, you haven't seen your kids, and you're calling me for help?"

"Yeah, that's about the size of it, Benny. I didn't know who else to call, except for Joycie, and I have no idea where she is or how to get in touch with her. I was hoping you could get ahold of her for me. If I can just get bailed out of here, I'll go home to my kids at Rene's. I promise. I can get a public defender, and maybe somehow, I can get out of this. What do you think?"

"Well, Louann, I wish I had the money to get you out. I don't know much about how the public defender thing works. I can talk to Mama, see what she says, but if I was you, I wouldn't get my hopes up."

"That figures. She's never done a thing for me my entire life. I don't know why she would now. But she is my mother, too. I thought maybe this time—" Benny stopped me before I could go on.

"Louann, listen. I'll talk to her. And if she can't do anything, I'll figure something out. She's not doin' so well, herself. All right? You just hang tight. Give me the details about where you are and how much you need, and I'll take care of it."

Two days later, the matron came and said I had a visitor. I looked horrible, but I didn't care. Anyway, who would be coming to see me?

In the visitor's room, there was Benny, sitting alone. Looking around, tapping his fingers on the table, shaking his leg up and down, so nervous, you'd think he was the one in trouble.

"Hey, Benny!" He jumped up, and we hugged. I might have even seen a smile twitch onto the guard's face as she watched us. "I can't believe it's you. Man—it's so good to see you. Look at you—a beard and everything. You're a real grownup. I hope you've got good news—"

"Yeah, well, I hope so too, Louann. Hey, you look pretty good. They taking care of you?"

"Well, it's clean, and there's food. Most folks are pretty nice, but it's not a vacation. I haven't run into any bitches, if you know what I mean. I want to go home and see my kids."

"And that's exactly what's gonna happen, Sis."

"What? Are you shittin' me? You mean Joycie came through?"

Benny looked away and rubbed his hand over his face. Not looking me in the eye, he said, "Not exactly . . ."

"I should have known better. She can't stand the sight of me, much less want to *help* me with anything. It'll be a cold day in Hell before . . ." I was getting agitated. Coming off coke and booze cold turkey had me pretty strung out. I wanted to get up and stomp around, but I could see the guard glancing my way as I got louder and beat my fist on the table.

Benny put his hand over mine and patted it. "It's going to be okay, Louann. Quiet down, now. You don't want to get in any more trouble than you already are. Joycie used that good-for-nothing husband of hers as an excuse, saying she couldn't help even if she wanted to, but that you were a big girl, coming up on thirty years old, and would have to take care of yourself."

"Of course that's what she'd say. She doesn't even know how old I am. Thirty? She's crazy. I just turned twenty-six. She's never wanted to do anything for me. Hell, she never even wanted me in the first place. I would have been better off dead." Covering my face with my fisted hands, my head sank, and all the breath went out of me. Tears started a slow crawl down my cheeks through my clenched fingers.

Benny pulled my fists away. "Look at me, Louann. Look at me. I'm going to get you out of here. I've already talked to a public defender, I'm getting the money together, and you have a court date next week."

I sniffed and wiped at my face with my arm. "What? You did all that?"

"Yes, I did. And you might as well know, I talked to Rene, too. Told her everything. She already suspected you were in some kind of trouble. Of course, she didn't bother Bessie with it. They've been passing the kids around, making sure they were taken care of, but Family Services has already been out to check on them. She said you were going to have to come to terms with what to do about them—said the caseworker was talking foster care if you didn't show up soon."

"Oh my God. My babies! I can't lose my babies. What am I going to do, Benny?"

"First thing's first, Louann. We're gonna get you out of here, then we'll figure out the next step."

"Thank you, Benny, thank you. What would I do without you?"

"It's all right, Sis. We'll figure it out. That's what real family is about."

The guard pointed at her watch. Our time was up.

AFTER MEETING WITH my public defender, we came up with a plan. She advised me on the best course of action. The next week, I stood in front of the judge.

"I, Louann Babcock, throw myself upon the mercy of this court. I am unemployed, homeless, an addict, and an unfit mother. I love my children but have no way to provide for them at this time. I wish to give their father, Morris Babcock, temporary full-time custody until such time as I am able to care for them." My voice was wooden, my face burned red, and tears rolled down my cheeks as I read the words to the court.

Benny had tracked Morris down and explained the situation. I was sure he had no idea what he was getting into, but he agreed to take the kids. Benny made all the arrangements. He got the money together for my bail, too. Going to rehab was a condition of my bail, so he took care of that, too.

At the rehab center, I ate their bland food, went to the group sessions, nodded politely, and said what my therapist wanted to hear. I wasn't really convinced I was an addict, but I was willing to do and say anything to get my kids back, so I went through all the motions and followed the program.

"My name is Louann Babcock, and I am a drug addict." *Okay, maybe, if you say so.*

"I will not associate with drug addicts." *This one shouldn't be too hard.*

"I will get a job." *If I can find one.*

"I will call my counselor if I feel overwhelmed." *Can they talk twenty-four-seven?*

"My worth as a person is not determined by how my mother treated me." *Yeah, right.*

"My life has value." *Who says so?*

Maybe because it was my first time, maybe because I was relatively young and healthy, and maybe even somewhere deep down, it was because I really did want to get better, but I managed to look recovered on the outside. I knew how to suck it up, play the good girl, and convince everybody I was getting better.

But behind the façade, hidden from the counselors, the therapists, the other rehabbers, the visitors, the probation officers, and even myself at times, my doubts were alive and well. I tried to convince myself there actually were people who loved me, people who wanted me in their lives, people who cared if I lived or died. But when you've been in the pit of Hell as an unloved child and young adult, then as a drug addict, the screams inside your head never listen to the truth. Now, I hated myself, too. What kind of a mother would give up her kids? I didn't deserve them, and I didn't deserve to get better. So why bother? I kept the screams hidden and quiet long enough and well enough to earn my release from the rehab center.

I got another job at a convenience store and moved around, staying with first one cousin then another. Every once in a while, I'd go see Mama. She was in her eighties and barely lucid, but being with her calmed me and gave me a tiny bit of purpose. Looking into her eyes, I would catch a glimpse of what mother love was supposed to be, and a little twinge would nudge my heart. *I love my babies. Where are they? They need me. I can do this! I can be a real mother to them.* It was like she was trying to tell me I was loved, that I had love to give. Real mother love was the therapy I really needed.

I didn't have a plan to get my kids back. The temporary custody was supposed to have been for six months, but at that point, I still wasn't settled enough to support them. Morris hadn't bothered to stay in touch. Months slid by like a snake slithering casually through the grass, pausing now and then to flick out his tongue for the scent of prey. My aimless existence kept me right on the edge of falling back into addiction. When I felt myself about to go over that cliff, I'd high-tail it back to Mama for a dose of her silent therapy. All I had to do was sit with her and look into her eyes, and my strength would grow. Each time, it got a little stronger than before.

LOUANN

1995

"**H**EY DARLIN', WHAT'S A PRETTY GIRL LIKE YOU DOING IN A dump like this?"

I eyed the man using one of the oldest pickup lines that existed. He didn't look like the kind of fellow who normally came into the store. He was wearing nice clothes, was clean-shaven, and was buying Coca-Cola, not beer.

"I might ask you the same thing, mister. We don't get many of your type coming in here."

"What do you mean, my type? How do you know what type I am, anyway?"

I nodded over toward the cold beer case. There were two scruffy-looking dudes in wife-beater undershirts, dirty jeans, and backward baseball caps. "That's what we mostly get in here, and it's pretty obvious you're not that type."

He turned and looked over the two dudes, then gave me a sheepish grin. "Well, I guess you'd be right about that. But that still doesn't explain what you're doing here. What's your story?"

"Oh, honey, you don't have time for my story, and if you did, you wouldn't want to hear it. That'll be four ninety-seven for the Coke and the snacks. Want some lotto tickets with that? Or maybe some cigarettes?"

"Nope, this will be it. Don't gamble, don't smoke, and don't drink nothin' harder than this Co-Cola."

I slapped my hands down on the counter. "No shit. What are you, some kind of preacher?"

At that, the man laughed. "No, ma'am, I'm no preacher. I'm just a man trying to live right. Ain't that what most of us are trying to do? You look like somebody who might be trying to do that, too."

I handed over his change. "I don't know about that," I said. "I'm probably too far gone to do that now."

He looked at me real solemn-like. "Oh, nobody's that far gone. You've got time to make things right—if you determine to make it happen. I know from personal experience."

"That so?"

"It's so. I tell you what. What time do you get off? I'll meet you at that Krystal across the street and tell you about it. I promise I'm not a serial killer. You'll be perfectly safe over there. The cops drop in all the time."

"Yeah, I know they do. They come around and look out for me over here."

The two grungy-looking guys came up behind the man with their beer in-hand. I don't know what made me say it. Maybe I thought, *What the hell? It can't hurt.* I slid the small bag with the snacks over. "Here you go, sir, thank you. Krystal at eleven. Come again soon."

DANIEL CHILDS SAVED my life. That night, we shared our stories in the Krystal.

"Tell you what, Miss, um." Leaning in to squint at my name tag, he said, "Miss Babcock, I'll go first."

"Fine with me. And please, call me Louann. Let me grab some coffee first."

"Oh, sorry, I shoulda offered you some. Need something to eat? And my name's Daniel, by the way. Daniel Childs."

"No, just the coffee. They know me here and give it to me free. You want some? I can get an extra cup."

"Oh, okay, yeah. That'd be nice."

I came back with the two coffees and sat down. "So, what's your story, Daniel Childs?"

"Well, I'll try to make it short. I grew up in Kentucky; been working warehouses and factories since I was sixteen. Married and had a kid by the time I was twenty-one. Wife found she liked heroin better than me and our little girl, ended up addicted. I never did dope, but I drank too much. I tried everything in the book to save her, but after five years, it took her. She died of an overdose. I got myself to AA and quit drinking. Haven't touched a drop in over ten years. I swore I'd never let anything like that happen again to anybody I loved. Me and my daughter Katie have been on our own since then. She's seventeen now, and that's what I live for. She's with my mom up in Kentucky right now, since I had to come down to Florida to set up a distribution center. But I'm headed home in about four weeks. That's my story, and I'm sticking to it. Your turn." He took a long sip of his coffee, winked, and smiled.

"I know some of that heartbreak," I said. I wasn't prepared to tell him my whole life story, but I decided I could share some of it. "I know what dope can do. As much as I hate to say it, I've been there. Thank God I went through rehab, and so far, I've stayed clean. That's because of my own daughters. I've got three girls—well, I don't actually have them right now. They're with their dad. He's in the Navy and has temporary custody until I get back on my feet. Let's see, they're about fourteen, nine, and seven now. I'll be getting them back soon as I find a permanent place to live and save up some money. I don't have much other family: one brother I'm fairly close with, another half-brother and -sister, a couple of aunts and cousins. No mama or daddy in the picture. I was raised by my great-grandparents, but that's another story."

We must have talked two hours that first night in the Krystal and made plans to meet again the next night. Something about this man was so kind and wise. He'd known addiction and heartbreak, just like me. The next night, he said he'd known we had something in common when he'd first seen me at the Quick Stop. "I know the signs," he said. "Now I try to help other people in similar circumstances. That's what drew me to you."

We met every night that week at the Krystal and talked at least an hour every time. I told him more about my mama and daddy and my girls. He told me how his own mama had been such help after his wife had died, especially with Katie. He never mentioned anything about other women or getting married again. We showed each other pictures of our kids. After five straight days, I was going to have the night off. I felt safe enough to take things a step farther.

"Daniel, I don't have to work tomorrow night. How would you like a home-cooked meal?"

"Are you sure, Louann? I could take you out."

"I'm sure. I'd rather cook for you. It's been a while, but I think I can come up with something decent."

"I'd love that."

I gave him my address in the little trailer park where I'd rented an old Airstream.

"Don't expect anything fancy, but it'll be edible," I told him.

The next night, he was there at six-thirty on the dot. When I opened the door, there he stood—and he had flowers in his hand. I think that was when I realized I could fall in love with him.

I'd made spaghetti and salad, and we had iced tea. We laughed and joked over supper, and he helped with the dishes. We sat outside on the steps afterwards. "So, all this time," I said, "you never thought about finding another mother for Katie or a wife for yourself?"

"Well, that's a loaded question, Louann, but I s'pose it's reasonable. Of course, a mother can't ever truly be replaced. I've let Katie know the truth about her mother in bits and pieces over the years. She seems to have come to terms with it."

"But what about you, Daniel? Don't you ever get lonely?"

He sighed and didn't speak right away. "You know, for years, I was so busy with Katie. She was involved in all kinds of activities—sports, horses, music lessons, dance lessons. All the things little girls love to do. I didn't have time to think about myself. Oh, there were ladies, if you want to call them that, who tried to catch my eye. None of them seemed sincere to me. More like they just wanted a man for his income, to have somebody around the house, and to help take care of their kids. They were willing to take on an extra kid to make that happen. I saw right through 'em. That wasn't what I wanted for my Katie, 'specially when she was younger."

"Yes, but she's older now, Daniel. What about now—and the future?"

He looked at me and smiled. "Louann, I could be askin' you the same thing. You've mentioned getting your girls back, but what then? It's hard for a single mother. Easy to fall back into old habits. How are you going to manage?"

I was a bit taken aback by such a direct question. I knew that Daniel was used to mentoring recovered addicts, but I hoped our friendship was more than that. I wasn't real sure how to respond.

"I'll just take it a day at a time. Right now, the main thing is finding my kids and getting them back."

Daniel nodded. "That's a pretty tall order to start with. I think you're going to do just fine, Louann. One day at a time."

He had deftly turned the conversation away from himself. I'd have to try another time to get more out of him. I knew I'd been thrown a lifeline. I wanted to grab it and hold on tight.

LOUANN

1995 to 1998

WE SAW EACH OTHER EVERY DAY FOR THE NEXT TWO WEEKS. I remembered he'd said that first night we'd talked that he was going back to Kentucky in a month. My brother Benny had recently moved to Kentucky. Was it a sign? My probation was up, and I'd stayed clean, but I had no idea where my kids were.

Benny'd said he hadn't heard from Morris in several months. Last he knew, they'd still been in Texas. And Morris would only communicate through Benny. He never returned calls or letters from me. Dan said he'd be willing to help me find them, but that he had to get back to Kentucky. There was nothing holding me in Florida, now. Bessie was still living, if you could call it that, but she had moved from her sister's house to Joycie's down in Coral Gables. Joycie had written that Bessie didn't recognize anybody, never ate, and slept all the time. She also said that she didn't think it'd be much longer before Bessie passed, but not to bother comin' to see her. *Yeah, right. You'd tell me anything just to keep me away. Don't worry. I'm not about to show up on your doorstep.*

It was Dan's last week. I had the feeling there was something he was holding back, but he was going to have to say it or do it, not me. On my night off, I made supper for us again at my trailer. We sat outside afterwards. The weather had cooled off a little bit in the four weeks he'd been there. He put his arm around my shoulder. I snuggled in close. He turned my face to his and placed a soft, gentle kiss on my lips. I didn't want it to end.

"Mmm," we both murmured.

"I've been wanting to do that for a while now, Louann."

I laughed. "I've been wanting you to do that for a while, Daniel."

We kissed again, deeper and longer this time.

"You know, Louann, I'm going back to Kentucky this weekend."

"Yes, I know. I'm going to miss you."

"I've been thinking, Louann."

"Oh yeah? I've been thinking too, Daniel."

"Well, um, we wouldn't have to miss each other so much if you came to Kentucky with me."

"Is that right? I was thinking the same thing. Is this an official invitation?"

"I suppose it is. Are you game?"

"Oh yeah, Daniel, I'm more than game."

I was soon on my way to Kentucky. I called Benny to let him know where I'd be and that me and Dan were looking for my kids. I told him to please let me know if he heard anything from Morris.

Dan was true to his word. We got settled, made calls, sent letters, and used every method possible to find out where Morris was with my girls. We got the runaround from most places, and nobody seemed to care that my children were essentially missing.

Dan had a good job as a plant manager. His daughter, seventeen-year-old Katie, lived with us, and we all got along fine. We kept hitting dead end after dead end, trying to find my girls. I had to do something to keep from going crazy when I got discouraged, so I ended up taking classes and getting my real-estate license. It was enough to occupy my mind. Me and Dan made it official and got married in July of 1998. I was thirty-four years old.

LOUANN

1998 to 1999

THE CALL CAME ON NEW YEAR'S EVE.

"Louann? It's me, Benny. Are you sitting down?"

Nothing good ever came out of a conversation that started with "Are you sitting down?" I sat down hard in a kitchen chair. "I am now. What is it? Are you all right? What about Mama? Is she okay?"

"Yeah, yeah, I'm fine, and Bessie's the same, far as I know. But I do have news."

"Okay, so tell me. What is it?"

"It's your girls, Louann. I found them."

I nearly dropped the phone. All I could do was utter, "Oh my God," over and over again.

Dan and Katie both came running to the kitchen. "What? What is it?"

Tears were now streaming down my face as I moaned. Dan grabbed the phone.

"Hello? Oh, hey, Benny. What? Oh my God! Where . . . ? How . . . ? Who . . . ? Wait a minute, let me get something and write this down." Dan motioned for Katie to find him paper and a pen.

"Okay, now tell me again. What's the number?" He scribbled on the paper. Katie put her arms around me, trying to calm me down. "Okay, I got it. Benny, we can't thank you enough. We'll let you know what happens. Yeah, you too, Benny. Happy New Year. Thanks again. Bye."

The three of us hugged like vines on a tree. We cried and laughed. Finally, I was able to talk. "How in the world? Where are they? Let's go—right now! I can't wait . . . oh my God! Let's see—Melissa's almost seventeen, and Miranda should be almost twelve, and Mikayla eleven. Oh my God, my babies."

Katie was crying now, too. "Oh, Louann! I'm so happy for you."

Dan sat me back down and pulled out chairs for himself and Katie. "Whoa, now, honey. It's not that simple. Benny says we got to call this lady in Oklahoma. She'll give us more information. Try to sit tight, and I'll see if I can get her. Don't know if she'll be in, since it's New Year's Eve."

"Oklahoma? Are they in Oklahoma? How did they end up there?"

"I don't know, honey. Let me call and see what we can find out."

I took a deep breath while he dialed the phone number. Katie heated up coffee that had been sitting out since breakfast and put it in front of me. Dan turned the phone volume all the way up, and I could hear the ringing on the other end. Then an answer.

"Jackson County Department of Family and Children's Services. How may I direct your call?"

I heard that clearly enough. Department of Family and Children's Services? What did they have to do with anything? Why had Dan called them? I grabbed his arm and clamped down with my fingers. He reached with his other hand to pat mine and spoke to the woman on the line.

"Yes, this is Daniel Childs. I have a message to call Ms. Lorraine Huff."

"Hold one minute, sir, and I'll connect you." Click, then ringing.

"Lorraine Huff. How can I help you?"

Dan cleared his throat. "Um, hello, Ms. Huff. My name is Daniel Childs. My wife and I had a message to call you."

"You did? Do you know what about?"

"Not exactly, ma'am, but we figure it must have something to do with my wife's children, Melissa, Miranda, and Mikayla Babcock. You see, we've been trying—"

"Hold on, wait a minute. Is your wife Louann Babcock?"

"Yes, ma'am, she is. Louann Childs, now. About the girls, are they—"

"Mr. Childs? Is your wife there? May I speak with her?"

I gulped and took a deep breath. "Hello? This is Louann Childs."

The woman was silent for a moment. I was afraid. Were my girls all right?

"Ma'am?" I said. "My girls . . . ?"

Ms. Huff finally spoke. "Mrs. Babcock, um—excuse me, Mrs. Childs—we were told you were deceased."

Now I was trembling. Dan's eyes had gone wide. "What? Told I was dead? Who said such a thing? When? Why?"

"I'm sorry, ma'am, Mrs. Childs. Are you the birth mother of Miranda, Melissa, and Mikayla Babcock and the former wife of Morris Babcock?"

"Yes, I am. That's me, and I'm not dead! I've been trying to find my kids for years."

"All right, I see. Your girls are fine. They are in foster care, custody of the state of Oklahoma. Their father, Morris Babcock, is incarcerated. You'll need to come to Jackson County, Oklahoma, as soon as possible. Bring your identification, marriage and divorce records, and birth records of the children. It may take a while to sort this out, but the sooner you can gather that documentation and get to us here, the sooner we can get your children back to you. Do you have other questions?"

I was so stunned I couldn't talk. I handed the phone back over to Dan. I knew from my own experience that foster care wasn't necessarily bad, but I also knew that wasn't always the case. "Ma'am? This is a lot to take in. We do have many questions, but they can wait for now. We just want to get these kids back. There is one especially important question. Are the girls really all right?"

Another pause on the other end of the line. "Yes, Mr. Childs. The girls are all right now."

I grabbed the phone back. "*Now*? What do you mean they're all right *now*?"

"Mrs. Childs, that's all the information I can release over the phone. I assure you they are well taken care of. Let me get some more contact information from you, and I'll let you get started on finding that documentation."

I numbly handed the phone back to Dan and walked out the back door into the icy Kentucky New Year's Eve.

LOUANN

1999

NEW YEAR'S DAY, 1999. DELIRIOUS WITH JOY, NERVOUS AS A CAT with a long tail in a room full of rocking chairs, I cooked our peas, collards, cornbread, and pork chops. I went for a walk in the freezing cold. I tried to watch football but couldn't sit still. I ate and ate and ate some more. Katie and me tried to play cards, but I couldn't concentrate. There wasn't a damn thing we could do about getting records on New Year's Day. When I called Benny and told him what we'd found out, he suggested I call Joycie and tell her.

"Why in the hell should I do that, Benny?"

"Just call her, Lou. It might do her some good to hear from you." He gave me the number.

Do her some good? What good had she ever done for me? I knew Benny kept up with Joycie and was the closest to her of all her kids. Maybe he knew something I didn't. Could this have something to do with Mama? After thinking about it most of the afternoon, I called Joycie's number in Florida. I knew she always took forever to answer her phone, so I let it ring and ring. Finally, she picked up.

"'Ello?" a low, slurred voice answered.

"Joycie? Is that you?"

"'Ello? Who's there?"

"Joycie, it's Louann."

"'Ello? Who is it? Speak up! I can't hear you."

Oh, hell. Was she drunk? Was she on some kind of pills? Was she beaten half-unconscious? There was no telling. I prayed Mama was all right. Raising my voice, I tried again. "Joycie! It's Louann!"

"Oh, hey, Louann. It's been a while. Whatcha callin' for?" She seemed to understand now who I was, at least enough to be annoyed.

"Joycie, how's Mama? Is she all right?"

"Mama? Oh, she's about the same. Guess she's gonna live to be a hundred, even if she is just a vegetable. Lord ought to go on and put her out of her misery."

I cringed. Here was Joycie, the mother who hated me, talking about the only mother who had truly loved both of us. "Joycie? You're taking good care of her, aren't you?"

Suddenly clear, Joycie sounded mad now. "Hell yes, Louann. What do you think, I want her to die? What makes you so worried about it, anyway? We ain't seen or heard from you in months. Why are you calling? You need money to get out of jail again?"

I swallowed hard and wavered between shame and anger. "Actually, Joycie, I have good news."

"Oh, you do? Good news? Well, it's about time. What is it?"

I ignored her dig. "I'm married now. To a real nice man named Dan. We live in Kentucky, not far from Benny. And guess what the best part is?"

"Oh, do tell, Louann. What is the best part?" It sounded like she was turning away to take a long drag on a cigarette, disinterested in anything I had to say.

"Well, we've been looking for my kids ever since, well, ever since Morris's temporary custody was up. It's been years, and we couldn't find them or him anywhere."

"Yeah? That sounds about right. Give a man his little girls, and you might as well send them all straight to Hell. If you ask me, you'll be lucky if you ever see them again."

What was she talking about? I knew about her own husband Dave trying to mess with my sister Barbie, but this sounded like there was more to the story. "What are you talking about? Oh, never mind. Anyway, we found the kids. I have to go to Oklahoma to get them, but we found them."

"Well, la-tee-da. Good for you. Maybe your daughters will be better to you than mine have ever been to me. Look, Louann, I gotta go. Come see your mama sometime. Bye now."

Click. The line went dead. Oh. My. God. I'd just shared the best news of my life with my own mother, and all she could do was berate me. That was it—it would be a cold day in Hell before I called her again. Then the guilt starting eating at me. Why did she sound so out of it? Was she sick? What about Mama? Joycie didn't sound like she was in any condition to take care of herself, much less anybody else. What had gone on with Barbie? Joycie had said *daughters*, which made me think she and Barbie weren't on the best of terms, either. Whatever it was, I was not going to allow her to destroy my joy at finding my girls. That was the most important thing, right now. I made up my mind right then and there.

In the living room, Dan and Katie were watching TV.

"Hey, y'all. Listen up."

Dan turned down the volume.

"I have an announcement to make. I'm leaving in the morning for Oklahoma. You can go with me or not. Stay here if you want and start tracking down those papers, but I'm going to see my kids come hell or high water. Goodnight." I stood there and hesitated, waiting for them to protest. They simply looked at each other and smiled.

Dan winked at Katie and said, "Told you so!"

I walked away, went to bed, and melted into the most peaceful sleep I'd had in years.

LOUANN

January 1999

THE CHEAP MOTEL BED WAS NOT COMFORTABLE. NOT THAT I'D expected to sleep. Driving fourteen hours and knowing that I was within fifty miles of my daughters had me too wound up. I sat in a Waffle House and drank coffee until just past daylight and was on the doorstep of the one-story brick office building that housed the Jackson County DFACS division when the first employee arrived at work at eight a.m. She unlocked the glass door with a key, turned, and started to say something to me, then thought better of it. She motioned for me to come inside and take a seat. The hard, molded plastic chair was no more comfortable than the motel bed.

I watched as the woman relocked the door, turned on lights, and punched numbers into a keypad on the wall. I waited patiently, following her every move, as she looked at me nervously. When she settled behind the counter at the receptionist area, pointedly ignoring me, I walked up right in front of her and cleared my throat.

"We are not open to clients until nine," she said. Two other ladies unlocked the glass door with keys and came in from the cold. They walked quickly behind the counter and disappeared down a hall.

"Is that so? Well, my name is Louann Babcock Childs. I'm here to see Lorraine Duff and my children." I had the woman's attention now. Her eyes widened. Apparently, word had gotten around about my resurrection. All that stuff about confidentiality? That was bullshit.

The woman started prattling. "I don't even know if Lorraine will be in today."

"Then get on the phone and call her in."

Ignoring my demand, the woman said, "If Ms. Duff doesn't come in, I'll find someone else to help you."

I leaned over the counter and pasted the meanest look I could muster onto my face. "I don't want somebody else. I want Ms. Duff. And I want to see my kids. Make it happen."

I went back to my seat. Flipping through ragged months-old magazines, I watched others come in to work. It was obvious they were employees by their attire, the way they greeted each other, and the questioning disdain of their lifted eyebrows as they glanced over at me. Only one was remotely friendly—a mature woman, graying hair in a French twist, who smiled and nodded. By eight forty-five, no more employees were unlocking the door to come through. A line of bedraggled-looking women, some with bundled-up children in tow, was forming outside the door. They looked at me sitting inside and talked among themselves, hands flying, faces scowling. I couldn't hear them, but I could imagine their conversation.

"Who's that woman?"

"How did she get inside?"

"What's so important about her?"

"It's freezing out here. You'd think they'd open early."

The receptionist disappeared down the hallway and was gone for about five minutes. When she returned, she went over and unlocked the door. As the cold women shuffled in, complaining loudly, she ignored them and came over to me.

"Mrs. Childs, you can follow me now."

I smiled sweetly at the women removing coats, hats, scarves, and gloves from themselves and their children, then followed the lady down the hall.

We stopped in front of a partially open door with the word "DIRECTOR" stenciled on it.

"You can go in. Ms. Duff is waiting for you."

The French-twist woman came around the desk. A dark-blue suit and pearls completed her look. No surprise that she was the director. "Come in, Mrs. Childs." She offered her hand. "I'm Lorraine Duff. We spoke on the phone. Please have a seat and I'll close the door."

I sat down and observed Ms. Duff as she closed the door, taking her own seat behind the desk. Her pale face was powdery, but her smooth red lips and nails matched. No rings on her fingers. Had she ever been married or had children of her own? I knew immediately that she ruled this office and probably had for many years.

"I must say I am surprised to see you so soon, Mrs. Childs. It is unheard of for one to gather all those documents so quickly, especially with the holiday and the weekend."

"It's nice to meet you, too, Ms. Duff. I don't actually have the documents with me. I drove yesterday from our home in Kentucky. I understand I can't take my children with me without the documents and court proceedings. But you must understand this: I haven't seen my girls in years, and I intend to see my daughters. I know my rights."

Ms. Duff folded her hands in front of her on the neat desk pad. "I'm sure you do, Mrs. Childs. However, it may not be quite that simple."

"I don't care if it's simple or not. I will see my daughters today."

Ms. Duff pursed her lips in a thin line. She reached into a briefcase on a side table behind her desk and took out a thick manila file folder. She opened the folder and looked over the first few pages. Finally, she flipped the folder closed and looked at me. "I believe that can be arranged, Mrs. Childs. I need to see your identification. Then I need to make some phone calls and set up the appointment. It may take several hours, but we should be able to facilitate a visit for late this afternoon or evening."

My stoic determination dissolved. Slumping in the chair, the realization that I would see my girls before the day was done rolled over me like sinking into a warm bath. "Oh my God. Finally! Thank you, Ms. Duff. Thank you so much!"

THE VISITING ROOM at the Jackson County DFACS office was right out of Better Homes and Gardens. I looked around at the plastic plants, the magazines fanned out perfectly on the coffee table, and the pillows on the sofa placed just so. Pastel-colored floral prints hung on the walls. The room was staged perfectly to encourage positive family interaction, seeming to mock the families that visited there. In contrast to the perfection of the room, the families that met there were broken and soiled, touched by violence, drugs, molestation, criminal activity, or all of the above.

Perched on the edge of the couch, my crossed legs swung wildly. My hands fidgeted, and my eyes stayed glued to one of the two doors. I had entered through the one on the right and was told my girls would be entering from the door on the left. Finally, I heard murmuring voices behind the door on the left. The door swung inward, Ms. Duff holding it open, and in walked Miranda and Mikayla. They were clinging to each other. I jumped up and covered the few feet across the room full-tilt.

For a split second, they were stiff as boards. Then it turned into one big group hug—tears and all.

From the girls:

"Mommy! Mommy!"

"We thought you were dead—"

"Where were you?"

"I love you—"

From me:

"Oh, my darlings—"

"I love you so much—"

"I've been looking for you—"

"You've grown up—"

We hugged and hugged and dissolved into laughter. Ms. Duff stood discreetly by the door. My eyes swiveled from one girl to the other. I wanted to drink them in. Miranda, at thirteen, was no longer a little girl. She had filled out, had on a touch of makeup, and her hair was long and straight. What had happened to her tangled curls? Mikayla, just a year younger, looked almost identical to her sister in size, but her hair was lighter, and she didn't have on lipstick or blush. They both wore earrings in their pierced ears, bangles on their arms, and rings on their fingers. My girls had grown up without me.

I couldn't keep my hands off of them, either. I stroked their hair, patted their cheeks, squeezed their arms, and rubbed their backs. I'm sure my silly grin never budged from my face. Very casually, they were throwing out tidbits of information.

"We lived in Texas for a while."

"One time, we were separated and had to live in two different places."

"One of the houses we stayed in was a mansion!"

"I won first place in the fifth-grade spelling bee!"

"We got to have a cat and a dog."

Once they got started talking, they didn't stop. Suddenly, it hit me. I stepped over to Ms. Duff, who was still standing by the door. The girls fell silent. I didn't have to ask the question. All I had to do was look into her eyes and say the name. "Melissa?"

Miranda was the first to speak. "Mama, is Melissa coming too?"

Then Mikayla. "Mommy, where's Melissa?"

I answered without turning to them, keeping my eyes on Ms. Duff. "I'm not sure. Maybe Ms. Duff can tell us?"

"Certainly," Ms. Duff said. "Let's all sit down, and we can talk."

I sat on the couch between Miranda and Mikayla. Ms. Duff took a seat across from us in an armchair. The girls stayed quiet. My heart was fluttering as I tried to keep my voice steady. "Where is Melissa?"

"Well, Mrs. Childs, while Miranda and Mikayla have been at the same home the last few months, Melissa has been in a different home. It's rare that foster families can take in three siblings together."

Mikayla piped up, "Who's Childs?"

I patted her arm, smiled, and said, "We'll get to that later, honey. Let's talk about Melissa for now. I understand, Ms. Duff, that Melissa is in a different home, but why isn't she here?"

"You know Melissa is seventeen, now, Mrs. Childs—"

"I know how old my daughter is, Ms. Duff. What I don't know is where she is. Can you please explain?"

"Yes, Mrs. Childs. You see, Mrs. Detter, Melissa's foster parent, said Melissa had a school function to attend this evening. You know how teenagers can be. She really did not want to miss the basketball game."

I sat back on the couch. My daughter had not seen me in years, and she didn't want to miss a ball game? I sensed some hesitancy from Ms. Duff, but I didn't want to dig any deeper in front of the other two girls.

Miranda spoke up. "Oh, Mom, Melissa loves basketball. She's one of the best players! She told us last week her team might win the state championship."

"You've talked to her?"

Mikayla broke in. "Oh, sure. We talk on the phone every Saturday. And sometimes we get to visit or go to her games. We got to see each other at Christmas and on New Year's Day, too."

"Is that so? I'm sure you two enjoy that. Maybe I'll get to one of her games, soon, too. Maybe we could all go together. Wouldn't that be fun? Ms. Duff, do you think we could arrange that?"

"Um, well, um, I'd have to see about that. I'm not sure . . ." Ms. Duff's lips were in a tight line, and her toe was tapping furiously. I changed the subject.

"All right, well," I said, "tell me more about what you two have been up to. How's school? Do you have friends? How do you like your foster mom? Are there other kids there? Is there a dad? Have you had any brothers around?"

The girls started chattering and talking over each other. They seemed genuinely happy and looked healthy. I said a silent thank-you prayer for that, but my mind was churning over Melissa. There had to be more to the story. Even so, I was absorbed in hearing my two youngest daughters tell me about their lives. We talked and laughed, and I told them a little about Kentucky, Dan, and Katie, saying we were getting everything in order so they could come home and live with us.

It seemed like only a few minutes had passed when Ms. Duff interrupted us. "I'm sorry, dears, but I'm afraid our time is up. It is a school night. Holidays are over."

There were groans all around as Ms. Duff continued. "Let's say our goodbyes, and I'll take you two girls out to Mrs. Murphy. She's been waiting in the lobby. Mrs. Childs, I'll come back, and we can talk about further arrangements."

Miranda, Mikayla, and I hugged and smothered each other with kisses. I promised I would see them again soon. Ms. Duff escorted them out amid cries of:

"I love you, Mommy!"

"I'm so happy you found us."

"Come back soon."

"I want to go home with you."

Tears streamed down my face as I reassured them that I loved them and that I would be bringing them home soon. I blew kisses as we were pulled apart. "Goodbye, for now, my darlings!"

As SOON AS Ms. Duff and the girls were out of the room, I sank down on the couch. I felt like a stuffed animal that had lost its insides and was now just a limp rag. The buildup to seeing Miranda and Mikayla had been intense, and putting on a happy face in spite of Melissa's absence had taken its toll. As wonderful as it was to see my younger girls, I was heartbroken that Melissa had not been there.

Ms. Duff returned a couple of minutes later. She sat on the couch about an arm's length away. She must have picked up on my despair. Patting my arm, she spoke softly, addressing me by my first name.

"Louann, how are you? The visit went very well, I thought. You never know how children are going to be after a separation, especially when it's been years, but your girls seemed at ease and comfortable with you. What did you think?"

"Oh, it was wonderful, and it was easy, like you say, like we'd never been apart. But oh, how they've grown. Not the little girls they used to be."

"Yes, girls at that age change very quickly. It's been a long time."

"But, Ms. Duff, what about Melissa? There's something you're not telling me."

"You're right, there is. Quite a bit more, in fact. Are you sure you want to hear this now?"

"Yes. I have to know."

"All right, then. Let me get the file from my office. Would you like anything? Coffee? Tea?"

"No, I'm fine. Let's just get this over with. I want to hear everything."

Ms. Duff was back in just a minute with the same file folder she'd had on her desk earlier that day.

"Okay, Louann, are you ready? This case goes back a couple of years."

"Years? Oh my God. What happened? This is all my fault. I should never have—"

"Louann, you cannot blame yourself. That doesn't help anybody at this point. Let's just go over what happened."

I took a deep breath. I had done my homework over the last three years. I knew about the welfare cycle and broken families. I knew about the damage done to kids whose parents are absent, either physically or emotionally. I knew that kids whose parents were violent and involved in drugs often resorted to the same vices. And finally, I knew about the probability that children who are molested often become molesters themselves. After all, my own mother was molested, then allowed her daughter to be molested, and look at the mess I had ended up in. Our family fit the classic example of dysfunctional. Bessie and Hampton had been the only stable influences Joycie or I had ever known.

"All right, Ms. Duff. Go ahead. I'm listening."

She opened the folder and flipped back several pages. "The case came to us about a year ago. Before that, it was adjudicated in Cleveland County, so I can't say a lot about what happened with the girls before they came here, understand?"

"Yes, ma'am. Go on."

"Back in September of ninety-seven, the case first came to Oklahoma Department of Family and Children's Services in Cleveland County. They were called in when the girls' father, Morris Babcock, was arrested and charged with lewd molestation."

"Wait. You mean Morris did something to his own daughters? That can't be possible!" I was shocked. I'd never seen Morris have any leanings in that direction. In fact, he had roundly denounced both Richard and Dave when I'd told him about all they'd done, even though I didn't know the full extent of Richard's abuse at that time. In all the time we'd been together as a family, I'd never known him to do anything inappropriate with the girls. This was hard for me to believe. Then again, he'd changed over the years we'd been together. Had he changed in other ways that I was not aware of?

"I know this is hard to hear, Louann. I'm just telling you what the record shows. May I continue?"

"Oh my God, you mean there's more?"

"Not exactly, but things tend to snowball. It was not all the girls— only Melissa."

"Melissa? Does that have something to do with why she wouldn't come here tonight?"

"I can't say for sure, Louann, but let's save that for now, okay? Let me go on with the details of the case."

I stood and paced the room, chewing my fingernails. "Go on."

"The case was brought to the attention of DFACS when a teacher overheard one of the younger girls telling about playing chase in the house, sliding around on the floor at home in just their panties, and Melissa's panties coming down, showing her bottom. Then her sisters and daddy laughed about it. DFACS investigated, talking to the girls and to Mr. Babcock. Even though they all admitted that's what had happened, the caseworker wasn't satisfied enough to let it go. She deemed there to be enough evidence to bring charges. Mr. Babcock was charged, arrested, and incarcerated. That's when he said there were no other relatives and that the girls' mother was deceased, so the girls were placed into foster care."

I stopped pacing, put my hands on my hips, and faced Ms. Duff angrily. "Why, that's ridiculous. First of all, they were just playing. What a self-righteous bitch to turn that into something ugly. Didn't she believe the kids when they said it was all in fun?"

"I'm sorry, Louann. I can't speak to that."

"Well, what about being told I was dead? Did anybody check on that? Ask for proof? A death certificate? For God's sake, nobody asked the kids? There's a grandmother, too, and a great-grandmother. Aunts, cousins, all kind of relatives. You say I have to produce documentation to get my kids back, but those assholes took the word of an alleged child-molester that I was dead? Something is wrong with this system." I was taking my anger out on her, but really, I had a gnawing sensation inside that I was at fault. Had I done the same thing as Joycie? Abandoned my girls to a child molester? Could I have been that blind? I'd always thought Joycie had to know what an evil man Dave was, but was it possible that I had been just as gullible?

"Mrs. Childs, please calm down. We know there is always room for improvement. We can't undo what's been done. May I please continue?"

Now I was really ticked. I marched over to one of the armchairs and plopped down, crossing my arms and fuming. Had this whole thing been one big mistake, or was I partially to blame? "Go ahead. I can't wait to hear more about how fucked up this is."

"Really, Louann. I know you're upset, but—"

"Oh, save it, Ms. Duff. Keep talking."

She cleared her throat and turned the pages again. "Mr. Babcock testified that he'd let the girls run around his apartment in only their under-wear. They would play, roll around on the floor, and turn flips, that kind of thing. None of the girls, including Melissa, claimed they were uncom-fortable or encouraged to do this in any way. As it turned out, the court did find him guilty, but only on one count of lewd molestation, and only upon Melissa. This was because Melissa was an adolescent at the time, and this was considered inappropriate behavior for a father to allow from a girl of that age."

I relaxed just a touch. "Well, at least that's one shred of common sense. So what happened next?"

Ms. Duff folded her hands primly. "Mr. Babcock was sentenced and served his time. The girls were in foster homes, and as far as we know, that was a good experience for them. When their father was released, he took custody again, and that should have been the end of the story."

"Except it obviously was not the end of the story, or we wouldn't be sitting here. Please continue."

"Yes. Unfortunately, when Mr. Babcock was released and moved over here to Jackson County last year, he failed to register as a sex offender. This is required anytime someone who has been convicted of a sexual crime relocates."

I shook my head. "Uh-oh."

"Sadly, yes. When he was discovered living here with his children and unregistered, well, let's just say the Jackson County DA is very tough on cases involving sex offenders. He revoked probation, once again, Mr. Babcock was incarcerated, and the girls went back into foster care."

I squeezed my eyes closed and rubbed my forehead. This story was getting to be incredibly stupid. "And of course, once again, no one fol-lowed up on the possibility of other family members."

Ms. Duff looked down at her daintily folded hands. "Well, it was already in the record, you see, so—"

"Yeah, I see. So what happened next?"

"Well, things were actually a little different this time. You see, Melissa had developed, well, shall we say, an attitude? She was very upset about what was happening."

"You don't say? Imagine that!"

"Yes. She threw tantrums and had to be subdued to transfer to the foster home. Under the circumstances, we thought it best to place the younger girls separately. We also arranged counseling for Melissa. At first, she was acting out in the home and at school, but she was always sweet around her sisters. In the last couple of months, she has calmed down considerably."

"At least that's good to hear. But that doesn't explain why she wouldn't want to see me."

"There's a little bit more, but we're almost done. It seems that in her counseling sessions, Melissa talked about the family and you specifically. She was extremely angry that you sent them to their father, then never came for them. Apparently, she said enough that for some reason, the counselor grew suspicious that you were, indeed, not dead. When the counselor broached this with Melissa, it was difficult. Melissa felt that if you were alive, you would have found a way to them. On the other hand, something made Melissa question if it was true. Many of her struggles stemmed from this contradiction. Anyway, we decided to delve a little deeper, and lo and behold, there you were, alive and well in Kentucky."

I had to laugh a little at this. "Well, it was about fucking time somebody figured that out."

Ms. Duff's proper façade cracked a little. She smiled. "I guess you could say so, Louann."

I heaved a sigh of relief. "So, what happens next? Especially with Melissa? Is she still mad at me?"

Ms. Duff shook her head side to side slowly. "I'm afraid Melissa's still got a ways to go to resolve her feelings. She did not want to be included in the reunion this evening, and I have to say I think that was best, too. It may take her a while to come around."

I hung my head. "Can't say I blame her. I was a pretty rotten mother when I gave them up, even if I thought I was doing what was best for them. I know how hard it is to feel unloved and abandoned."

Ms. Duff tilted her head. Her eyes softened, and she smiled slightly. In a quiet voice, she said, "It may take some time, Louann, but she may come around."

I thought of Mama, trying time and time again to reach Joycie, then me. I remembered looking into those eyes and drawing strength from her mother love. Could that help now? I sniffed and straightened up. "I understand. So what happens now?"

The kind, sympathetic look on Ms. Duff's face was replaced with her standard professional mask as she went back into character. "First of all, you still need to get the documents. You will also need to engage an attorney. There'll be a court case to resolve the custody issue. Mr. Babcock will have an opportunity to testify, also, even though he is incarcerated and will be for several more months. We can set up a visitation plan in the meantime, until the hearing takes place. I think it best if your visits with Melissa and the younger girls are separate at first. Then, depending on how it goes, we can see about having the visits all together. How does that sound?"

I wanted it to be resolved yesterday. Patience had never been one of my virtues. "About how long is this going to take? Are we talking days, weeks, months?"

"Usually, the most time-consuming part is your gathering of the documents and getting on the court calendar. Once we have the documents, we can most likely get a court date within a couple of months."

"Months? It's going to be months?"

"I'm afraid so, Louann. But as I said, we can arrange visitation in the meantime."

"Oh. Yeah. Okay. I'll be here every weekend from now on until I have my girls back on a permanent basis. Go right ahead and set that up."

Ms. Duff beamed. "I will do that. Now, let's go over some papers and other information, and you can be on your way."

We went over to her office. As I was leaving with a big envelope of forms, I turned to Ms. Duff. "I'm sorry about my outbursts. It's just been so, well, so hard. I'll be in town overnight and head back home first thing in the morning. Please call me if there is anything I can do. And I promise you'll have those documents as soon as possible. Thank you so much for everything."

I almost reached out to hug her, but something held me back. Then, she looked me in the eyes and placed both of her hands on my forearms. "Oh, Louann. Thank you. It's not often we have happy endings in my line of work. I'm glad we can reunite a mother with her children. Isn't this how everything's supposed to turn out?"

I'm not sure which one of us made the first move, but we embraced each other.

LOUANN

January 1999

MY KNEES WERE SHAKING THE NEXT SATURDAY WHILE I WAITED in the DFACS "living room." Melissa had agreed to see me, but Ms. Duff had warned me not to expect too much. There was a soft knock, the door opened, and in stepped Melissa. She was about my same height, wearing jeans, a T-shirt, and sneakers. Her long, dark hair was pulled back in a ponytail. She did not have on any makeup, jewelry, nail polish, or anything girly. She looked like a wholesome, scrubbed kid who'd just been listening to music or playing Nintendo, except there was a scowl on her face. Her frowning eyebrows made deep furrows on her forehead.

I couldn't help it—I ran to her. I saw a wild look in her eyes and was afraid she was going to turn tail and run back out the door, but I was on her before there was time for that. I knew Ms. Duff was watching our every move. I threw my arms around Melissa, hugged, kissed, stroked her hair, patted her back, all the things a mother wants to do when she has been separated from her child. I spoke the words I'd been wanting to say; they came tumbling out of my mouth without giving her time to respond. "Oh Melissa, my baby—honey, you're so beautiful—are you okay—I'm so sorry—I've missed you so much—I love you."

Melissa stood stiff and still as a tree trunk. She never lifted her arms, never softened under my hugs, never spoke. As I stepped back and released her, tears flowed down my face, but her face told an entirely different story. She was still frowning, her eyes narrow, her lips in a tight, hard line. Her head began to shake back and forth, from side to side.

I brought my hands together under my chin, prayer-like. "Melissa? Honey? Please? Please say something? I've been waiting for this day for years."

She crossed her arms over her chest, set her feet apart, and lowered her chin. Finally, she spoke. "So have I, Mother. So have I."

"Oh, baby, can't we sit down and talk this over? I'm sure it's all been a big misunderstanding."

Melissa brushed past me and planted herself in one of the armchairs. I looked hopelessly at Ms. Duff, who closed the door, took my arm, and walked me over to the couch.

"I think that's a good idea," she said. "Let's all sit down. I'm sure both of you have things you want to say to each other, so let's get comfortable. Melissa, would you like to go first?"

"Actually, no, Ms. Duff. I'd like to hear what my mother has to say about why she abandoned us."

"But, Melissa, I didn't abandon you!" My voice raised and quivered. Ms. Duff placed her hand on my arm.

"It's okay, Louann. Take it easy. Start at the beginning and tell Melissa what you want her to know about how we ended up here today."

Melissa pasted on a bright, fake smile. "Yes, Mother, dear. Tell me how your three daughters ended up in foster care, our father in jail, and you running around the country doing drugs and sleeping with men. Tell me all about it!"

I buried my face in my hands. Ms. Duff rubbed my back and passed me a tissue. She spoke to Melissa. "Melissa, please let your mother have her say, then it will be your turn. All right?"

Melissa huffed, crossed her legs, and looked away. "If you say so," she responded.

My body was now shaking uncontrollably, and my breath was shallow. I felt lightheaded. I had not expected to be attacked like this. I tried to compose myself. Taking a deep breath and straightening my back, I started. "All right. Here goes. I'm not sure where to start. As you know, Melissa, I never really had a mother—not a real mother anyway—although Bessie did the best she could. When Morris and I married, and you were born, I was determined to be the best mother in the world, and I did a pretty good job for a while. Don't you remember? When you were small? All the fun times we had in California?"

She was still gazing off to the corner of the room, not looking at me or Ms. Duff.

"Well, anyway, then Miranda and Mikayla came along. Morris worked hard. When he got assigned to Rhode Island, he said it would be best if we stayed behind, there in California, or went back to Florida, where my family was. I laughed to myself when he said that, like my family was going to be of any help to me. But I figured, better to be with the people you know, so I packed you girls up, and we went back to Florida. Melissa? Are you listening?"

Her eyes flicked over to me momentarily, then looked away again. "Yeah."

I went on. "It was hard being alone with three young kids. My aunts and cousins helped some, and I tried to make it work, but I couldn't. Bessie was sick, and Joycie was nonexistent. I was depressed and lonely. I was scared that it was in the cards for me to be a sorry mother, just like Joycie had been to me. I was unlovable, unworthy, and didn't deserve to have beautiful, sweet children like you and your sisters. I pretty much gave y'all over to Aunt Rene and went my own way."

Now, Melissa looked me in the eye. "Yes, you did. That's exactly what happened. Do you know what that was like? Never knowing where you were or when you were going to come back? Maybe Miranda and Mikayla were happy with all the little cousins to play with, but I was older. I knew something wasn't right. I knew it wasn't supposed to be that way—a mother abandoning her kids."

"You're right, Melissa. It wasn't right, and I should have known better and done better. I can't explain it, but it was like I was doomed to repeat the same mistakes my own mother made. Men, drugs, you name it. Eventually, when I was arrested and the drugs dried up, I came to my senses. I told that judge I was not a fit mother. I asked to give custody to your father temporarily, and only temporarily, so I could recover and make a home for us. The judge agreed."

Melissa snorted. "Yeah, right. We know how that turned out."

"Melissa, I swear, I didn't have any idea your father might be that way. There was never any indication. He loved you girls. He was a good daddy when he was around. I couldn't believe when they told me about—"

"Mom, stop. You don't know what you're talking about. It's not true. Daddy was not 'that way.' He never laid a hand on us. That whole story was so screwed up, he never had a chance in court. I tried to tell them, but those sorry-ass lawyers turned it all around and made everything sound ugly."

Melissa was crying now. I couldn't just sit there. I knelt beside her chair, putting my arms around her. She softened and sobbed into my shoulder for a few moments, and then it was like she caught herself. She shook me off and stood up, at first turning her back on me. Then she whirled around, lashing out. "It's still your fault! All of it! If you hadn't run away, if you hadn't got on dope, if you hadn't sent us to him. Maybe if you'd stayed in California? We were happy out there. But, oh no, you had to come back to your crazy family in Florida. That's where everything went wrong."

I understood she blamed me, just like I'd blamed my own mother. I knew it was my fault. Once again, I was not worthy of being loved. And now my daughter hated me. But one thing was for sure: I loved her, and that would never change. I had to make damn sure she knew that so she wouldn't be cursed, as I was. I came up behind her and placed my hand on her shoulder. She tried to shrug it off, but I kept it there. Ms. Duff had gotten to her feet and came over near me, but I put my other hand up, palm out, for her to stay away.

I spoke quietly, softly. "Melissa, I know I've done some bad things in my life. But I want you to know I'm on a better path now. I'm clean, and I have a man who makes sure I stay that way. He doesn't even know you girls, but he loves you, too, because he loves me. And that's the most important thing right now. I love you. I love you, Miranda, Mikayla, Dan, and his daughter Katie. I love you all and want us to be a family. I will do everything in my power to prove this if you will only give me the chance. Please, give me that chance. That's all I can ask."

Melissa sniffed. Without turning to look at me, she said, "I don't know, Mom." Then she turned to face Ms. Duff. "I want to go now. Can I go? Please?"

Ms. Duff looked from me to Melissa. I nodded a yes.

"All right, Melissa, I think this is enough for today. Hopefully, we can talk again next week. Come on, I'll walk you out. You can visit with Miranda and Mikayla a few minutes before I bring them back to see your mother. All right?"

"Yes, ma'am."

As they went to the door together, I called out. "Goodbye, Melissa. I'll be here next week. I love you!"

Melissa stopped but again did not turn to face me. "Goodbye, Mother."

LOUANN

February 1999

B Y THE END OF FEBRUARY, WE HAD ALL THE DOCUMENTS AND A court date for April first. Only four short weeks until I could bring my girls home. When I brought up the possibility of the courts not awarding me custody, Ms. Duff assured me the court hearing was just a formality. There was no doubt in her mind that I would regain custody of all three girls. We had four weeks, essentially four visits, to get the girls acquainted with Dan and Katie. We also had four weeks to convince Melissa that she could be comfortable with us. At seventeen, she had no choice as far as custody, but she could make things difficult for all of us if she maintained her attitude of blame and hatred. We had not talked since that first time.

Ms. Duff set up the visits, just like before. Me, Dan, and Katie took off work and school on Fridays and drove straight through, getting a cheap motel for Friday night. That way, we were rested, and we could start the visits earlier on Saturday and have more time. We decided to start with the same format as before, bringing Melissa in on her own first, then the younger girls. If things went better with Melissa, then we would get all of us together. Melissa's counselor had indicated to Ms. Duff that she had made some progress, so we were hopeful.

I tried to prepare Dan and Katie in case Melissa was still angry, but we were all edgy. Dan paced the room, and Katie's eyes were as big as saucers. I found myself holding my shoulders clenched and tight. When Ms. Duff brought Melissa in, I relaxed immediately. She walked in leisurely without hesitating. Her face was relaxed. She looked each of us in the eye, then, lo and behold, she smiled. "Hi, Mom."

It was all I could do not to rush to her, but I knew taking it slow and easy would be better. I did not want to overwhelm her. I relaxed, smiled, and took a step towards her. "Hello, Melissa. It's so good to see you again. I have a couple of people I'd like you to meet."

"All right," she said.

I placed one arm through Dan's and the other through Katie's on either side of me. "This is my husband, Dan Childs. You can call him Dan."

Dan removed his arm from mine, took a step toward Melissa, and put his right hand out. "Hello, Melissa. It's nice to meet you. I've been looking forward to this."

Melissa hesitated, and I held my breath, but Dan did not waver. He continued to stand with his hand out and a smile on his face. I'd never loved him more. Then Melissa reached out her hand. "It's nice to meet you, Dan." Their hands came together in more of a gentle grasp than a shake.

I was able to breathe again. This wasn't so bad. Now I gestured to Katie.

"And this is Dan's daughter, Katie. She's about a year younger than you."

Bless her sweet heart, Katie stepped forward. She put out her hand, and Melissa did, too. They held hands, not shaking, and Katie spoke. "It's so nice to finally meet you, Melissa. I've been looking forward to having a big sister. I hope we can be friends."

Melissa's eyelids rose in brief surprise that changed quickly to conditional acceptance. With a small, barely there smile, not too warm, she responded, "I hope so, too, Katie."

I was relieved to have the introductions over with. Ms. Duff suggested that we all sit down, and then she initiated a generic conversation-starter. "So, Melissa, I know you've been playing on the varsity girls' basketball team. How is that going? Isn't the season almost over?"

I had to hand it to Ms. Duff; she'd done her homework. Melissa started talking. I mean really talking, not just answering yes or no questions. She rambled on about how it was such a surprise the team was doing so well, they were heading into tournaments next weekend, and they had a good chance of placing at least second in their region. Melissa was acting so differently from our first meeting that I couldn't say a word. I just stared in amazement. Dan and Katie picked up the slack, interjecting questions and comments, commiserating and laughing at all the right times. At some point, I realized Melissa was addressing me, and I startled back to reality.

"Mom? What do you think? Could y'all do that?"

"What? Could we do what? I'm afraid my mind was wandering!"

They all laughed, and Ms. Duff joked, "But, Louann, you're far too young for that!"

I was embarrassed that I'd lost track of the conversation. "What is it you want us to do, Melissa?"

She looked younger, more innocent, and a lot like the loving younger child I remembered.

"Come to my game next weekend? Could y'all do that? Lots of the other kids' parents come. That'd be awesome if you could."

She was inviting us to be a part of something important to her. I wasn't sure about the protocol for such things, so I looked at Ms. Duff. "Well?"

Ms. Duff looked pleased. "I think that could be arranged. We can work out the details on this end, and I'll give you a call this week, Louann."

We all clapped and cheered. I jumped up, rushed to Melissa, and hugged her. "That sounds great, honey. I can't wait."

Melissa appeared to suddenly remember she was supposed to be mad at me. After briefly returning my hug, she straightened her shirt and put her shoulders back. In a more mature voice, she said, "All right, then. I have to get to practice if I expect to play in that game. I guess this means I'll see you all next weekend. It was nice to meet you, Dan, and you, too, Katie."

Ms. Duff stood to walk Melissa out. As they neared the door, Melissa looked over her shoulder. She smiled and looked straight at me. "Bye, Mom. See you next week!"

I collapsed on the couch, grinning so big I felt downright foolish. She'd called me Mom, smiled at me, and talked and laughed with Dan and Katie. Praise God—we were all on cloud nine. I'd set Dan and Katie up for a sullen girl with an attitude, but Melissa had charmed them both. I hoped and prayed that it wasn't a fluke.

We took a short break, and Ms. Duff brought Miranda and Mikayla in. The introductions went well, and our visit was just as good as Melissa's, if not even better. Before we knew it, it was time to say goodbye.

"Go, Melissa, go! Rebound! Way to go!"

When the kids yelled her name out over the crowd, she spotted us but looked away. Was she embarrassed? The game did not go well for her team. Although she was doing great, the rest of the team didn't hold up. As the coach led the team off the court, she scowled and stomped and brushed off fist bumps from other players that were meant to console and encourage each other. We stood around a little ways off from the other parents, waiting for the girls to come out of the locker room freshly showered and dressed. After about ten minutes, Melissa was the first to appear. She had pulled on sweats, and her face looked like a thundercloud.

"Melissa?" She walked right past me without a word. I looked to Ms. Duff for help.

"Let me try," she said. "Melissa, hold on a minute, please."

Melissa stopped and whipped around. Her voice harsh, she said, "What? What is it? Can't y'all just leave me alone?"

We all stopped dead in our tracks. Sweet little Mikayla, bless her heart, was so excited. She hopped in a circle around Melissa, trying to grab her hand. "But, Melissa! We're all going together for a celebration dinner. It's all planned. There's going to be pizza and wings, and—"

Melissa stepped forward, right in front of her baby sister's face. "Don't you get it? I don't want to go anywhere with any of you—especially her!" Pointing straight at me. "She ruined my life. I don't ever want to see her or any of the rest of you ever again."

Stunned silence except for Mikayla's hysterical crying. A young, professional-looking black woman in a tailored suit joined our little group, gazing sympathetically at Melissa.

Ms. Duff spoke. "Oh, Ms. Partain, I'm so glad you're here. What on Earth is going on?"

Ms. Partain answered, "Let me see what I can do." She stepped beside Melissa, who had turned her back to us, and placed an arm around her shoulder. She led her over to the bleachers and sat down with her a few rows up. We couldn't hear them and tried not to stare.

Ms. Duff gathered us into a close group and explained. "Ms. Partain is Melissa's counselor. She called me this afternoon and warned me that Melissa had a setback in their session this week. I was afraid something might happen today, so I asked her to be here."

Dan, ever the peacemaker, responded uncharacteristically. "What in the hell just happened? That wasn't just a setback. It was more like a possession! That was not the same sweet kid we met a week ago."

"I don't know the whole story, Mr. Childs. Let's wait and see what Ms. Partain has to say." After a minute or two, the counselor patted Melissa's shoulder and came down the bleachers to where we stood.

She put her hand out to me, then Dan and Katie, introducing herself. She gave Miranda and Mikayla hugs and exchanged looks with Ms. Duff. "I'm afraid this is not a good time for the planned family visit. Melissa is in quite a state, and I don't think it is in anyone's best interest to force a visit at this time. I am hopeful we can resolve the issues with more counseling this week, but I can't make any promises. I'm so sorry you and Melissa have had to go through this."

My stomach was in knots. I asked Ms. Partain, "What happened this past week? A kid doesn't change from day to night just like that. She was perfectly happy last Saturday. Something is going on here, and I don't like it. What happened?"

Ms. Partain and Ms. Duff exchanged looks again. They both took a step or two towards me and stood on either side of me, linking their arms with mine. They walked me away from the others, out of their hearing range, and Ms. Duff spoke softly. "Louann, your ex-husband is out of jail."

Oh my God. Well, that explained it. But how did Melissa know? Did Miranda and Mikayla know? Had he tried to contact them? Where was he exactly? If I got my hands on . . .

"Louann? Are you all right?" Ms. Duff was looking at me, her forehead lined with concern.

I snapped back to reality. "I'm not sure. What does this mean? Is he responsible for Melissa's change of attitude?"

Dan was standing with us now. "What's going on here?"

I spoke up. "It's that goddamn Morris. He's out of jail."

Dan's hands, at his sides, balled into fists. I'd only seen him angry a few times, and it was not a pretty sight. In fact, it was downright terrifying. His jaw was clenched, and a vein throbbed in his temple. "That's what this is all about? If that scumbag has been near these girls, I swear to God I'll—"

Ms. Partain placed a hand on Dan's arm. "Mr. Childs, please, let's talk about this. I think the best thing right now would be to get the girls back to their homes, and then let us adults discuss what needs to happen next. I can take Melissa with me, you all can go ahead with your plans for Miranda and Mikayla, then we can meet up later. Don't you agree, Ms. Duff?"

"That sounds good. Let's see—we should be through with dinner by six-thirty. Why don't we meet back at the office about seven?" suggested Ms. Duff.

"Sounds good," said Ms. Partain. "I'll go ahead and get on my way with Melissa. See you all in a little while at the office."

Dan put his arm around me, and we watched as she went up to where Melissa still sat in the bleachers. Ms. Partain spoke briefly to her, then led her down the steps and out through the gym doors without so much as a glance in our direction. Miranda and Mikayla looked at us, their mouths turned down, chins trembling, and eyes welling up with tears. Katie was looking on, helpless. My mother instinct kicked in. "All right, girls. It looks like Melissa's not up to joining us, but we're off to Pizza Hut. Who wants pepperoni?"

Dan picked up the theme and chimed in. "I'm all for pepperoni, just hold the mushrooms."

Plastering a smile on her face, Ms. Duff spoke up. "My only request is for thin and crispy crust, please."

We went out into the cold and piled into the car. The girls sang along to the radio. It was dark in the car, and I was glad for it. The kids wouldn't be able to see my eyes brimming with tears.

I made it through the meal and drove Miranda and Mikayla back to their foster home without exploding. Now, back at the DFACS office, waiting for the counselor to show up, I was seething. While Katie waited in the lobby, Dan watched me march around the pretend living room, mouthing off to no one in particular. "How could this happen? What idiots let an accused child-molester out of jail? Why was Melissa mad at *me*? Where is that son of a bitch? When I get my hands on him, there will be hell to pay."

I was interrupted when Ms. Partain came bustling in, but I didn't let that stop me. I turned on her. "How could you let this happen? You were supposed to be helping her. Now she's angrier and hurt more than ever. You need to fix this—now."

Ms. Partain stood silent and calm and let me finish my rant. Ms. Duff suggested we all sit down. Dan and I sat on the couch, and the two women sat in the armchairs. Ms. Partain was the first to speak.

"Mrs. Childs, as you know, Melissa has never believed that her father was actually guilty. She has maintained all along that it was just a misunderstanding. She expressed her anger towards you on that first visit. The following week, we had two sessions that helped her understand that her anger at you was misdirected. She seemed to come to terms with that. Then, last week, her father was released. They spoke on the phone. I don't know the exact conversation, but her anger came back with a vengeance."

Dan showed little patience with the counselor's patronizing tone. "Vengeance? I'd say that's an understatement. What we witnessed today was more like a raging psychopath! How do you explain that?"

Ms. Duff spoke this time. Was she trying to divert our anger off the counselor? If that was the case, it wasn't going to work. "Mr. Childs, Mrs. Childs, we are dealing with a seventeen-year-old girl who has been traumatized, separated from her mother, father, and siblings, as well as experiencing a multitude of upsetting experiences over just the last few weeks. Under the circumstances, it's not unusual for an adolescent to exhibit extremes in behavior."

I wasn't having any more of this psychological babble talk shit. "Yes, as you say, Melissa has experienced all those things. Let me remind you, however, that most of that occurred while she was under your care, especially this most recent upheaval. I want my daughter back, and I want her back now."

Ms. Duff and Ms. Partain exchanged knowing glances again. What was it with them? Were they telecommunicating or something? It was rude and condescending to act as though they were aware of things we weren't and that they knew better than us what was best for my daughter.

Ms. Duff turned on her false sympathetic voice, smooth and crooning. "Now, Louann, you know that decision is up to the judge. You will have your say in court. Until then, I think it's best to let Melissa be. Ms. Partain will continue to work with her, and hopefully, she can bring about a resolution."

I jumped up. Dan put his hand on my arm, stood with me, and spoke before I could retort. "Ms. Duff, I understand. Ms. Partain, we hope this can be resolved. I think it best that we leave now. The next time we see you will be in court, right? Come on, Louann, let's go."

Ms. Duff looked relieved. "That's right, Mr. Childs. Just a few more days and this will all be resolved."

I knew Dan well enough to understand he meant, *Louann, shut up and let's get out of here.*

Back at the motel, there was one more thing I needed to do before I could resolve myself to waiting on the judge's decision. Close to midnight, after two hours of dead ends, one of my phone calls hit pay dirt. I recognized the grizzly voice on the other end of the line immediately.

"Babcock here. Whaddya want?"

No introductions were needed. "I want to know if you did anything to my daughters."

Silence.

"No, Louann. I swear I never touched those girls."

"That better be the truth, Morris, because if I find out you did, I'll kill you, and you will burn in Hell."

The line went dead.

LOUANN

March 1999

Back home in Kentucky, we prepared the house for Miranda and Mikayla's arrival. I wasn't happy about Melissa staying in Oklahoma, but there was little I could do about it at this point. We all hoped she would have a change of heart and decide to join us, but we weren't counting on it.

Our plan was to arrive in Oklahoma the Sunday before the Thursday court date. We would visit with the girls, get their things together, and give them a chance to say their goodbyes, including to their sister Melissa. We wanted to leave for home as soon as possible after the hearing, but realistically, we knew it could be a day or two before we left the state. We talked every day with Ms. Duff to make sure there were no snafus, and she assured us everything should go smoothly—no surprises.

I hadn't spoken with Joycie since New Year's Day, when she'd been so cruel about me finding my children, so I was more than a little surprised when she called the day before we were to leave for Oklahoma.

"Louann? Is that you?"

"Yes, it's me. Joycie? You sound different."

"I should sound different, considering we haven't spoken in months."

"Yeah, well, as I recall, our last conversation was not too friendly. I'm surprised to hear from you."

"Well, maybe you wouldn't be so surprised if you called to check on me and Mama now and then."

"Mama? What's wrong? Has her condition changed?" Hoping against hope, I took a wishful leap. "Is she getting better?"

"Oh, get real, Louann. She's never going to get better. In fact, that's why I'm calling. She's worse. She's been moved to the hospital, and the doctor says she only has a day or two left. Thought you might want to know."

My heart fell. Bless her soul. I was ashamed that I wasn't there for her when she needed me most. Sure, at one time, I'd been determined to take care of her, but I'd been only a kid, then. Life had happened. It was when I'd lost her guiding love and wisdom that I'd lost my way. If not for Dan Childs, I might still be lost—or *actually* dead—and where would my children be then? I had not one iota of sympathy for Joycie, but I did owe Mama for the lessons she'd taught me about mothering and love.

"Oh, Joycie, no! Here I am, finally about to get my girls back home after three years. I was planning to bring them down for a visit. Our hearing is next week, and I'm getting them back."

"Well, good for you. That's your usual selfish nature. Well, I've got news for you. The world does not revolve around you, and I can hardly tell the doctor to hold off and not let her die until it's convenient for you to get here."

"Joycie, you know that's not fair—"

"Listen to me, Louann. You go right ahead with your life. I won't even bother to call when she's dead. Goodbye."

Life sure has a way of lifting you up then slamming you on your butt.

Dan knelt down and took my hands in his own, looking into my eyes. God, I loved that man. "Louann," he said, "I know this is tearing you up inside, but if there is anyone who wants you to get those girls back more than me, it's Bessie. She knows what a mother's love truly is. She understands your heart. We're going to go ahead with our plans and accept her blessing."

So that was exactly what we did. We drove to Oklahoma, then spent the next day with the girls. We returned to the motel around ten p.m., and the message light on the phone was blinking. It was Joycie's number. I called back, but Benny answered. Thank God it was him, even though I knew that if he was there, it could only mean one thing: Mama was gone.

In that sweet cusp between sleeping and waking when we are still in a dream, the smell of hot coffee edged me over to wakefulness. That moment of blissful unawareness was dispelled, and reality came crashing through. It was time to face life and death. Dan brought coffee over to the nightstand.

"Thank you, honey. What would I do without you?"

"You're welcome. And don't worry, you'll never have to find that out. I promise I will be here for you, always."

I lay back against the pillows and sipped my coffee. We didn't have to be anywhere until we met the girls after school about three that afternoon. My mind was swirling with so many thoughts that it hurt to think, much less speak. My two girls joining our household, my mama gone. My mind bounced back and forth from joy to sorrow, sorrow to joy. Dan, being the sensitive soul that he was, did not force conversation. Every half-hour or so, he'd ask if he could get me anything or did I need anything or was there anything he could do. I'd just smile and answer, "No, thank you, darling."

Around two, the phone rang, and Dan answered. It was Benny. "Oh, hey, Benny. How y'all holding up? Is that so?" I reached out my hand for the phone. "Uh-huh, she's right here. Hold on a sec."

"Benny? Hey, honey. How you doin'?"

"Louann, I know this is bad timing, but the funeral's going to be Thursday the first."

I sucked in my breath. *Damn!* "Benny, you know what happens on Thursday?"

"Yeah, Louann, I do. I tried to get them to change it, but—"

"Look, I know Joycie's probably doing this just to spite me. But I'll tell you what, I know good and well that Mama would want me to be in that courtroom on Thursday morning gettin' my babies back. And that's exactly what I'm going to do. If Joycie doesn't like it, she can kiss my ass, and you can tell her I said so. I've waited this long, and I'm not going to chance a delay of this hearing."

"I understand, Louann. We're all really happy for you. You take care of things up there, and we'll talk again in a few days, all right?"

"Thank you, Benny. I love you, and Barbie and Bobby, too. Tell them all I said hello, and we'll all get together soon. Bye, now."

"Bye, Louann."

LOUANN

April 1, 1999

W E HAD ONE MORE DAY OF VISITING, AND THEN IT WAS THURSDAY morning. April first, 1999. Me, Dan, and Katie wore our best dress-up clothes and were in the courthouse lobby at nine a.m. Miranda and Mikayla were there with Ms. Duff. Melissa was there with Ms. Partain, but they stood a little ways off and didn't bother to greet us or even glance our way. I'd wondered if Morris would be there, but Ms. Huff had assured me earlier in the week that he just had to make a statement and did not have to be there in person. She said the assistant district attorney who was presenting our case had already taken Morris's statement and had it ready to present.

About 9:20, a clerk came out, greeted Ms. Huff, and spoke to our little group. "All right, folks, it's time to get settled in the courtroom. Ready?" She moved away to speak to Ms. Partain, then rejoined our group.

I gulped. My knees felt like Jell-O, my stomach roiled like a bubbling pot, and a lump rose in my throat. I couldn't speak, so I nodded. God, I hoped I wouldn't throw up. Dan put his arm around my shoulders, and I sank against him. I managed a weak smile at Miranda and Mikayla. They were both fidgeting—flipping their hair back over their shoulders, licking their lips, shifting their weight from one foot to the other. I mouthed words to them. *I love you.* After that, they both flashed a grin and gave me a thumbs-up.

Ms. Duff took each girl's arm, and, walking between them, followed the clerk. Dan, Katie, and I were next, and Melissa and Ms. Partain followed a little distance behind us. We entered the hushed courtroom and were led to the first row. The clerk indicated for our group to sit on one side of the aisle, then motioned for Melissa and Ms. Partain to sit on the opposite side. Katie and Dan slid in first, then me and Ms. Duff with a girl still on either side, Mikayla on the aisle.

Once we were all seated, I couldn't resist a glance at Melissa. My firstborn, my darling, who would not be going home with us. I noticed Mikayla holding her hand low in front of her body, making a waving motion and smiling towards her sister across the aisle. Melissa shifted her eyes toward Mikayla, gave a brief hint of a nod, and looked straight ahead. My heart was breaking. It wasn't just me she was rejecting. It was her sisters, too.

On the other side of the rail, three men sat at a long table, a court recorder was settled at her station, and a uniformed bailiff stood near a door. The clerk spoke to all of them individually, moved to take her place near the judge's podium, and nodded to the bailiff. Then she turned forward and spoke.

"All rise. The honorable Judge Marilyn D. Dickson."

It was all I could do to stifle a gasp. It was a woman—I had not been expecting that. I had assumed the judge would be a man. Even though Ms. Duff had said she was certain everything would go off without a hitch, I couldn't help but wonder if this could make a difference. The woman stepped briskly up to her bench. She had dark hair in a bowl cut, had big-rimmed black glasses, and looked to be in her fifties. She wore no makeup, and the lines on her face were barely visible. She smiled pleasantly around the room, said, "Good morning," and picked up the gavel.

"I now call this court to order. We are here this morning to adjudicate the custody of minor children Melissa, Miranda, and Mikayla Babcock, who currently reside in the custody of the state of Oklahoma's Department of Family and Children's Services. Counselor for the State, you may make your statements."

One of the men at the long table stood up and stepped to the open area before the judge. "Good Morning. Your Honor and ladies and gentlemen of the court, this is an unusual case, yet one that can be resolved quickly in a manner satisfactory to all parties."

He proceeded to give the entire history of all that had transpired, including mine and Morris's marriage, separation, and divorce, then moving on to my addiction, jail time, rehab, and subsequent search for my children. At this point, he gave the background on Morris moving around with the children, the questionable charges that had landed him in jail, and his telling the authorities the children had no living relatives, thereby resulting in them being placed in the custody of the state.

He also read the deposition that Morris had recorded, where he denied the sexual molestation charges but admitted he'd lied about the children's mother being deceased. It stated that he willingly released the girls to the full custody of their mother, with the condition that the oldest daughter, Melissa, be allowed to choose her place of residence with either him or her mother. I had resigned myself to that condition, despite knowing that Melissa would choose him. I'd had to sign a statement to that effect myself.

The judge proceeded to ask a few clarifying questions, which the assistant DA answered confidently. Finally, she said, "So, Counselor, what is the recommendation of the State of Oklahoma?"

"Given the circumstances of this debacle, the district attorney recommends the custody of Melissa, Miranda, and Mikayla Babcock be remanded to their mother, Louann Walker Babcock Childs, subject to the condition regarding Melissa Babcock, to which Mrs. Childs has previously agreed."

The judge shuffled papers on her desk. The assistant DA stood quietly. I held my breath. *Thirty seconds seems like an eternity when the fate of your children hangs in the balance.*

Finally, the judge spoke. "Is Mrs. Childs present in the court?"

The assistant DA answered, "Yes, Your Honor, she is present." He turned and indicated me with his hand.

Judge Dickson spoke again. "Please approach the bench, Mrs. Childs."

I did not expect this, either. Absolutely no one had warned me that I might have to say a single word in court. Was I going to be questioned? Accused? Dan gave my arm a squeeze, and as I passed Ms. Duff leaving my seat, she did not meet my eyes. Anxiety gushed over me like an open fire hydrant. I teetered on the heels I rarely wore to stand in front of the judge.

She bent her head and looked at me. I was surprised to realize she had a kind look on her face. She spoke softly so that only I could hear her words. "Mrs. Childs, I know that you have made mistakes in your life. We all have done so. The important thing is that we accept punishment and learn from those mistakes. I believe you have served your punishment by being separated from your children. I believe you have learned from your mistakes, as is evidenced by your sustained sobriety, rehabilitation, and willingness to let Melissa choose her residence. I want to return your children to you, according to the law, and allow you to bestow on them the fullest realization of a mother's love."

She rapped the gavel, whispered to me, "You may return to your seat," then spoke aloud to the court as my tears flowed and I made my way back to my seat. "My ruling is to concur with the recommendation of the state that these children be returned to the full custody of their mother. So be it. This court is now adjourned."

LOUANN

1999 to 2006

THE NEXT FEW DAYS WERE A WHIRLWIND AS WE MADE ALL THE final arrangements to move Miranda and Mikayla home with us. Dan was a trooper among all those female hormones. My girls were taking to him and Katie like a pig takes to a puddle, and he and Katie were just as at home with them. Once we got home, we enrolled them in school and introduced them around to friends and neighbors. Dan was offered a new job at a plant in Missouri in early 2000, including a promotion and more money. It was our chance to start a new life in a home in the Southern Ozarks. I was so wrapped up in being a mother, I couldn't think about being motherless myself.

I stayed in contact with Benny, and occasionally, I'd talk to Bobby, too. I never talked to Barbie and hadn't since she'd moved out from Joycie's in the late 1970s, when she'd been eighteen. Benny always said he didn't understand why Barbie still came around to Dave and Joycie's, even after she'd moved out—like she was drawn to them. He said the way her and Dave acted when they were together gave him the creeps—there was something downright strange about it. And of course, I hadn't spoken with Joycie since right before Mama had died. I had long ago stopped trying to understand anything that went on in Joycie's life. Trying to maintain a relationship with her just wasn't worth the pain that came with it.

ONE SPRING DAY in April of 2000, after we'd moved, Benny called to tell me that Richard, our grandfather, had died. Neither of us had any feelings for Richard, but Benny said that Joycie was really torn up about it. As far as we could tell, all of her life, Joycie had loved her daddy. Richard's wife, Helen, had died three years before. I hadn't kept up with them but had heard that Richard had not been kind to Helen over the years while she'd suffered from cancer. No surprise there. He'd never taken care of his daughter Joycie, so why would he take care of his wife? Their son, Richie, had taken care of his mother until the end. Now his daddy was dead, too.

I only got news from Joycie through Benny. She was still with Dave off and on, even though Dave and Barbie, who was thirty-one now, still saw each other. I know it sounds weird, and I can't explain it, but somehow, Joycie still wanted him in her life just like she'd wanted Richard there up until the day he'd died. She and Dave had divorced at one point, but she'd never given up on him. She'd even gone so far as to have stomach reduction surgery, trying to lose the weight she'd put on over the years to be more attractive, trying to compete with her own daughter, I supposed. During those years, she'd become sicker and sicker and ended up addicted to pain pills. I wasn't going to waste any effort on Joycie.

Those last few years with my girls and Katie went by like lightning. High school, sports, dances, boyfriends, and the horses and dogs we raised kept me, Dan, and the girls busy. Before we knew it, the girls were all out of school and mostly on their own. Soon, it was just me and Dan. I still dabbled in real estate, and he worked at the plant. In our spare time, we took care of the animals and got together with the kids. Life was good.

ONE COLD WINTER day in 2006, Benny called. "Louann, I need your help."

He sounded horrible. "Oh my God, Benny. What's wrong? Are you all right?"

"It's Mama, Louann. I just can't . . ." Sobs choked out his words.

This was about Joycie? I took a deep breath and let Benny cry. Eventually, he got it out and calmed down.

"Benny? It's going to be okay, baby. Try to tell me what's going on."

He gulped and sniffed, and I could picture him wiping his eyes. "Okay. Well, you know Mama hasn't been well for a while now."

"Yeah, you told me."

"So, I brought her up here to stay with me."

"Oh, Benny, no."

"What was I supposed to do? That piece-of-shit Dave and Barbie weren't taking care of her. And you're not going to believe this, Louann. Barbie is pregnant. I would bet money that Dave's the father. None of them would say so, but I think that's what put Mama over the edge. What else could I do? She's my mama." He was crying again.

"Shh, Benny, it's okay. I know she's your mama, and you love her. What's going on now?"

More sniffling. "Well, she's been here for about six weeks, and I just can't do this no more. Either she's screaming and carrying on at me to take her home, or she's passed out on the pills and I'm afraid she's dead. Louann, I need help."

Oh, hell. I didn't want to do this. Me and Dan were happy on the farm. Life was good. What had Joycie ever done for me? I didn't owe her anything. Apparently, my silence scared Benny. He screamed into the phone, "Louann. Are you there? Louann?"

Defeated, I sucked in a long breath and kneaded my brow. "Yeah, I'm here, Benny. I hear you. I'm not making any promises, but I will try to do this for you. You understand? It's not for her—it's for you. Can you meet me halfway in Paducah? I can be there at noon tomorrow."

Benny had not been exaggerating. If anything, he hadn't told me the worst of it. It was clear driving back home from Paducah that this was going to be hard.

"Where in the hell are we?" Joycie slurred. "Looks like goddamn middle of nowhere. I want to go home to Florida. I thought you was gonna take me home. I wanna see Dave and Barbie."

"No, Joycie. I'm taking you to my house."

"Your house? I don't wanna go there, Louann. Take me home right now." She beat on the dash of the car.

"Stop it, Joycie, right now. I'm taking you to my house, or you can get out right here on the road. It's your choice."

"Oh, hell. Guess I'll go to your house. But then I'm going home."

For the three weeks that Joycie was with me and Dan, she was either vomiting all over my house, shittin' herself, or falling down drunk, all between fits of rage and bouts of unconsciousness.

I'd put her in one of the extra bedrooms. Every morning, the bed was wet.

"Dammit, Joycie. The bathroom's right there. You're worse than a two-year-old."

"I can' help it. Gimme my pills. I need my pills."

"No more pills for you, Joycie. That's what knocks you out so you can't even wake up and go to the bathroom. Now get up so we can change you and this bed."

"You ain't gotta change me, Louann. I'm not a baby. You was a baby once, you know. Somebody had to change you. And hell, it sure wadn't gone be me. I didn't want to have no baby. If it weren't for my daddy—"

"What did you say? Joycie? What do you mean if it wasn't for your daddy? If it wasn't for Mama and Daddy takin' care of me, I wouldn't be here. You're crazy."

Then she was out again. Hell. She could just lay there in her own piss. Talkin' out of her mind one minute, then passed out the next. Why in the hell was she bringin' up Daddy? It didn't make any sense to me.

It was even worse when she got into a diatribe against me. "You know, Louann, I coulda had a whole different life if it wasn't for you. You came straight outta Hell. I never did want no baby—hell, if I coulda stopped him, I woulda, but there you were. I wadn't but thirteen. What did I know? Daddies are s'pose to love their little girls. Yes, ma'am. You're the daughter from Hell. Born straight outta evil."

Most of the time, I tried to ignore her, but it still hurt. I was the daughter from Hell; she'd never wanted me, never loved me. No surprise there. None of that was news to me; I'd lived with it all my life. Only since I'd been with Dan did I feel like I was worth more than a piece of shit. I couldn't have stayed sane those few weeks if it hadn't been for him.

One night, Joycie left the house without our knowledge. The cops brought her back the next morning, muddy feet, shitty nightgown, and all. She said she was going home to Florida, and if we didn't let her, she was going to kill us and herself. That did it. She had to go. As much as I hated Dave, it was me that had to make the call. I did not give him a choice. "I don't care what you have to do, but you have to take her. I'll meet you halfway in Montgomery."

Dave and Barbie did not want her, but they were responsible for her condition. Plus, Joycie wanted to go back to Florida. That was her home. I didn't care what they did with her. Take her in, put her in rehab, whatever. Whatever they did, it wouldn't be for long. I knew what addicts looked like when they were close to the end, and she was getting closer every day. After I got off the phone with Dave, I called Benny and told him. He wasn't surprised.

LOUANN

2006 to 2008

BENNY CALLED ABOUT ONCE A MONTH WITH AN UPDATE. HE SAID from what he could tell, Joycie kept getting worse. He didn't think Dave or Barbie did much to take care of her; they just kept her supplied with pills so she'd stay out of their hair. Even though it was sad, and there was nothing I could do, it didn't ease my guilt. Daughters were supposed to take care of their mothers. Just like mothers should take care of their daughters—an idea that had been ingrained in me from birth, but God knew I'd never been cared for by Joycie. I'd tried so many times to understand, to make peace, only to be shot down repeatedly. Why couldn't I let it go? Would I ever get over wanting, wishing for, and dreaming of a mother's love?

The final call came in November 2008.

"Louann?"

My stomach dropped. I knew Benny's voice beyond a shadow of a doubt. I also knew it had to be bad news. He'd called just three days before, so he wouldn't be calling again so soon unless something was wrong.

"Benny? What is it?"

"Mama's gone, Louann. She's dead."

The room was spinning, and I felt sick. Whatever it is that keeps us together in such situations kicked in. My mothering instincts took over once again. "Oh, honey, I'm so sorry. What happened?"

"Dave called just a little while ago and said she was gone." Benny sounded strangely vacant. I suppose that same sense of calm had come over him. That surprised me. He was so soft-hearted I couldn't believe he wasn't breaking down.

"Is that all? When did this happen? Where was she? Was she at home or in a hospital? Was anybody with her? What exactly happened? What did she die from? What about arrangements? I can leave within the hour and be down there by this evening." I was rattling off questions and making plans.

Benny yelled into the phone, "It doesn't matter, Louann! None of that matters. She's gone."

I was stunned by the harshness in his voice. "What do you mean? Of course it matters. She's our mother. We have to go."

There was a quiet sobbing on the other end of the line. "No, Louann. There's nothing to go for. She died a week ago, and they already cremated her. That son of a bitch burned our mama before he even let us know she was dead."

My control evaporated. "Oh my God, oh my God, oh my God—"

"Louann? He said something about her dying in her sleep, too many pills, and they couldn't afford a funeral, so they just did the quickest and cheapest thing. It happened on November third."

I was trying to take in what Benny was saying. It made no sense. "Listen, Benny, I love you. We gotta stick together. I need to go. I need to talk to Dan. I need to . . . I need to . . . do something . . . I'm not sure what. I'll call you back later, okay?"

"Okay, Louann. I love you. Call me later. Bye."

"Bye, Baby Brother, bye."

I WAS ALONE. Dan wouldn't be home from work for another hour. All I could do was walk around the house in circles. I threw on a coat and went outside, where I walked in more circles, beating my fists at the cold air and screwing my face up to stifle the screams. I lost it. My mind, my sanity, my whatever. That control that takes over in emergencies was gone.

My eyes landed on my car. Running back to the house, grabbing my purse and keys, I got in the car and slammed the door. Dirt and gravel flew as it fishtailed down the long drive. I didn't know where, but I was going somewhere, anywhere. I came up on Highway 99 and turned north. I drove miles and miles, speeding, swerving, makin' curves into straightaways. It was getting dark, and the sky was soon as black as an iron skillet. When I saw neon red lights that said "Mini-Mart," I pulled over. It didn't take but a minute, and I was back in the car with bottles—glass ones with a variety of booze and little plastic ones with pretty-colored pills. I opened one of the glass bottles and took a swig.

Looking around, I saw another neon sign across the road. This one was blinking green: VACANCY. For the first time since I'd left my house that afternoon, I knew where I was going. I swung across the road without bothering to look. A horn blasted, and my car shuddered from the wind of the passing semi. God, if I was gonna kill myself, I didn't want it to be on the road. I checked in to the shoddy little motel. The room stank of mold, and the bathroom smelled like pee, but it didn't matter to me. I didn't plan to be conscious for long.

As it turned out, I was somewhere I had been before. It wasn't the physical place I recognized, but the state of mind was all too familiar. The same place of mind I'd been in all those years ago down in Florida. It could have been a flophouse, some guy's shitty apartment, or even another roach motel, but this time, it was a cheap place on a backroad in Missouri, and I was strung out on pills and booze.

I DON'T KNOW how long I'd been there—could have been days, could have been weeks. Somebody was beating on the door.

"Louann? Open up. It's me, Dan."

"Go away."

"Louann, let me in, or I'm going to break down this door."

"Dan, you don't wanna see me. Go the hell away and don't come back."

I dragged myself over to the window and peeked out. It was twilight, and there was my darling Dan, head against the doorframe, fists resting on the sides of his head, sobs wracking his body. *Shit.* I cracked the door. "What is it? Dan?"

He wiped at his face and looked at me with sad eyes. "Thought you might want to know that you're a grandma, Louann. Miranda had her baby today. That's all." He turned around and shuffled off. I closed the door and went back to the rumpled bed.

Grandma? Me? Oh, my Lord. Illusions of babies flooded my mind: my own girls, my brothers and sister, cousins, babies I'd seen on the streets. They somehow got mixed up with images of Joycie. But she was dead. Was she haunting me? Was I sacrificing the family life and love I could have with Dan, my girls, and my own grandbaby because of her? Now it was Mama who loomed in my mind.

If I had learned anything from her, it was how important it was for a baby to feel loved. Now those memories took over: Mama telling how her and Daddy had taken care of Joycie when her own mama had left her. Mama recounting how they'd taken care of me when Joycie had been so sick after I was born. Mama teaching me to count to one hundred while we'd sat on the porch shelling peas. Mama making chocolate milk just for me. Mama looking after me, Benny, Bobby, and Barbie, even though she'd been bone-tired. Mama saying how I could help Joycie look after my brothers and sister that time she'd sent me to Jacksonville 'cause I'd always been such a good little mama. And then, just like she was standing right beside me, I heard her say, *You'll have to make it on your own one day. Now's as good a time as any. One day, when you're a real mother yourself, you'll understand. Children have a hard time understanding why their mamas do what they do sometimes, but it'll all make sense in the end.*

I must have drifted off. When I woke up, everything came flashing back. I looked around, halfway expecting to see Mama right there in the room with me. I ran to the door and jerked it open. Bright sunlight came flooding in. There was no sign of Dan. *Oh my God. What now?*

It was time. I vowed that no grandchild of mine would ever lack love in their lives. I understood exactly why Mama had become the mother Joycie and I had needed. Even if it looked like I might have to live the rest of my life not knowing why Joycie had been the way she had, I knew in my heart that I needed to come to my senses and go home.

I called Dan. "Hey, honey, it's me," I said.

"I know it's you," he said. "I ain't forgot your voice."

"I just wanted to let you know I'm sorry. I went off the deep end. I really lost it, but I've found it again."

"Louann, why couldn't you let me help you? I've helped you before. It didn't have to be this way."

"You make things sound easy, Dan. It's not. Letting go of Joycie is the hardest fuckin' thing I've ever done, and I had to do it by myself. Don't you get it?"

"Yeah, honey. I get it."

"I want to come home now."

"All right, darlin', you come right on."

After a few days back at the farm, I can't describe the joy it brought when I saw Miranda's baby. The love that overflows a grandmother's heart goes a long way towards filling the void left by the lack of a real mother's love.

LOUANN

2017

S O MANY OF MY EXTENDED FAMILY HAD PASSED ON, BUT AT LEAST
Benny, Bobby, and me stayed in touch. We lived in different states
but managed to get all the cousins together once a year for a reunion.
This year, 2017, we were in Florida at Aunt Rene's. She was in her eighties
now, but Marybeth and her family lived in her house and took care of her.

This year seemed extra special since it was the first time Richie had
made any of our reunions. Sittin' around, telling family stories, we talked
about how everybody hated Richard, but anybody that had known Helen
had been fond of her. Richie chuckled and said he could understand that.
He was kind of quiet most of the time and didn't reveal much about his
life growing up or his mama and daddy's deaths. I told him I'd worshipped
his mama ever since she'd saved my life that day of my daddy's funeral.

I was thinking a lot about Joycie this year, since it was coming up on
ten years since she'd died, back in 2008. As we talked, I got to thinking
about Richie being one of the only living links to my grandfather, Joycie's
father. After all, Richie and Joycie were half-brother and -sister. Could
he know anything about the strange affinity Joycie had had for Richard?
Was there even a small chance he could have some insight into why Joycie
had hated me so much?

Like a presence whispering in your ear that you can't ignore, something told me he might have a clue. I was always afraid to mention it to
anyone in the family because it seemed like Richard was a taboo subject.

Maybe Richie knew something he didn't even realize was significant but that could help me understand Joycie better. I stewed on this possibility. I made up my mind that I had to talk to Richie privately. I promised myself that if I didn't learn anything helpful, I would let it go and resign myself to the unanswered questions that had plagued me my entire life.

Something told me I would know when the time was right. We only had that evening and the next day before everybody would go their separate ways, so I couldn't put it off too long. Dan knew something was up. He would catch me smiling to myself and comment that I looked like the cat that had swallowed the canary. Another time, he said that I had that "Mona Lisa" smile on my face. I just grinned and said, "Can't a girl smile and be happy without being accused of something?"

He would laugh it off, saying, "A woman like you? Hah! With a smile like that, I know you're up to something. Guess I'll just have to bide my time until you're ready to tell me."

The next morning, I noticed Richie sitting outside his RV that he'd driven up to Williston. He was by himself, with a steaming cup of coffee in one hand and his other hand resting on the head of the dog next to him, gently kneading the dog's ears. This was my chance. There was even an empty fold-up chair right next to him.

I walked over. "Mind if I sit and visit?"

"Go right ahead. Duke likes company," he said, referring to the dog.

"Hey, Duke—you're a handsome boy. But what about you, Richie? You don't mind company, do you?"

"Aw, naw, Louann. That's fine. What's on your mind?"

"Well, I've been hopin' to get you by yourself, Richie. I've been thinking."

He grinned. "Uh-oh. This sounds serious."

"Well, maybe it is. I was thinkin' about my real mother, Joycie. You know, we never were very close. I was wondering if . . . well . . . since you two were half-brother and -sister, maybe you could shed some light on something that's been bothering me."

Richie shifted his eyes away and set the coffee cup down on the ground. He leaned forward and put his hands together, then looked directly at me. "Go on," he said.

"Well, you know I always had a turbulent relationship with Joycie. Bessie and Hampton pretty much raised me, and Joycie never took any interest in being a mother to me."

"Yeah, seems like I was always vaguely aware of that."

"Well, it gave me lots of problems over the years. I've dealt with addiction and depression, all kinds of horror stories, but I'm better now. Finally got my life together."

"I'm glad to hear that, Louann. I really miss my own mom. I had to help her out a lot in the last few years of her life."

"Well, I tried with Joycie, but it just wasn't meant to be. Anyway, I was never told who my father was. If I asked, I got different stories from different family members. It was always something vague. Joycie's been gone almost ten years, and your mom and dad have been gone longer than that."

"Yeah, a long time since then. So what?"

"Well, I've been struggling to understand why my own mother never could stand the sight of me. I need to make peace with her, and I never got that opportunity before she died. It still bothers me. I always sensed something strange in her relationship with y'all's daddy Richard. I was wondering if you ever heard or knew anything that might help me. Maybe some little insignificant thing that you thought nothing of but that could shed some light for me? Is there anything you remember?"

I held my breath. Again, Richie seemed hesitant.

"Louann, I'm not sure if—"

I interrupted. "Rich, please. I've got to know. There's this feeling that a key piece of information is missing that would solve this for me. I've been trying my entire life to understand."

"Well, Louann, I can tell you this. I never understood the strange relationship between Joycie and Richard, either, and neither did my mother. You know he was a mean son of a bitch."

"Yes, I always knew that. And your mother was so sweet—she took a real interest in me and said she loved me. Even saved my life that time your daddy tried to kill me back when I was a kid! But what was it about Richard and Joycie?"

Richie shifted in his chair. "Well, um, there was this one time I overheard a conversation. Richard was being his usual bastard self, and he told my mother he loved Joycie more than her."

I got a sick feeling in my stomach.

"Louann, are you sure you want to hear this?"

"Yes. I have to know."

"Okay. Here goes. Well . . . I guess I'll just spit it out. Richard told me if I ever told anybody what I'd heard, he would kill me, but since he's dead and gone, I suppose you deserve to know."

"Oh God, Richie. Please, just tell me."

He took a deep breath. "You sure nobody's ever told you anything about this, Louann?"

"Yes—I mean, no, nobody's told me anything, Richie. Please, just say it."

"Okay, here goes. Richard said he raped Joycie when she was just thirteen, and you were born as a result."

My breath stuck in my chest. Bile rose in my throat. I swallowed hard, and just as suddenly as it came, it went away. A sense of relief flooded over me. I couldn't speak for a moment.

"Louann? Are you all right?"

"Yes, I'm all right. Oh my God. I knew it. Somehow, I'd always suspected. Why didn't she tell me?"

"I don't know, Louann. When they realized I'd overheard the conversation, I was sworn to secrecy. Richard said he'd kill me if I ever told anybody, and I believed him. I'm sorry. I pushed it away with so many other unspeakable things I never wanted to relive. I always knew Joycie and Richard had a strange relationship—something more than just a father and a daughter, but it seemed dark and secret. I didn't want to know."

"I can't tell you what this means to me, Rich. It finally explains so much. No wonder she couldn't love me as a mother should. I've blamed her all these years when it was really that piece of shit evil Richard that was at fault . . . sorry, I know he's your daddy too, but I can't help it."

"There's no love lost between me and him. But all that was years ago, and I've moved on. You have to learn to let things go or they'll drag you down forever. If this can help you make peace with Joycie, then I'm glad."

"Richie, somehow I knew you would be able to tell me something, even after all these years. We're family, and we need to stay in touch more often."

"Yeah, I know. There's no telling what all we don't know about. Hey, by the way, did you know Richard has another son? His name's Richard, too, but they call him Dickie. He lives in Alabama."

"You're kidding. No, I didn't know that. That bastard. We've probably got half-sisters and -brothers all over the country. Maybe I'll look him up sometime. For now, I need to focus on coming to terms with him and Joycie."

"I guess so, Louann. Glad I could help you out, but sorry about the circumstances."

"Yeah, I know, Richie. Love you, and thanks so much again. We'll talk again soon, okay?"

"Sure, you're welcome. Love you, too."

We both stood up and hugged. "I can't tell you how much this means to me, Richie. Thank you so much."

He patted my back as we hugged. "You too, Louann, you too."

Finally. It all made sense. I understood why Joycie couldn't love me the way a mother should. She'd lived a life of hell from the time she'd been a very little girl to the day she'd died. Now there was just one more thing I had to do to make peace with Joycie and for myself. Just like Bessie had said, it'll all make sense in the end.

I went back inside and found Dan. "You know how you said I was up to something?"

"Yeah, did you do it?"

"Do what?"

"Whatever it is you were gonna do."

"Oh, yeah, I did it."

"I could tell. You almost look like a different person. You're standing up straighter. You're smiling. You look like somebody took a load off your shoulders."

"Well, I guess you could say that's exactly what happened. Are you ready to listen to a long, long story?"

AFTERWORD

A COUPLE OF YEARS EARLIER, IN THE MIDDLE OF WINTER, I'D received a small package in the mail from my sister Barbie. I moved to throw it out, but I could swear a voice in my head said *Don't throw me away!* Barbie and I hadn't spoken since before Joycie had died, and I couldn't imagine anything she would be sending me that I could want. As I stared at the little package, about four by six inches and an inch thick of crinkly brown paper sealed up with clear tape, an odd feeling came over me. I picked it up, and it was warm in my hands, despite the cold outside. It weighed almost nothing.

I carefully undid the tape and opened the wrapping. There was a single piece of folded paper inside and a small Ziploc bag with what looked like tiny white pebbles and dust. Unfolding the paper, I read,

Dear Louann,

Was going through some things and came across this. I had put it aside for you after mother died, in case you came around some time, but guess that's not going to happen. Thought you might want to have part of her remains.

Your sister,
Barbie

At the time, I had clutched the bag and cried. The crumbled remains were all I had of my mother, and they would never supply the love and acceptance I had wanted from her my entire life. I tucked the bag away in the back of a dresser drawer and never laid eyes on it again until the day we got home from the reunion, after I'd talked to Rich. Now I knew exactly what I needed to do.

I sat down with paper and pen and started pouring out my heart to my mother.

Dear Mama,

I finally feel like I can say that—dear Mama. I have learned the truth about what you lived through, and now I know why you weren't able to show me the love a mother normally does for her child. In your own way, you showed me love by protecting me from your awful truth. I want you to know that I forgive you for that, and I know that in your heart and in your own way, you did love me. You gave me life. I will never understand the relationship between you and my real father, but that doesn't matter now. I know the truth, and I love you. I am placing this tiny part of you with the only real mother and father you ever had, same as me. I hope now you can rest in peace away from the horrors of this world.

Always your loving daughter,
Louann

I took the Ziploc bag and the letter into the kitchen. Placing the paper in an old pan, I set it in the sink. Striking a match, the flame burned bright as I touched it to the edge of the paper. It took only a moment to turn those words from my heart into ashes. When they cooled, I dusted the burned words into the same Ziploc bag, sealing my words of love and my mother together.

I explained to Dan where I was going and why. As always, he was completely understanding. I left early in the morning and cried nearly the whole ten-hour drive to Albany. The next day, Benny and Bobby met me at the City Cemetery. It was a sunny day, and a slight breeze swayed the high grass that surrounded the gravel plot. Flat white slabs with Mama and Daddy's names lay side by side. Next to Mama, a small, gray, unmarked stone marked Joey's resting place.

My brothers stood behind me as I knelt down. I held the bag close to the ground and let the ashes of my mother and my words drift down to rest forever on the earth between Bessie and Hampton, the people who had loved us both the most in this world.

POSTSCRIPT

By the Real Louann Childs
2021

I FINALLY UNDERSTOOD WHY MY MOTHER COULDN'T STAND THE SIGHT of me, why my grandfather/father tried to kill me, and why I was always missing something important in my life. I spent from the age of fourteen, when I lost my daddy, to the age of fifty-three searching for something. So many things. I won't be defined by my birth or my past. I have nothing to hide. I did a lot of things I wish I could change, but that is the past. I am proud that I beat addiction and that I was finally able to make peace with myself and with my mother. Now I am no longer a victim.

Most of my life, I allowed people to treat me badly, talk crap about me behind my back, and use me to get what they wanted. All because I wanted to be loved and have a family. I may never again be close with my sister Barbie, and I struggle with reminding myself that she, too, was a victim and still is in many ways. I am sad that my oldest daughter and I still find it difficult to have a positive relationship. I won't say that I don't believe my own children, but I may never know the truth about what happened between her and her father. I love my brothers Benny and Bobby. They have each faced their own demons. Sadly, Bobby's were the same as Joycie's and mine. He battled addiction most of his adult life and lost that battle last year, in August of 2020. I love my half-brother

Rich—without him, I would have never learned the truth. Now I have what I've always wanted in life: the love of a family.

There is one thing I will never understand: the evil and sickness that exists in this world. Why men or women can abuse children and wreck lives and get away with it, like what happened in my family, I will never comprehend. It is a horrible cycle. Joycie's real mother treated her the way Joycie treated me—like a plague you had to endure. I survived, scarred but alive. Others are not so fortunate. I can't explain the hatred and sixth sense I have around men who are abusers. I feel it in my very soul and actually become sick to my stomach. It is a black and evil thing.

I hope and pray that telling my story can help someone else who may be caught in this evil, wicked cycle. The unknown raw truth I lived with for most of my life nearly destroyed me, as it did my mother and may still yet do to other family members. Although the revelation of that truth brought anger and heartache, it had to be exposed. Truth, no matter how painful, must be revealed. Only then can healing take place.

The **National Domestic Violence Hotline** *aids victims of domestic violence 24 hours a day. Hotline advocates assist victims, and anyone calling on their behalf, by providing crisis intervention, safety planning, and referrals to local service providers. The hotline receives more than 24,000 calls a month.*
800-799-SAFE (7233)

Childhelp National Child Abuse Hotline. *1-800-4-A-Child or 1-800-422-4453*
www.childhelphotline.org

Find your local **Child Protective Services** *number:*
https://www.childhelp.org/wp-content/uploads/2018/01/CPS-Reporting-June-2018.pdf

National Sexual Assault Telephone Hotline

1-800-656-HOPE (4673)

https://www.rainn.org
/about-national-sexual-assault-telephone-hotline

Prevent Child Abuse America

https://preventchildabuse.org/resource
/preventing-child-sexual-abuse/

Centers for Disease Control and Prevention; Preventing Child Sexual Abuse

https://www.cdc.gov/violenceprevention/childabuseand
neglect/childsexualabuse.html

ACKNOWLEDGMENTS

There are so many people who have played a part in my journey to publish Louann's story. First and foremost is the real Louann. Thank you for trusting me to reveal your story to the world. Let us hope and pray it will lead other women to overcome their pasts and move forward to save themselves. Also, to her extended family who helped corroborate and fill in gaps, thank you for your part in telling Louann's story.

To my writing community, for that is truly what it is: a kinship like no other. My author friends and colleagues are such encouragers who support my desire to tell the real-life stories of strong women. My writing and critique friends who read and reread drafts, providing critical feedback and reassurance, are also a part of that tribe. I don't dare list names for fear of leaving someone out, but you all know who you are.

To Steve McCondichie and all the staff at Southern Fried Karma, thank you for believing in the value of this book and making it possible for me to make it available. It has been a long road, and I am thankful for your guidance and willingness to take on a relatively unknown author. Finally, to my own family, especially Joe. You all enable me to tell stories that need to be heard. Without your patience and support, I could not be the Bohemian Southern Belle, empowering strong women through the written word.

ABOUT THE AUTHOR

Janet Hogan Chapman was born and raised in Atlanta, Georgia. She has worn many professional and personal hats, but throughout them all, she has been a writer. She has published professional education materials, essays, poetry, novels, and a memoir. She is a founder of the Southern Crescent Literature and Libations literary group, an award-winning independent author, and a member of several professional writers' associations and has been a featured speaker at book clubs, festivals, and other literary events. Janet holds five college degrees, including a doctorate in education. She enjoys spending time with family, travel, reading, and genealogy. Janet has published two previous novels (*Madam May: A Tale of Madams, Morphine, Moonshine, and Murder* and *Dorothy May: Can She Find a Forever Family?*) and one novella (*After Madam May*). Though these books and *MotherLove* are not a series, there is a character thread that runs through them: all are based on real people and true stories. They are available through your favorite online bookseller and can be ordered by independent bookstores. As the saying goes, truth is sometimes stranger than fiction, and nowhere is that truer than in the South. Learn more about Janet as the Bohemian Southern Belle at www.georgiajanet.com.

BOOK CLUB
DISCUSSION GUIDE

1. What feelings did this book evoke for you?

2. This book deals with difficult issues. How could it encourage or provide hope to readers? Specifically, how could this book help mothers and daughters who struggle in their relationships?

3. What strengths do you see in each of the narrators? (Louann, Joycie, Bessie, Hampton, and Richard.) Likewise, what do you see as their greatest faults?

4. How could Louann have improved her own relationships with her daughters, especially her oldest, Melissa?

5. Bessie was a positive influence on Louann and a model mentor for her as a mother. How do you think the lack of contact with extended families affects parenting in today's culture?

6. Research suggests that one in 20 families with a female child has experienced father-daughter sexual abuse. Do you believe this is a valid number, or do you suspect it could be a higher or lower incidence?

7. Share a favorite quote or scene from the book. Why did this stand out?

8. What did you think about the format of different first-person accounts? Could any one character have told the story effectively?

9. What do you think the author's purpose was in writing this book? What ideas was she trying to get across?

10. Are there lingering questions from this book that you are still wondering about?

SHARE YOUR THOUGHTS

Want to help make *MotherLove* a bestselling novel? Consider leaving an honest review of this book on Goodreads, on your personal author website or blog, and anywhere else readers go for recommendations. It's our priority at Brown Chicken Books to publish books for readers to enjoy, and our authors appreciate and value your feedback.

OUR SOUTHERN FRIED GUARANTEE

If you wouldn't enthusiastically recommend one of our books with a 4- or 5-star rating to a friend, then the next story is on us. We believe that much in the stories we're telling. Simply email us at pr@sfkmultimedia.com.

Do You Know About Our Monthly Zine?

Would you like your unpublished prose, poetry, or visual art featured in The New Southern Fugitives? A monthly zine that's free to readers and subscribers and pays contributors:

$40 Per Book Review

$40 Per Poem

$40 Per Photograph or Piece of Visual Art

$15 Per Page for Prose (Min $45 and Max $105)

Visit NewSouthernFugitives.com/Submit for more information.

ALSO BY
BROWN CHICKEN BOOKS

Lacrimosa (Shadows of the Mind: Book One), Mandi Jourdan

Parker's Choice, Mike Nemeth

CPSIA information can be obtained
at www.ICGtesting.com
Printed in the USA
BVHW041357190622
640125BV00018B/147